D0013073

Praise for Robert J. Begiebing's *The Strange Death of Mistress Coffin*

"Not since Kenneth Roberts has anyone written of early New England life in such vivid and convincing detail."
—E. Annie Proulx, *The New York Times Book Review*

"It turns and twists upon itself, revealing complications and complexities of truth and character in suspects and sleuth. *The Strange Death of Mistress Coffin* is also a contribution to the ranks of fictional solutions to unsolved true crimes, such as we find in Tey's *Daughter of Time*, Satterthwait's *Miss Lizzie*, or Dexter's recent Gold Dagger–winning *The Wench is Dead*."
—*Mystery News*

"Begiebing illuminates 'the dark and wonderful intricacy' of the human heart."
—*Yankee*

"Like a good wine, this book has an aftertaste that lingers in the mind well after it is finished. It will not be quickly forgotten by any who read it."
—*Mostly Murder*

"This is not ordinary mystery. Just imagine *Peyton Place* as Hawthorne might have written it."
—*Booklist*

"Begiebing brings warmth and passion to a people who are often remembered for their rigidness and superstitions, as in *The Scarlet Letter* and the Salem witch hunts."
—*Portsmouth Herald*

"There is the stuff of a compelling motion picture in this imaginative and carefully written work. Great summer reading."
—*The Keene Sentinel*

"Begiebing has made bold use of conjecture and imagination, changing names and inventing characters to recreate a time and a place far removed from our own—but peopled by men and women whose emotions and motives are entirely recognizable today."
—*Valley News*

"A lean and supple tale of Puritan New England."
—*The Virginia Quarterly Review*

"This admirable first novel is dotted throughout with startling accounts of the tribulations suffered by superstitious Christians who settled the alien territory called America."
—*Publishers Weekly*

"A great achievement of imagination and research."
—*Boston Magazine*

"It is a riveting read—the crime's historical interest is as thrilling to ponder and compare with recent murders as it is to experience in fiction."
—*New Hampshire Premier*

"Tightly written and engaging."
—*The Seattle Times*

"A fresh look at the all too stereotyped Puritans."
—*Asheville Citizen-Times*

The Strange Death of Mistress Coffin

For Linda

The Strange Death of Mistress Coffin

a mystery

Robert J. Begiebing

Algonquin Books of Chapel Hill   *1996*

Published by
Algonquin Books of Chapel Hill
Post Office Box 2225
Chapel Hill, North Carolina 27515-2225
a division of
Workman Publishing
708 Broadway
New York, New York 10003

Design by Deborah Wong.

I would like to thank four good friends whose encouragement
and advice helped me to change the direction of my life and
write this novel: Bob Hoddeson, Loftus Jestin, Lawrence Kins-
man, and Wesley McNair.

LIBRARY OF CONGRESS CATALOGING-IN-PUBLICATION DATA
Begiebing, Robert J.
    The strange death of Mistress Coffin : a novel / by Robert J.
Begiebing.
      p.   cm.
    ISBN 0-945575-56-4: $17.95
    ISBN 1-56512-145-7: $ 9.95 paper
    1. Massachusetts—History—Colonial period, ca. 1600–1775
—Fiction.   I. Title.
PS3552.E372S7   1991
813'.54— dc20   90-19528
                                                       CIP

10   9   8   7   6   5   4   3   2   1

The wife of one Willi[x] of Exeter was found in the river dead, her
neck broken, her tongue black and swollen out of her mouth, and the
blood settled in her, the privy parts swollen, etc., as if she had been
much abused . . .
—The Journal of Governor John Winthrop of Massachusetts, 1648

The Strange Death of Mistress Coffin

Prologue

To Richard Browne, Esq.,
at the Sign of the Red Pony,
Salem.

Sir—

It was a most signal pleasure to regain the acquaintance of
so able a young man who proposes to venture among us in this
New England, a wilderness of riches sufficient to enable you to
restore that portion of your patrimony which agents of your
late father have so lamentably squandered. And though it was
a great sorrow to learn of the death of my old friend and dis-
tinguished associate, yet I came away in the firm hope that his
son might choose to cast his lot with us. Upon certain inquiries
into the especial advantages just now of our Pascataqua region
for the forest trade, I can report not only abundant opportunities for a young man of parts, but an occasion of some urgency that doubtless shall be the foundation of your engage-
ment with our plantation, of the settlement upon you of such
lands as those we discussed, and of your credible entrance into
the forest trade. In brief, you shall have the occasion to mark
your distinction among us. Just as I saw upon our meeting in
Salem on the twelfth day of last month that you, like your father, have grown into manhood with a quick and compassion-
ative mind, so do I hold in high confidence your uncommon

capacity and your occupation in the Inns of Court; for your familiarity with instruments and courtesies of the law equips you for such an errand as I have in mind and promises such welcome and excellent assistance as that which, I do freely confess, I just now stand so in need.

I refer to an incident that came to pass last spring, but the effects of which still linger among us, viz., the strange death of a local woman, Mistress Coffin, whose body was found after long search in the waters of our great inland bay. She had been stripped of every shred of clothing and tormented in a most unspeakable manner. We have been unable to gain an exact view of what occurred or who was the instrument of such violence. Our desire for resolution to this outrage has met with bitter disappointment. The dead woman's husband, you see, mysteriously withdrew his action against the man deemed likely to be responsible, directly or indirectly, for the poor creature's demise, one Jared Higgins. More, there was a certain lack of demonstration and thereupon the Courts and magistrates became otherwise occupied. Hence it is that litigation has insufficiently advanced, nay has entirely vanished. As a magistrate, however, my personal interest in justice concerning these events has rejuvenated, particularly in consideration of certain late occurrences. Jared Higgins has disappeared, his wife lives in a dark web of afflictions from causes unknown, and some are roused to fear and anger as much by the incapacity of the Court to assign guilt as by lingering circumstances that issue from the woman's death.

Our foremost concern will be the afflicted woman, Elizabeth Higgins. We must uncover the source of her torments and assuage them, and throw light upon the strange disappearance of her husband. Then perchance we may search the death of Mistress Coffin to its truest source.

It would seem but dark ambage were I to belabor the myriad

details in this epistle. I shall tell you what we have uncovered when we next meet, and Goody Higgins shall relate her trials and situation to you herself. Can you lay down your affairs and come away directly?

Now as to the merits of life in our plantation, several of which I touched upon when we met, I doubt not that you have discovered by your sojourn in the Bay Colony even unto this day the wealth that awaits those who would labor in this wilderness, far removed from the amenity of Mother England. If more bereft of comfort even than certain of those settlements through which you have passed since your landing at Boston, our small plantation, I assure you, is most excellently situated, well above the mouth of the Merrimac, upon the fish-laden river at Robinson's Falls which contributes to our great inland bay and, ultimately, the fine harbor at Strawberry Banke. We are merely a journey of a day or two, first by ship out of Boston or Salem and then by boat up into the bay and river. You need but hire your passage upon your arrival at the Banke and the boatmen will deliver you to us.

We boast the advantages of the most flourishing plantation of the Pascataqua, a region if remote yet furnished with good woods, springs, rivers, fish, fowl, game, fruit, the nearby multitudinous seas and commodious bays, harbors, and islands. The seaport, hardly a half-day's journey by water, thrives and cannot but continue to prosper in future Atlantic trade. The great pine dominates our forest, yet are there plentiful maple, ash, oak and other choice woods to increase the gathering trade in lumber, staves, and naval stores. To the rising prosperity of our plantation at the Falls let me recommend to you likewise the orderliness of our community itself—founded as it was by learned men of God who established laws, magistrates, and church from the outset—that might well serve as exemplar to less fortunate settlements in our region. Found to be within the patent and choosing to become allied with so prosperous and successful a benefactor, we, moreover, have lately come under the additional protection and regulation of Massachusetts Bay.

I shall not adventure to make this epistle any longer than to say how much I enjoyed all your news of England and have related these same to Mistress Cole, who even now remains struck by wonder. She sends you most affectionate greetings and lives in high anticipation of your likely arrival. She craves to speak further of news from Mother England, and to see again the son of one so cherished, a son now in the flower of his manhood but who, upon our last seeing him, was barely more than a child. Do say you will come to assist us.

Awaiting your reply, I remain, Sir, your affectionate servant,

JONATHAN COLE   Robinson's Falls, October 10

1648

Part I

Stay not among the wicked
Lest that with them you perish,
But let us to New England go,
And the Pagan People cherish.

—Song, "Invitation to
New Plantation," 1638

I

≋

"There is a man in town," Elizabeth Higgins said. She was watching Richard Browne carefully. "I do not think an Englishman by birth. Mr. Coffin, or so he is called. Last May, he hired my husband to convey Mistress Coffin in his canoe to Dover market."

"I do not know that settlement well," Richard Browne said.

"There's a large market there in early summer, by Third River. Some dozen miles from where we sit. She had been trading cattle, and other things. When her affairs were settled, she returned to the landing, or so it was said by one, and could not find my husband, Jared. Although he had said *he* looked for her! The hour grew late; he finally returned home."

"Was your husband not alarmed?"

"Of course! He went to Mr. Coffin. The man grew distracted, made accusations, raised a search party. It was later he finally laid charges. As a first step against my husband's breaking contract. Victory would have brought more serious accusations to the higher court. If she were forced overland, there were those who knew she carried on her some Indian wheat seed and other currency."

A four-foot back log settled in the fire. Elizabeth Higgins rose, moved farther to one side and opposite certain trivets and skillets and braziers standing on their spindling legs, and then adjusted the logs with a hay fork that had been leaning in the corner.

"And she never returned home," Browne stated.

"That's so. They finally found her ill-used body in the water. Whoever it was took more than her kernels and coin." She paused. The fire boomed from its adjustment and the wind at the chimney. "Pray spare me describing," she said. "Thus do our first parents bring calamities upon us."

He nodded, then said: "And thus we add unto them by cruelty in our own persons."

She looked narrowly at him. "Her husband was, I say, outraged. In all the back and forth, Jared made it clear that here was a woman to find her own trouble—I don't know just what he told them. Then Mr. Coffin added 'raising an evil report' to his list of charges." Elizabeth Higgins stopped and looked down.

"She was, in truth, a high-spirited woman," she finally continued. "Clever, more fond than her husband of trade and town affairs. And loose-tongued, Mr. Browne."

"I don't see why the unfortunate man would not pursue the satisfaction of saving his murdered wife's name, at least," Browne said, as if to himself.

"Perhaps he received satisfaction otherwise. Jared had done nothing. This man has powers others do not. Who can say where they end? He is respected for much learning." He saw hatred in her eyes. "The Devil will pick his bones!"

"Do you charge him, Goody Higgins, with *maleficium?*"

"I am tormented, Sir."

"Tormented?"

She paused to test Browne's eyes again, then added: "And signs. You might think me crazed if I speak everything."

He waited.

"Here's one then." She seemed suddenly defiant. "One night a strange animal—one I had not seen before but *like* a rat—got into the house and woke me. Its movement was sluggish. But its eyes shone hideous by the fire, and it had rows of terrible little sharp teeth. I dared not go near but woke young Jared, who after much effort drove it out. Since that night we have sweet bays by the door stoop."

"Your torments are by this man's hand or word?"

"Can you not see it, Sir?"

"You believe his ways darker than the Court. By what do you justify this belief?"

"The loss of my husband! Illness of children! Blasted fields! Do not such things justify?" She nearly spat out her list of injuries.

"Not always in themselves," he said calmly. "God's hand is at times ferocious."

"Yes, God's invincible fire may scourge any of us, Mr. Browne." She seemed near tears. "But I can only tell you, and Mr. Cole, my beliefs. I have seen and felt things no Christian woman should. My husband and many others the magistrates examined. But the proceedings are hidden."

Browne got up out of his chair and walked about the room. "The Lord too fires upon us, as you say. And there may be danger in assuming malignancy. Moreover, are not malignant persons His agents too, sent to try us, when He but loosens the chains? I wish to discover what is hidden, Goody Higgins, and by such pursuit to aid you. If as you say I discover some black corruption, so be it. But we must divide the day from the night."

She made no reply. He paced, looking at her from time to time. Noticing now also the shelves displaying her pewter and other ware, catching half-consciously the flicker of light off the brighter pots and kettles, the warming pan, the whitewashed walls between the brown timbers, he thought that despite her torment she managed to keep her house in order, the floors well sanded and scrubbed. In the corner beside the shelves stood her washbench, her broom, some large wooden tubs and

three baskets. In the shadows there seemed to be other implements of housewifery. Only the woman herself appeared disordered.

Was she beginning to trust him finally? Her resistance, her
suspicion, seemed to be slackening. They had been wary of
him, this woman and her son, from the very moment of his
arrival.

He compared her willingness to talk now to an hour ago when
he had arrived with Mr. Cole—a selectman and a magistrate,
now under the General Court of Massachusetts—at her small
gambrel-roofed house by the river. The boy had opened the
rough door just wide enough to peer out with both eyes and
hold a firebrand toward the faces of the snow-covered intrud-
ers. At Mr. Cole's voice, the boy opened the door and they
stepped in quickly against the storm. The woman, sitting directly before a voluminous fire, rose, placed some sewing work
on the settle, and turned toward them without speaking.

He had not been able to see her clearly by the light of the
fire and two knotty slices of burning candlewood held low in
the wall, their smoke rising slowly into the chimney. She pulled
the bedrug, draped over her shoulders, around her apron and
skirts.

But Cole, a large forceful man who dominated a room or a
conversation, immediately introduced Browne as "the newcomer
we spoke of, who has come to help."

Then she and Browne nodded at one another and the boy,
perhaps fourteen, moved closer to his mother. The brand he
held illuminated her face, and Browne noticed that her pale,
probably hazel, eyes were vivid, yet her face was that of a
woman who had gone without sleep, or had passed a dangerous
travail. Her erect body did not conceal her fatigue. As Cole
spoke with her of the storm, the state of her cordwood, the
town's desire for a minister, Browne watched her. In a better

moment, she might be a striking woman, he thought. She was perhaps thirty-one or two.

"It's all right, Jared," she had said to the boy as Cole made ready to leave. "You go to sleep now."

Browne now looked at Elizabeth Higgins again. "It must be very late," he said. "You need to rest, Goody Higgins."

"Sleep is a stranger to me." She began reciting from the Psalm: "'I am weary with my groaning, all night make I my bed to swim: I water my couch with tears.'"

He took up some further lines to encourage her: "'Let all mine enemies be ashamed and sore vexed: let them return and be ashamed suddenly!'"

She looked up at him, her face now like one returning from the dullness of sleep.

"I'll stop awhile if that would help," he said. "I can spend the time until daylight watching in that chair." He smiled. "You've given me much to think on."

"You will help me?"

"I will look into these matters. I will do everything I can to discover your husband and put your sufferings to rest. I am disquieted by these events, as is Mr. Cole. Why not sleep now, Goody Higgins, and let me wake?"

She had asked at first, before he had removed his great cloak, if he were to be their minister. But he had explained that he was called not by the Lord but by Mr. Cole, as an assistant in a certain Higgins-Coffin matter.

Then he added: "I am not a dissenter after the good Lincolnshire folk who settled here when the Synod banished Mr. Robinson and others." She had said nothing, so he continued. "I came over later to see after my father's ventures, which turned to losses."

"And just how is it Mr. Cole believes you may help, Sir?"

"I believe I may."

She looked unsatisfied. He continued: "I never took my degree at Cambridge, but went to Lincoln's Inn. Nor did I stay long enough to be called to the bar. Mr. Cole believes, however, that I might be of use here in divers ways, as I had been briefly at Salem. And to you."

"So you are among us now," she said. "You will not be asked to leave with such a protector as Mr. Cole." She stopped as if resting a moment. The glow of the fire fluttered over her face. "He has smoothed your way, Sir, just as he hopes you shall smooth mine." She looked him over and he quietly bore her scrutiny.

Must she not, he thought, see that he was a man of substance? His manner, after all, was gentle. His plum waistcoat and suit of full leather breeches, his indigo doublet lined with silken cloth and much brightly slashed cutwork must, he assumed, reassure her. He noticed her eyes on his embroidered gloves, which he had removed and placed in his lap. And did not his age speak to her in his favor as well? After all, unlike Mr. Cole he was of her own generation, conceivably her very age.

It was then that he had asked her whether she might tell him of her present troubles.

Now she was getting up and unwrapping the bedrug from around her. She placed it on the settle and looked at Browne.

"You have provisions for this season?" he asked.

"Yes. Some from planting grounds untouched, some in trade." She glanced upwards toward a single small chamber above. "Some bushels of grain, barley, and rye. Peas and beans as well. And some Indian wheat." She glanced toward the north end of the kitchen area at a small door. "And several flitches of bacon; there is cheese, cider, and butter in the dairy house." She sighed, as if the further words had fatigued her completely.

"Good then," Browne said. "This is all most curious. That

seat by the fire will comfort me while I think. You join your children now in sleep yourself. I'll be just here."

She settled some coals into a bright warming pan, saying as if speaking to herself: "Jared and I laid a fire in the other room this night." Then she turned and walked toward the open entryway to the only other room, or parlor, at ground level. At the threshold she turned again to Browne slowly, like one sleepwalking, and said: "I am very thankful, Mr. Browne; just now I need to sleep."

He was about to speak, but she slowly turned away. Just before disappearing into the room, she loosened her headcloth, and a thick coil of dark blond hair escaped to the small of her back. In the firelight the hair was abundant and lustrous, seeming to him so vigorous as to exist separately from the exhausted woman herself.

He glimpsed the shifting light of flames against the entry wall from a fireplace in the second room. He thought he heard the murmurings and turnings of sleeping children also. There was a soft rumble of firewood from the other room. Then the house grew still enough to redouble the noise of the snowstorm.

Browne pulled the bedrug around himself now and settled into the rude chair. He looked about the room, noticing more of the implements and materials of her labors. Her spinning wheels had been moved from the small chamber above, he imagined, closer to the hall fireplace. Bits of flax and what might have been cotton wool lay about by the wheels. He now saw on the floor a child's poppet made of some kind of straw or rags lying below a rough little go-cart of the sort toddlers would use to scoot about under their working mother's eye. These children, he thought, would have much more work to do in the absence of their father.

The fire swooped with a gust of wind. He smiled and murmured ironically:

> Let my Enchantments then be sung, or read.
> When Laurell spirits 'ith fire, and when the Hearth
> Smiles to it selfe, and guilds the roofe with
>   mirth. . . .

At times a child stirred or groaned in its sleep. But otherwise the compact house grew as quiet and concealed as the brackish shifting river hidden under its new cover of ice and deepening snow.

II

≈≈≈

Browne found the house of Balthazar Coffin upriver from the Higgins' house, well above the falls where the river turned fresh. It was an imposing house of two stories with an overhang in the front, a further half-story in the gable tops, and a long lean-to roof steeply sloping low into the first story in the rear. The central chimney was the largest in this settlement of houses with generous chimneys. The clapboards had turned an unusual light gray, as if made of unfamiliar wood, but the neatly riven roof shingles were burnished to a more familiar gray tinged with deep browns. Upon the front door lay a heavy iron knocker in the shape of a fantastical rampant boar.

Once inside, Richard Browne sat with Balthazar Coffin at a long library table constructed of a single plank of wood nearly three feet wide. The room was disordered by books lying about in trunks, in cases, and on the floor. The table top was cluttered with manuscripts and dried plant specimens. They had exchanged some desultory talk before sitting, and now a cup of warmed rum sat before each man. The late daylight that penetrated from without tinged the room with a solemn golden hue.

Coffin's beard was neatly trimmed after the Flemish style, and his eyes, though intelligent, were bleary. His dress was somber and plain, after the manner of grave doctors or ministers. And despite his leanness there was about him a certain solid self-possession—a force of identity that perhaps a master would have captured in the man's portrait—which was to Browne the most extraordinary thing about him.

"You have spoken to many others about the matter, Mr. Browne?" Coffin asked.

"Only to Mr. Cole and Goody Higgins."

"Has the woman gossiped every manner of tale?"

"She's much troubled."

"Ah, she is troubled."

"There is sleeplessness, some pain, and visions. Much trouble in head and heart."

"Mopishness," Coffin said. "Suffocation of the mother." He flipped his hand in dismissal. "Any number of things."

"I think not," Browne said. "But we shall see. Her losses distress her, certainly." Browne hesitated but there was no reply. "She's my first charge, so to speak. Mr. Cole asked that I look after her and the strange disappearance of her husband."

"You are staying with the Coles?"

"Just this first week until I arrange lodging. I come here to Robinson's Falls by way of mutual acquaintances, at Mount Wollaston, between my father and Mr. Cole. I seek to regain a substantial portion of my own lost patrimony. I would, you see, make my way here anew, make this wilderness yield up its riches. So I've placed myself at the service of Mr. Cole. I mean to plant a property to be granted me in the spring. My father had long prepared me to manage his estate."

"Your father is a peer?"

"He is now deceased. But was in the House of Commons, a man educated by the marketplace in the 'Exchange of Christendom,' as they say."

"Ah, you are frank, Mr. Browne."

"I do not relish subtleties in such circumstances. I have learned, moreover, that it's best to be direct when you seek information."

"Indeed. Well, Cole is a good ruler. The people respect him.

His concern is for all of us. Goody Higgins and her husband are another matter. There has been much talk of this, as you say, disappearance."

"And so will I have to speak with many others to gather direction. Of course I have heard of these tragic events of last . . . June? My deepest sympathies, Sir.

"There is much hidden," Browne went on. "And there may be a connection to Higgins' disappearance. I do not even know how people regard him now. Might he have been forced to flee by some? His culpability remains at issue, I take it."

"Indeed!"

"There are records of proceedings, inquiries? I understand you withdrew your action against him. . . ."

"Mr. Browne, you are an educated man. It is ever a joy to meet such a one in this wilderness. My household welcomes you. My library, such as it is, is at your disposal. But this matter of my murdered wife I cannot dwell on with good humor. She was my wife but five years. As your training tells you, where certain evidence is lacking or in contradiction with other testimony, and accusation is countered by less supportable charges, and so on into voids of speculation, then withdrawal is the better part of justice and sense. And where the name of one's wife is at stake, and a deceased wife at that, one's duty is to withdraw. Who murdered my poor Kathrin in such a manner I know not. That Higgins was negligent at the least, at fault in our contract, and ultimately slanderous is plain. But my case against him did not proceed as it should—too little to incriminate him.

"Higgins is a practical man, Mr. Browne. He is esteemed for his skill, not of mind but of hand. He has many cohorts, a strong reputation, audacity, courage. He has explored much in these parts, trades with the natives, wrests his living from this wilderness by shrewd doings and labors. Indeed, many owe him a debt. I may be the first to doubt his credibility."

"I see."

"I have absolutely no idea where he has got off to. But it is not unlike him. He has often been at some curious adventure or discovery."

"But on such occasions of absence he would tell his wife of his intentions, would he not?"

"So one might expect. Yet I cannot answer for their habits, for what is between them."

Browne sipped his rum. This man Coffin seemed forthright. There was, however, a sorrow that seemed to hang like a vestige of illness about his vigorous body.

"I can tell you little more, Mr. Browne. My wife was as good as any, but a sharp wit and without reticence."

"Can you tell me of the inquiries arising from your action?"

"The inquiry became protracted. I will supply you a list of those connected with it." He got up to gather pen and paper. "Might you not discover something in my favor as well?" he said, seating himself again.

While Coffin wrote in a flowing, clear hand, Browne asked: "Where are the records of these inquiries now? Among the Norfolk County Court papers?"

"Whatever records remain. A magistrate of the Associate Court, one Dr. Cotton, seems to administrate these sessions and records. Without sufficient cause to pursue action for more serious crimes—for 'trials of life, limbs, or banishment,' as the magistrates say—the records at Boston would bear no fruit. The absence of a criminal case must be why Cole called upon you. My initial action was heard at the Hampton Quarterly Session. You might inquire there, or try Salisbury if nothing turns up." He finished writing his list and handed Browne the paper.

Browne rose. "I'm sorry to have troubled you with painful events."

At the front door, Browne added, "*Absit invidia*, Mr. Coffin."

"Of course not, Mr. Browne. My household and library welcome you."

Browne stepped over the threshold to the ground. "That is pleasant indeed, having left behind in England my own library, which I plan to recover at some later time. I have a particular collection of our English poets—famous and unknown—that perhaps one day I may show to you."

"Of course, you won't find much of that here I'm afraid; few of our recent poets, certainly. But what I have is at your pleasure. Our plantation needs men like you. *Age quod agis,* Mr. Browne. Wisdom go with you."

As Browne made his way back to the Cole's house, the snow on the frozen river, burying the marsh grass and covering the thickets, was reddened by the final rays of sun. The air was turning sharp, and a flutter of small wintering birds was gathering the thin warmth and protection of hemlock trees. He recalled now how it was the air that had struck him most upon his arrival in the New World two years ago. The peculiar, pleasant odors at each season enlivened him as if medicinal in whatever month of the year.

He passed the gristmill, now quiet in the freezeup, its huge wheel and buckets hung with snow and icicles on the opposite, east bank of the river. Higher up by the second falls on the west bank the new sawmill, long and narrow, open at both ends, was glowing and still in its sheath of unweathered shingles.

Goody Higgins' accusations puzzled him now. Could this man he had just met have presented nothing more than a mask? The man reveals no more than he has to, Browne thought, but I think there is no *maleficium,* not by this man's hand. He would have to search the court records.

III

~~~~~

The Examination and Deposition of Jared Higgins,
This Fifteenth Day of June, Anno Domini 1648,
Being Sworn, saith:

My name is Jared Higgins, planter at Robinson's Falls since
1640. I have thirty-four years, am married, and previously of
Nottinghamshire, England, Parish Gotham; thence of Charleston, Massachusetts Bay in New England.

Assistant Magistrates: Now, Goodman Higgins, the events at Dover
Market suggest on the face of them negligence on your part.
You are aware of the divers actions to be brought against
you at the next session of the Court. Would you explain, as
you understand them, the terms of your agreement with
one Mr. Balthazar Coffin.

Higgins: It was all plain, Your Honors. I to receive three percent of the sale price of several head of cattle upon completion of her affairs. For that sum, I was to convey Mistress
Coffin by my canoe along the river and bay to market at
Dover, and home again. Twenty-fifth of May, I believe it
was.

Mgts.: And you discharged such agreement?

H: I could not, Sirs.

Mgts.: Could not?

H: She never returned to the wharfs, Your Honors.

Mgts.: You both had appointed a time?

H: Roughly, Sirs. I was there early and stayed late.

Mgts.: Had you looked well? Had you made inquiries? Had you any conjectures from such inquiries?

H: I went to market myself, Sirs, on my own accounts. Then I bought a dram at the ordinary, spoke with some who know me. When at the time we agreed to meet she did not appear, I tied my canoe aways beyond the wharf and went back to seek her, guessing she dallied at market once the trading was over.

Mgts.: You had no success?

H: I saw her not, Sirs.

Mgts.: What thought you? And what were your actions when you found her not?

H: I was in the dark, Your Honors. I asked after her. Some had seen her at market, but not leaving, alone or with anyone. But she had her ways, Sirs, to charm the beard from Beelzebub, ask me. Proud of her sharp bargaining and of her husband's faith in like accomplishments. She wasn't the kind to hide her skill. More like to hold it up for all to know. And more than that, she wasn't above the pride of woman, truth be known.

Mgts.: But her absence, Higgins, how considered you that?

H: Darkness, as I say, to me, Sirs. I searched; I waited. I presumed a sudden notion took her to be away. Why? With who? I know not. Perhaps she struck a passion in one among the crowd. In time, I came to trust only that she lost herself.

Mgts.: You insinuate, man? Be clear on these matters. Keep to what you know to be true, by your sworn oath.

H: Sirs, I left for home without payment promised me. Thus am I also out my fee. I know only what I have said, Sirs. The day was hot, as if Nature had been wrenched in May to some late summer's noon. Once we were well upon the water she dropped her cloak. Then unfastened her cap.

Loos'd her bodice, free as that. There was such heat I pulled my shirt loose as well. But you, and Mr. Coffin too, ought to know she left herself too undone, and caught the eye of more than one waterman and planter along the quay.

And I to wait for such a one 'til the sound of Doomsday? Agreements are kept so long only as both parties keep to measures.

I know nothing more. I heard her fate like all the rest. The marks on her body once found, the sores of lust, the bite of serpents old as the earth.

Mgts.: Enough.

You know nothing more of what became of Mistress Coffin, upon your oath, Higgins?

H: That is so, Your Honors.

Be there much mystery here? Pride, Sirs. And Vanity. A woman's curse, Devil's tools, man's humiliation, as we know. What temptings might not lead to what sorrows? What might not befall one so near the snares and pits?

Wait, Sirs.

Had you seen her you would agree Balthazar Coffin must be unwitted to let such a woman, a widow and his wife, stray so far to market. He had best think on his own suit in such light. Would not your own advice and wisdom steer him toward his own negligence?

Ask those who know me—there are many. There is no evil done this woman, or any other, here!

Mgts.: Neither the causes nor the wits of Mr. Coffin are the question at this moment.

H: Indeed so, Sirs! But, with respect, he paints her a model Christian soul. So she may seem to him. Yet if in the sight of others that which one takes for truth is not upheld, then neither Truth nor Law stay sightless to let such accusations fall against me.

Her nature was otherwise, Sirs. Ask after that.

Mgts.: Cease this rant. You know nothing more of this woman's disappearance and end?

H: Only that there was some enchantment over her ripe and plucky beauty, Sirs. I make no mistake: something in her ways to disturb Christian men and women, truth be known.

Mgts.: Your answer is no, Higgins? Nothing else? Is that so?

H: Yes, Your Honors, my answer is I know nothing more.

Mgts.: Then keep yourself available for further examination at the pleasure of the Court. You are scheduled for the September session in Mr. Coffin's action.

IV

~~~~~

By early March, Richard Browne, wrapped against the cold, sat at a small table poring over court records, searching for any possible clarification of Mistress Coffin's death. With his gloved hands he occasionally scribbled notes to himself. On still another piece of paper he listed document numbers and titles as he flipped through them, reading rapidly. On top of a separate small set of papers he had placed Higgins' deposition.

He sat alone in the cold room, his breath smoking before him. An elderly clerk had unlocked the door for him after Browne had completed a lengthy interview with Dr. Cotton. Cotton—a large, gouty, red-faced, magisterial person—was a fellow Cambridge man. Although he had in common with Browne, as it turned out, several academic acquaintances, his Cambridge years predated Browne's. Cotton had attended Sidney College as a classmate of Cromwell.

At the moment Browne was feeling discouraged. He was surprised at how little he had been able to discover here. There was nothing to explain more fully Coffin's sudden retraction of his cause against Higgins. Nor was there anything to clarify Higgins' reciprocal retraction of his counter action for slander against Coffin. Nor was any greater light, finally, shed upon the woman's disappearance and death. Higgins was indeed implicated in nothing more than possible negligence and contractual failures. The examination and deposition of Coffin clarified further only certain relations between families in the town and certain features of the settlement's governance.

Only the examination of one Darby Shaw, a cohort of Higgins, intrigued Browne. He could not say just why he was so intrigued. But he placed Shaw's deposition on top of those papers containing Higgins' deposition and sat back. He was tired from picking his way through it all, not only the record of the Court but the waste books filled with preliminary records. He had passed through deeds, inventories of estates, contracts, attested copies, apprentices' indentures, inquests, and writs. His mind wandered; his body grew slack with fatigue.

There had been, of course, moments of entertainment. He had stumbled here through all the ancient passions and vanities, the comic oddities, the upstart rebellions and enduring desires given expression in the New World. Many had been presented for being disguised with drink. One dissident woman appeared again and again among the pages. She had threatened to tear one man's flesh to pieces; she had displayed her contempt of the Court and magistrates. Browne had skimmed through charges and counter charges of abusing the watch or other persons as proud saucy boys, malapert boys, rascally and jackanapes boys. There were persons brought up for failure to train or attend meeting; for stealing and vandalizing cocks of hay; for making an uproar in the street (wives as well as husbands); for theft of apples, petticoats, and money; for "second drunks," selling strong waters without a license, excessive drinking, vain mirth and singing with frequent oaths, lascivious songs and gestures; for suspicion of adultery; for sleeping in time of public ordinances and breach of Sabbath; for beating wives, husbands, or neighbors.

One wag was sentenced to the whipping post for saying he intended to join the church to have his dog christened. There was a group of young husbands presented for going into the woods with liquors to sing and shout at an unseasonable time of night, thereby occasioning their wives and some others to go out and search for them. Another wife told the Court to kiss her arse.

Amidst all of this Browne had found Higgins v. Coffin for slander and Coffin v. Higgins for defamation, raising an evil report of his deceased wife, and breach of a promise to carry his wife in a canoe to market, yet not bringing her up in the canoe again. And he had discovered, eventually, three preliminary depositions relating to the case.

But it was Shaw's deposition alone that Browne paid the clerk to copy for him at the end of the day, promising to return in a fortnight for it with the remainder of the clerk's fee. Browne was due to return to Robinson's Falls the next day.

His notes bundled in his bag, Browne hurried in the cold, murky evening to the ordinary where he had also been able to engage a room through the keeper's wife. He thought of his supper by the fire, of a bowl or two of sack, of his bed and warming pan.

Later, his belly full, his body relaxed from the drink and the fire, Browne lay curled up in his bed under thick bedclothes, squinting by dim flickering light one last time at his documents list, hoping for some hint of an unseen pattern, or some missed connection between the players in the Higgins-Coffin drama.

He saw the labor before him. He now found a certain pleasure in trying to tease out meaning and order. He saw that he would have to cast a wider net of interviews. He would have to probe Coffin and Goody Higgins far more than he had, come to know them and draw out all the implications of their stories, and compare their stories more closely with others'. All the implications, all the hidden turnings of past actions, seemed to demand of him some resolution now. And the missing Jared Higgins seemed to beg for pursuit. That was the major task his benefactor Cole had set him to, just over a month ago.

He knew well enough that despite his friendship with Cole, any outsider had to demonstrate his usefulness to a settlement, any newcomer would be accepted only after scrutiny. Yet the violent death of this woman had already begun to take on a force of its own in his mind. Here was something worthy of his solution. Each interview and document, however unrevealing, deepened his fascination with these people, their circumstances, their relations. He felt intuitively just now that the solution would be shockingly simple, like some soon-to-be-grasped mathematical principle still teasing about the portals of a theoretician's mind.

Browne snuffed out the lantern and slid deep into the warm bedclothes. His drift toward sleep glowed with wine-touched confidence. Find the woman's husband. And the truth. The very thing to do.

After all, he had seen his family's fortunes squandered in considerable measure on New World ventures, had journeyed to reclaim his losses from the hands of incompetents or, worse, thieves, and had failed to recoup a single loss yet had resolved to begin remaking that fortune in a world free of the props and limitations of homeland and family. He, therefore, upon his arrival at a remote plantation in mid-winter needed something worthy to fascinate and represent him while awaiting the promises of spring.

V

THE EXAMINATION AND DEPOSITION OF DARBY SHAW,
this twentieth day of June,
anno Domini 1648,
Being Sworn saith:

My name is Darby Shaw, carpenter and trader, of Robinson's Falls since 1641. I am thirty-five, widowed, previously of Nottinghamshire, England, Parish Gotham.

Assistant Magistrates: Are you not an acquaintance or associate of Jared Higgins?

Shaw: Known him most of my life, Your Honors. We were boyhood friends. After my second wife, Mary, died in childbirth he helped me settle at the plantation. It was our first child, and we but married two years.

Mgts.: Your association with Higgins extended to trade, did it not?

Shaw: It did. We'd hunt and explore together. We've claimed some intervals and upland meadow together, know the best hunting lands from our travels and from the savages. Yes, he has helped me in the fur trade now and again.

Whenever one of us needs help in some labor we ask one another first, provided there is payment enough for two.

Mgts.: You have trusted each other completely?

Shaw: Aye to that, Your Honors. Better than any other.

Mgts.: Your trade is directly through the savages? And you, as well as Higgins, consort with them and are welcomed by them?

Shaw: You can find better quarter with most savages than with some English plantations, Your Honors. More than one have remarked on that.

Mgts.: So they may have, Shaw. But our question is the extent of your trafficking and living with the savages.

Shaw: Well, in my case, much. Fur is my trade, now, Sirs. When I first came to the plantation I built and enlarged fair houses and mills. Fishing shallops even, everything there was to be built. But the fur proved ready and sovereign. Beaver, otter, musquash, martin, fox, raccoon—anything that'll bring the price.

Higgins comes along when he can spare the time, for about a third of my return.

Myself, I travel and live with the lords of the soil weeks at a time, mostly in these parts. But I've been known as far as the interior lakes and all up the coast of Maine.

We run a trading wigwam too. Moved some thousands of skins through last year on the beaver trade alone. Most of our corn comes in that way—worth five or six shillings a bushel.

Mgts.: Was Higgins well known among the savages?

Shaw: Times he has lived with them as I have. With some there is deeper trust than with others. But we've always abided the law—no trade in strong waters nor firearms, if that's your meaning. Where trust is sound by proved trade, there is no necessity to break English law. Higgins' relations with savages are less than mine. But he knows their ways well.

Mgts.: Then it is true as has been said of you that you have lived as a White Indian?

Shaw: I don't deny that. For a time. But I live at Robinson's

Falls. When I return to the savages it is for the sake of my trade, and theirs. All benefit. I do, the savages do. I need not tell Your Honors the gain to England, to all Europe, from the wealth of these forests.

Mgts.: And Higgins too has lived as a White Indian?

Shaw: That too is true, though not so much as I. No one calls him so, as some have called me.

Mgts.: Shaw, now think you hard upon your oath. Might there be some savage barbarity here in this violence to Mistress Coffin?

Shaw: For a pound or two? A few kernels? They live not by such need. Nor inclined to such doings as befell the good woman. To what purpose? Our trade and relations with the savages is good. Better here than in plantations to the south. Even where peaceable relations are maintained. There is less treachery because more sharing the return.

Mgts.: Higgins had no entanglements to bring on such barbarity? Had Higgins, to your knowledge, ever pursued this woman? Sought her favors?

Shaw: To my knowledge there were neither adulterous favors sought, denied, nor granted. These are matters I know nothing of. Nor did he ever speak of her particularly.

Mgts.: To your knowledge was there ever an instance of Higgins soliciting the favors of any woman?

Shaw: Any woman?

Mgts.: Upon your sworn testimony.

Shaw: Well, 'Honors, he was as true to his good wife as most, I believe. To be honest, I know only of an instance with an Indian squaw. There was a misunderstanding. He had thought the woman a maid. And having been away from his family so long, was tempted that her company would do no harm. Yet later the woman confronted him with her husband. Higgins saw his mistake and sought reparations. With my help we made the husband understand Higgins' mistake. He, the husband, had threatened to carry the matter to our own magistrates, saw it as an assault. He knew adultery to be a serious crime under our laws.

Our explanations along with some gifts in peace and good faith prevailed.

Mgts.: And there are no other adulterous instances to your knowledge?

Shaw: None, Sirs. He was, like any, likely to turn his eye on a beauty. Or like any other to comment on some passing jade or goodwife who caught his eye. But no instances such as this one.

Mgts.: Nor any bestial or sodomistical filthiness?

Shaw: None, Sirs. None.

Mgts.: Keep yourself available for further examination, Shaw. And to bear witness at the pleasure of the Court. Take no journeys mind you, even for your trade.

VI

~~~

Upon his return to Robinson's Falls, Browne spoke with Cole further about certain inhabitants of the settlement and then interviewed Darby Shaw. He found Shaw in his one-room bachelor's cottage, sullenly awaiting the approach of weather warm enough to make extended travel to distant fur trading outposts practical. The inside walls of his cottage were hung with clean, well-oiled tools—hand saws, whip saws, files, wrests, augers, chisels, gimlets, froes, hammers, felling and broad axes.

Thin, compact, tawny, Shaw was a peculiar-looking man. His appearance was less that of an Englishman than a French trader or cross-breed. His long hair was kept in place by a leather mechanism. His clothing was made of coarse animal skins worn with the fur side against his body, just as an Indian would reverse his clothing, fur inward, during cold seasons. Yet at the moment he also wore over the skins an English laboring man's short brown fustian frock.

Shaw seemed fatigued to Browne, despite his wiry strength, from his day spent building a new gristmill. And he was not pleased to have a stranger questioning him again about his friend Jared Higgins. He knew nothing about this, nothing about that. Browne knew better, so he tried another tack.

"You know Goody Higgins well?" Browne asked.

"I do. She is my friend's wife. Why would I not?"

"Indeed. Have you any idea of her torment over the loss of her husband?"

"Of course. What do you take me for? I feel much for the woman. I help as I can."

"So she has told me," Browne said.

"Have you questioned Coffin and Mr. Cole?" Shaw asked.

"I have."

"And you see no greater torment from that direction?"

"Coffin? Thus far, I have not."

"Then you had better look deeper."

"What do you know of the matter?" Browne asked.

"Only that the woman is unnaturally tormented."

"And such torments you lay to Mr. Coffin?"

"He would have reason, by his lights."

"Yet you have no other or clearer reason to believe these torments come from Mr. Coffin?"

"You need ask me that, Mr. Browne? From what you have said you know all the circumstances. You offer some other explanation of the source of her torments?"

"Such things do not always arise from dark arts."

"Then you lay to God these horrors?"

"I do not presume to lay anything to God, Shaw. And I am careful in laying mischief to anyone. I have seen no horrors. Have you?"

"No. But I trust the word of Higgins, and of his wife."

"So I understand."

"You understand?"

"I have been on these researches for some time now, as you see. My belief is that Higgins is alive. I come for your help, Shaw. I am here to help Goody Higgins. That is my charge from Mr. Cole. I wonder if we might not do better, even for her sake, to quit this play of wit and be direct."

"I know nothing of Higgins' disappearance. You think I would not have told his wife if I did?"

"Might you at the least tell me of these torments as you understand them, Shaw?"

"They belong to Goody Higgins. I'll not tamper with them."

"I seek only to learn more about the nature of your laying their source to Coffin. A woman is murdered. The man most recently associated with her, and then his wife, experience ill fate and visions. Does that lead us to the victim's husband? Does that demonstrate his necromancy? It is a possibility, of course. But might not murder, suit, investigations all distract minds? Might not nature kill and blast?"

Shaw's body seemed to rise up out of his fatigue. "Here is a dream, then," he said. "Tell me it comes from nature, or God. It is Higgins', not his wife's. Those she can tell you herself."

Shaw leaned back on his bench against the wall. He looked directly at Browne. "In his sleep Higgins dreams he is planting an orchard. He takes care in the cultivation of seven trees that they might bear autumn fruit. Still, one tree dies, and it is not clear why. This tree bleeds a little, real heart's blood. The other trees flourish.

"Another night the dream returns, yet only after one of the children, little Mehitabel, is taken away by violent illness. This time Higgins returns to the dream orchard and another of the six remaining trees dies off. It is exactly as before—sudden, the bleeding, without clear cause."

"Then a second child?" Browne interrupted.

Shaw ignored his question. "Higgins wakes up crying. He tells his wife. They are confused. Helpless and filled with sorrow. They examine the children. Each of the six seems well in his sleep. But each night Higgins cannot sleep. He fears the dream, another dead child. He sleeps briefly each night and wakes up sweating, exhausted. Just when he and his wife begin to believe death will not follow, the second child falls ill, Anne, his youngest daughter, and dies of the same fever and bloody flux within a week.

"It was then that Higgins fled. It was as if he were killing his own children by his dreams. He wasn't going to wait for another dream, and death."

"These two alone died, finally?" Browne asked, although he knew the answer.

"Two of their seven. That he fled seems to have worked it. He felt as if some poison were in him. Might not his far and sudden removal put a stop to this power from wherever it came? What other way lies before a desperate and helpless father?"

"His dreams have stopped?" Browne asked.

"I know not where he is, alive or dead."

"Come, Shaw. If you can't tell me where, at least tell me whether the dreams have stopped. The children are alive now. We may need to watch and protect them. Surely he would wish us to!"

"They have stopped," Shaw said. He looked down at the table board.

"Ah," Browne answered. He remained silent. After some moments he asked: "He has not returned?"

"He *cannot!*"

"Can we help him?"

"He has decided to help himself."

"How so?"

"That I am pledged by my life not to say. And will not. I have broken my promise. Tell *no one* he is alive. The lives of his wife and children depend on our silence. Speak nothing of this to a soul."

Shaw looked up grimly. His face told what agony he was in to regain his secret and promise.

Browne felt a murderous moment pass between them and shifted his legs to brace himself. But Shaw only slammed his fist on the table. Then Shaw lay his head, face down, in the circle of his arms, and Browne left without another word.

VII

≋

In late April when scattered groups of coastal New England Indians returned to fishing encampments on the seaward reaches of the rivers, and when the first tumult of spring run-off had subsided enough to make canoe travel practical, Browne and Shaw set off by river and bay to find Jared Higgins among the Indians. Early in the voyage down the tidal river into the bay they were tracing the exact route Jared Higgins and Kathrin Coffin had traveled nearly a year before.

Browne had kept Shaw's secret. Not even Elizabeth Higgins knew from him anything of her husband. Between Shaw and Browne there had grown a trust, if no friendship. Gradually, Shaw had come to agree to take Browne in search of Higgins. Might not Browne and Higgins together, Shaw had been persuaded to believe, find a way out of the apparent dilemma that Higgins must either remain in secret exile or condemn his family by return?

They had passed the estate of the wealthiest man in the Piscataqua Plantations, one of the original pioneers sent by no less than Captain Mason himself to oversee the settlement and exploitation of the region. It seemed an estate in progress, but even now the most imposing monument to civilization in the wilderness that Browne had seen north of Boston. The owner's expanding manor house, his gardens, cornfields, orchards, pastures, timber lots, barn and outbuildings—all sweeping along the gently-rising grassy west bank of the river—struck Browne as the realization of what would have seemed until now an impossible ideal. He was unaware of his gaping until Shaw, behind him, laughed.

They had passed down through the thousands of alewives running upstream. Now on the first summery morning of the year, their canoe floated into the mouth of the river opening into Great Bay. Sunshine glittered off the spreading water with intolerable brightness. Salt marshes spread wide the margins between forest and water. The men saw the huge distant trees of the forest, open and parklike, the home of deer and fowl. In the labor and heat of paddling, Browne had removed his linen shirt. The cool, rank air from the water and marshes bathed their bodies. Across the bay thousands of geese were taking off and landing on the bright water. Swans glided by, their wings whistling overhead.

From time to time one of the men would dip into a small cask to drink cider from his earthen mug. As their canoe slid along one shore of the bay, birds croaked, chattered, and sang their spring polyphonies. Big trees with moss-covered trunks grew closer to the water's edge now, only occasionally pushed back by an interval of marsh or mead. As the canoe approached several white pines two hundred and fifty feet tall, three great herons broke from the tree closest to the shore.

But for a hunter's isolated and empty wigwam, there was no sign of humanity in this portion of the bay. As the morning wore on towards noon, the men spotted an occasional, distant fishing shallop, and once they saw a lone man fowling from a canoe, but they traveled in the signs and sounds of wilderness only. At midday they paddled to a small island to eat and rest.

They ate in silence, at times drawing from their rundlet of beer. Browne lay back on a soft rotting log to doze. They were both anxious to complete the search for Higgins, yet they lazed a while longer in the sun. Shaw was miserable in his leisure, a man who had been protecting his friend from evil, who had broken the ring of protection, and who now had to face the friend. Wouldn't the friend lash out, like an animal protecting its family? Yet Shaw, like Browne, lay in the sun, digesting his food, relaxing his muscles and back. Each man waited for the other to suggest they take up the journey. The spring sunlight was the narcotic through which they contemplated the encounters ahead and the hoped-for resolutions.

Browne dozed in and out of consciousness. He breathed the scent of brackish water mingled with pine, hints of spring blossoms, and damp earth. Sea gulls keened overhead. A fish hawk called out over the water from a tree on the island. The three-beat moan of some creature, perhaps a dove, eased across the water from the nearby shore. Then Browne fell completely asleep.

He was somewhere on the Mediterranean, in a white house with open windows and doors. Sunlight and warm wind stirred through the building. He was entirely alone in the bright house, which he now realized was situated on a hill or cliff overlooking the sea. There was a noise outside, as if someone had kicked stones. An old man whose hair, skin, and tunic were completely white entered the house, ignoring Browne. The old man began to paint dark murals on the white walls and to speak in a language unknown to Browne. Browne tried French, Italian, and Latin on the old man, who only laughed. Finally, he turned his pallid face on Browne and said in English: "Even though you are entering the middle of life, see how you must still struggle, fight, and learn. . . ." There was a sharp kick to the sole of Browne's foot, and he woke up.

"You snore worse than the lean of an old ship," Shaw was saying. He kicked Browne's boot again. "We must be moving. I fell asleep myself."

Browne did not get up at first. He wiped his face with his hand and breathed deeply. Then he struggled into a sitting position, still confused. Finally, he managed to stumble to the edge of the island and splash water against his sweaty face.

Later, they began to move inland up one of the several tidal rivers that emptied into the bay. The river gradually narrowed and the trees began to arch above them into a shadowy canopy. Shaw threw in a line to catch their evening meal. They surprised more than one bear wading about in the shallows for teeming fish. Within half an hour the empty spaces in the bottom of their boat were so filled with fish that they pulled in their line. Shaw said that they would make camp below a falls he knew just ahead, and portage around the falls in the morning. As they moved closer to the falls the men heard cheering and singing.

"They'll be there," Shaw said.

"That noise?" Browne asked.

"Indians. Spring encampment; they're celebrating."

By the time they arrived at the Indian camp the Indians were awaiting them. Browne saw a large cleared area beneath a few giant trees, about which reed-covered wigwams were scattered. The only noise he heard now was the falls, which the English had not yet dammed for their mills, and where now and then a fish leapt out of the boil. The Indians were brightly dressed, especially the young women and certain of the men (whom Browne took to be sagamores) whose bodies and hair were bedecked with fine blue and white beads. Children in turkey-feather cloaks scurried about the camp or giggled at these Englishmen in the canoe.

Once the canoe landed the Indians greeted Shaw as one they knew. There were preliminary courtesies; then the Englishmen were shown to a central fire by which fish on racks were being smoked and cooked. The games and contests were ended, Browne conjectured, by their arrival. But it became clear that feasting would soon begin. Most of the women, still in a playful mood, began to cook with a menagerie of pots and kettles—some of clay, some of copper and French in design, others of iron and more distinctly English. Only the children continued to chase one another and play, their laughter breaking the relative quiet now.

Shaw contributed their own catch to the feast. He spoke to a group of men in Algonquian dialect, translating bits of conversation for Browne when it might be of interest. As they began to be seated, the men produced clay and stone pipes painted with fantastic designs and almost human images. As they began smoking tobacco, Shaw turned to Browne and said: "I doubted they might be here this season, things have changed so much for the Indian these last ten years."

"English and disease," Browne said.

"And tribal war. Some have removed farther west," Shaw said. "Eat your fill."

Browne could not join in the talk that continued throughout the eating. He might have been a deaf man at a stranger's marriage feast. But once the eating abated, Shaw turned to Browne again and said: "Higgins is not among them. They tell me he is with the Penacooks, several days journey upriver and through the forest. They will likely be by the lakes. How far up country are you willing to go to find him?"

"As far as need be," Browne answered.

"There is no other choice," Shaw said and turned away.

Browne heard owls and wolves far away in the woods. Then the dancing started, absorbing the sounds of the night. Shaw joined in the celebration, seeming to abandon himself to the chants and rhythms as completely as the Indian men and women. There was much in their adorned nakedness, in their gestures and movements, that disturbed and excited Browne. But he merely watched, eating some final portions placed before him. Much later, both Englishmen grew tired and, at their request, were led to a wigwam where the opened area met the margins of the deeper woods.

Pleased now with the sweet fullness of his stomach and his dry, comfortable bed of animal skins thrown over flooring raised a foot off the earth, Browne felt his exhausted body glide toward dreamless sleep as he listened to Shaw's deep breathing and to the songs of Indians celebrating the renewal of their earth's gifts.

VIII

≋

Able to travel by canoe only part of the distance to the village of the Penacook, Shaw and Browne finally had to strike out through the wild woods. During their three-day journey Shaw explained some of what he knew of this tribe. The two men talked during their breaks for rest or meals, conserving their energy while they moved by saying little and concentrating on their way through the woods. What intrigued Browne most during these conversations was what Shaw said of the sachem Tantpasiquineo, a true Indian prince and powah, or magician, who could raise a living serpent from a snakeskin, create ice in summer and fire from ice, make trees dance, and heal the dying back into life.

Browne also wondered how Shaw kept track of where they were going. They were moving at a near trot without any apparent hesitation.

"Indian path," Shaw said. "Thousands of years old. Unless accustomed, white men don't see these paths. They lead in every direction through the forest."

"I see no paths, no markings or indicators."

"Just as I say," Shaw returned. "You'd as well look for churches and fair houses as for milestones and way markers among the Indians. Although such is what many English do."

They never stopped for long because of the swarms of black-flies. In the interior these "black devils," as Shaw called them, were a worse plague even than the mosquitoes in the humidity of mid-summer near the coast. Browne especially suffered, until Shaw gave him some greasy, malodorous ointment out of the little he had left in a container made from a small animal's skull.

When they finally approached the village Browne saw wigwams along the lakeshore and, far into the forest, cooking fires and groups of people. There were scores of fish and pelt-drying racks scattered about; in certain places of the visible lake were fishing weirs. Here was an Indian city, unlike any of the clusters of savage dwellings Browne had ever seen. Were they all gathering here under the great sachem against the onslaught of their afflictions? Or was this an ancient city? Certainly, he thought, as they moved into the village, this might well be the place for a man in search of anonymity and security from his white brethren.

Here too Shaw was known. The men Shaw spoke to seemed to understand and accept the Englishmen's purpose. They agreed to a meeting on another day with Higgins. For now the Englishmen were again invited to join the seasonal celebration.

When the eating ended that night, an old man rose before Browne and began to chant. These, Shaw explained, were ancient Indian tales he was reciting. To Browne they seemed mellifluous and strangely rhymed, yet incomprehensible.

"This is the story of the father deer," Shaw told Browne in a quiet voice. Browne looked at him blankly.

"The deer has power for them. These people have gathered into one of the last strongholds of the northern forest in the territory of Massachusetts and the southern Province of Maine. Many groups still spread throughout the forests, but here is a settlement impregnable by its numbers and most powerful leader. Not even the Mohawks dare provoke them now."

"The Mohawks are enemies of these savages?" Browne asked.

"And the most feared. But Tantpasiquineo defies them. He pays no tribute. And when two Mohawks were caught skulking nearby, they met their end. Tantpasiquineo returned a severed hand from each man to their own prince."

"What became of these wretches?"

"They were tortured to death, in the savage manner. It is worse for an enemy who falls into their hands for they are masters of keeping him alive under his torments."

"May we never become their enemies!" Browne said.

"We are brothers in trade. It is only the English who may break the partnership, as some even now have. There must be trust on both sides."

"Or we will be subject to their barbarisms."

"Reap as we sow."

After a moment Shaw added: "But their practices can be no worse than the torments of the Turks or Persians, or Christians come to that. Yet these Indians may exceed them all in prolonging an enemy's misery."

"By what method?" Browne asked.

"By divers practices. The common thing is to bind the victim to a tree and begin by cutting off one finger and toe at a time, then the hands, feet, arms, legs at each joint, until only the trunk remains. The flow of blood is each time stanched by searing the wound with fiery coals. Near the end they flay the flesh from the head and place more embers like a cap on the head. If his heart is still alive they cut it from his breast."

"A fiendish horror," Browne said and shook his head.

"More so for anyone awaiting similar treatment, who must watch and hear the screams of the victim, whose songs increase the next victim's terror."

Browne grew silent. The old poet's melodious chant flowed into the night. Browne recalled what he had been told of Boston and the southerly reaches of New England during the Pequod wars, a limited uprising the English had been able to beat down.

It seemed to him at the moment an historical eccentricity rather than a prophecy of the relations between the light and dark races. They cooperated in a trade now that the English were extending to the marketplaces of the world, a vast market, Browne believed, that could only grow in size and stability.

But Shaw's words recalled for him stray images of the old war. A man had once described for Browne the conditions of vigilance in the dank, gray-clouded Boston of late August, 1637. He saw again the smoke blowing about the town where grim, armed men received and displayed the gruesome trophies of war sent by friendly tribes and British excursions: the wampum, the squaws, the blood-clotted heads and hands of Pequod chiefs and warriors. And these sights and odors of war had stirred men to greater religious fervors, the trials and banishments resulting from the Antinomian controversy. Fast upon Shaw's talk of savage mutilations, Browne could not help recalling the descriptions of similar grotesque tortures matched back and forth between the English and the Pequod.

The night pressed in from behind him and millions of orange sparks leaped from the fire toward white stars. The only sound above the rush of the fire was the old poet's music.

IX

≈≈≈

The next morning the two Englishmen were shown into a wigwam where they met an Indian seated alone on a heap of animal skins. The Indian rose and embraced Shaw, then, at first in slightly hesitant English, asked his visitors to sit before him.

Browne soon realized that the man before him must be Higgins himself despite the greased and dyed flesh, the savage's clothing and hair.

In the course of early conversation, Browne also came to understand that there was some mild restriction placed upon Higgins at the moment, some discipline he was enduring, for he was required to reside and eat alone, and to avoid close contact with women. He joined the savages, however, in their daily work and entertainments, treated, it seemed in this sense at least, as a member of their community.

Higgins asked questions about the plantation and the condition of his family, and Shaw offered detailed answers. Yet Higgins showed some uncertainty toward Browne. It was not, to Browne's surprise, any particular anger over Shaw having broken his oath of secrecy. Higgins seemed to understand that Browne wished to help his family, seemed to accept Browne's arrival as some necessity in the unfolding of events. But there was a tail of suspicion, an animal watchfulness in the darkened face and steady eyes.

When his questions revealed nothing new about the circumstances of Kathrin Coffin's death, Browne suddenly turned to the question of necromancy. What, Browne asked, was the role of Tantpasiquineo in all this?

"I met him, as the sachem, two years ago," Higgins answered, "while trading with Darby here. We saw that he was a powerful man. So we worked through him our trading. We made sure the others we traded with knew we were trading under his care."

"With success?"

"With much success. We kept our trade honest. Darby could tell you the wealth he has put aside. I too was seeing my way to such gain in the fur trade when Mistress Coffin met her end. No one knows what we gained in trade but ourselves. There is wealth to be taken here, Mr. Browne, if one knows the ways of this New World."

"I don't doubt it. But what of Tantpasiquineo?"

"There was trust between us. There was profit on both sides. So when I came here in my afflictions, he grew interested in these torments and took me in, saw the danger immediately."

"Are there not other and more efficacious sources of help in affliction for Christians?" Browne asked.

"The source of salvation becomes less important when you are running from evil, from the death of all you know and love. My household cursed, my children dying. I myself under unjust suspicion. I had no other source within the plantation."

"Nor the polity of Massachusetts Bay?" Browne asked.

"You have to ask me that, Sir?" Higgins retorted. "The choice was death or flight. So I left, told no one. Except Darby, of course. This seems to have worked until now."

"For now," Browne agreed. "What is the role of this savage magician?"

"He has provided for my comfort and life. We also work together to understand the events and dreams attached to my affliction. I've placed myself under his protection."

"And he has offered you hope of deliverance?"

"He would learn something of Englishmen's magic. And he has labored in my behalf."

"By his chants and spells?"

"By whatever power he has."

"You would traffic with the Devil, his consort?"

"I'm a Christian, Sir. But I've been held over the pits of Hell, and have watched my children begin to tumble into the pits. Do not the Liberties of New England allow a tormented, innocent man to save himself and his own?" He hesitated, looking from Browne to Shaw. "I am no Separatist, no Opinionist, no Sectary of any color. I am a poor planter like so many others who has lived by his skill, Mr. Browne, and who has now found the fur trade to be good."

"But through necromancy, Higgins? Through black arts and heathens? One need not be a Separatist nor even bound under the Liberties of Massachusetts Bay, as we all now are, to see the dangers that way. If you would speak of the terrors of Hell's Pit, speak of maleficence, speak of the battles of necromancers."

"Tantpasiquineo has applied his powers in my behalf. That is all," Higgins said. "To do so is what he has chosen. And there seems some relief in it."

"Yet nothing is resolved," Browne said. "Still less the circumstances of your abandoned family. Your wife grows distracted, Higgins. With good cause. Might we not rejoin you and them and seek some Christian solution to these trials? Even granting there are black arts against you—which I do not—surely we could search them out."

"You would take that chance now? Have me take it?" Higgins asked. "I would not."

"Mr. Cole would bring in whatever pastors or teachers or physicians are necessary to relieve your burdens."

"Mr. Browne, I don't know you. But I believe your purposes honorable. I trust Mr. Cole's judgment of you. And Darby's.

But I mean to stay here for now. I don't know when I may return. Too much dear to me is at stake. And there's an end of it, Sir. I have to place myself in your hands also. I trust you to speak to no one of this meeting. No one. Else the blood of others is upon your hands. Exile under Tantpasiquineo has saved me and mine. Pray, do *not* cross me now." He rose to indicate that the interview was over.

That night Browne's sleep was punctuated by wakefulness and dreams.

"Was there someone in the wigwam with us last night?" he asked Shaw the next morning.

"No. I sleep hard, but I wake if someone comes near. Who?"

"I don't know. He stood by the dying fire, and but for one slice of moonlight in the smokehole, that spark was the only light. I saw a black shape; arms like wings. There seemed to be someone with him, behind him, a woman white as the moon."

"A dream," Shaw said, pulling his leather jacket over his head. "I saw nothing."

"Perhaps. What chance do you think we have of convincing Higgins to leave with us?"

"None. But that's something he must decide for himself. We'll give him a week, as we agreed."

Throughout that week Higgins never came any closer to leaving, and Browne never met Tantpasiquineo. The under-sagamores were, however, completely accommodating.

It was on their journey home that Browne began to understand Higgins' position. There was a certain logic to his adamancy, if one accepted his version of events. That version, of course, shed no light upon Mistress Coffin's death. Were he, Higgins, the guilty party, there would be reason enough for his flight from his own people and law, to become one of the lost or dead. But was Browne to discount the deaths of children, or even these accounts of sinister dreams?

X

≈≈≈

Jonathan Cole was a large, competent man who had risen from a long line of commoners. Unlike Browne or Coffin he had not been a university man, but had started as an apprentice and journeyman printer in London, had taught himself French and Latin, and had ultimately bought a printing shop, which he sold in middle life to go on an adventure to the New World with a new, and first, wife. Not unlike Higgins, he was a man of varied talents and practical skills that had stood him well on his adventure. But to these practical abilities Cole added a keen intelligence and a shrewd administrative capacity to manage community affairs. Everyone respected him and many sought his advice. He was one of the original, elected rulers of the settlement.

His manner with orderly people was just and kindly, almost (as he passed well into his fifties) avuncular. Yet when he was aroused over some breach of courtesy, modesty, or justice, he was like a black August storm suddenly piling in from the western sky bearing a blast of hail and a menace of high winds.

These qualities and a debt of generosity and friendship to Cole caused Browne discomfort as he sat in Cole's library withholding the solution he had discovered to the riddle of Higgins' disappearance.

The decision to withhold information from Cole had been long and tortuous. But finally Browne reasoned that there were lives at stake, including children's lives, and that he was growing less rather than more certain of the nature of Balthazar Coffin. Furthermore, the evidence against Higgins was riddled with faults.

"At this point it would be best, Mr. Cole, to speed up this search for a minister," Browne said. "Provide ample remuneration and bring in an excellent man. Perhaps the sickness here is more spiritual than legal."

"Are the two so separate, Richard?" Cole asked. There was an edge of good humor in his voice. "And our offers have been lucrative, including some of our choicest lands. Two of the recent candidates we rejected: one a narrow fanatic, the other an old goat whose sole vigor was, by reputation, concupiscence. Our best candidates have so far lacked, finally, sufficient interest to join us. Thus our search continues."

"Might not some pious and courageous man now be sufficiently intrigued even by Goody Higgins' dark circumstances?"

"That is a possibility, but of course if we discount the suffering that arises from a missing husband, her torments seem to have ended. Mostly this reduction in afflictions has occurred since your arrival, Richard. She tells me she has great faith in your abilities. So you have helped her greatly, as I believed you would.

"It is precisely because of your many talents and abilities— nay, even sympathies—that I encouraged you to join our plantation and asked for your help and judgment in this Higgins affair. My former associations with your father were not my only considerations, you see. It is, however, perhaps time for you to consider your other purposes here as well. Your acceptance is assured, there is the grant of property about which we have spoken, the trade in wood and other commodities flourishing all around us. 'If this Land be not rich, then is the whole world poor,' eh?" Cole chuckled. "What more propitious time for a young man of parts to regain his family's losses? Between us we know many people here and in England who can help you to great advantage.

"Moreover, the magistrates of Boston will be delighted to learn such a man as Richard Browne has become one of us here. They raise continual complaints about those of us in the whole Pascataqua region—accepting all their reprobates and outcasts!" Cole laughed. He leaned back in his chair and enjoyed himself over the idea. Then he stood up and said, "More cider, Richard!" and held out his hand.

He left the room. Browne, nervous, got up from his chair and paced about the small room. Cole was right, he did have overriding responsibilities to himself and his relations back in England. There was wealth to be made here, to be replenished.

When Cole returned holding two noggins full of cider, Browne began: "I cannot deny my responsibilities, nor my desire to settle and begin here, Mr. Cole. And I can never repay your aid and kindnesses to me. But if I may, I would dwell somewhat longer on this Higgins matter. I believe Coffin wants testing, for one thing. And if Coffin be innocent, then Higgins has much to answer for. Should he be found. I believe him alive."

"Alive?" Cole sipped his cider, musing. "You may suit yourself, as to that. And I would have you probe these matters so long as you may release truths out of darkness, so long as your efforts repay us. It is a mysterious business. Have they told you of the light over the meetinghouse the night before Mistress Coffin's death?"

"The light?"

"It is not uncommon. The Indians see them, and they have appeared near Boston. 'Corpse fires' some call them because they are sure to produce a corpse next day. Like a flame, hovering above a wigwam, church, or house."

"I had not heard of such a fire in this particular connection."

"Whatever the invisible world may answer for in England, Richard, it has much more to answer for in this wilderness where the English have planted. A gentleman from Cape Ann entertained me with his mouth full of marvels half the night on my recent visit there. Nearly twenty years ago many would swear to a great, snaky sea monster coiled like a cable upon a certain rock. Woe to the mariner who strayed too close!" Cole laughed, not the laugh of incredulity, but of curiosity in security, of men exchanging stories. Cole was known for taking pleasure in tales of wonder and human folly.

"One providence he told me was of an incident on that Cape, about a decade ago, which happened to a ship's master, a fisherman, one Mr. Foxwell. He had put off from shore to a night anchorage and was awakened at midnight by the calling of his own name, 'Foxwell—Foxwell,' coming across the water from the beach. He rose and looked out upon a great fire on the sands. Men and women were holding hands to form a ring and dancing around the fire. Again he heard his name, but finally there was only the dancing and the fire until the fire burned low and the dancers vanished. Exploring ashore the next morning, he found the footprints of men, women, and children. And an infinite number of brand-ends had been tossed up by the surf. The footprints were of people who wore shoes, but he could find nowhere any other traces of people, English or Indian."

"There is much that cannot be answered for in this world," Browne said.

"As there is in this case you pursue?"

"Perhaps the solution is beyond our understandings."

"Then we had better resort to prayer and fast," Cole said. "But Mr. Coffin is a man of parts. I believe he is to be trusted. Of course I have not had the opportunity to study the case as you have. Goody Higgins is at some peace now. Her oldest son, Jared, especially helps with a man's work. But life is difficult here alone. If her husband intends to keep absent, or if he is as I believe dead, we may have to provide her the opportunity to marry again. It comes to the same thing whatever the cause of his absence." He looked at Browne and smiled. "I can imagine no lack of suitors." He rose and stepped over to a series of little cupboards and drawers built into the wall beside the fireplace and pulled forth his pipe, which he proceeded to pack methodically as he ruminated. Then he turned around, waved his pipe generally about the room, and said: "Sup with us this evening, Richard. You have been away much too long. Mistress Cole has been asking after you. No need to dine out, as I've told you."

He then stepped within the great hearth and, with a coal snatched and held by a particularly slender pair of smoking-tongs, lit his pipe. "We are happy to have you with us," he went on. "We see so little of you, now you've taken lodgings. You'll have your own life soon enough, once you build. Then I'll wager we shall never see you! Come sup then."

XI

≋

On his way to consider once again the property to be granted him, Richard Browne passed Elizabeth Higgins' house and noticed the woman dressed in summer calico moving about in her kitchen garden. Although he had not spoken to her since returning some weeks ago from the village where Jared Higgins hid himself from the society of Englishmen, Browne knew instantly that he could not prolong his own silence.

He went up to the sturdy board fence that enclosed her garden, hearing the shunk-shunk of young Jared chopping wood on the opposite and shaded side of the house, and saw that she was now on her knees over weedpatches in the peas and lettuce. Bean leaves and blossoms stirred in the slight morning breeze. Browne saw coriander and dill plants underway, and one other plant that struck him as having the complete freedom of her garden—the large gillyflower. This, he guessed, to encourage hummingbirds. But here was a ripe profligacy by any garden standard, a crowding neighborliness of all manner of edible, herbaceous, and flowering plant.

Kneeling in the morning sunlight, caught amongst her floral charges, she had yet to notice Browne. He toyed with the thought that he had surprised the very deity behind the glorious golden profusion of English gorse that some time ago had crept and spread through certain nearby fields, as it had in so many fields among the settlements to the east and south. Flora herself. "To come forth, like the Spring-time, fresh and greene; And sweet as Flora. . . ."

But no, this woman wiping the perspiration from her face was real flesh entirely. And, come to think of it, was not Flora's sweetness itself tainted? Loved by courtesans and common whores? Enshrined beside the Circus Maximus?

She turned quickly, sensing someone behind her, and began to rise. He in turn was startled back from his wandering thoughts and approached to lean on the fence, confirming in that instant his decision not to tell her, not yet, of her husband's true condition. He spoke immediately in his embarrassment over being caught watching her.

"Good morning, Goody Higgins! Fine morning to be out in such a garden." It was all he could think to say. He smiled and waved an arm over the garden.

"Lovely," she said, catching her breath now that she recognized her onlooker. Her hand, which had been over her heart, rose to wipe her damp face.

"'Awake, O north wind; and come, thou south; blow upon my garden, that the spices thereof may flow out.'" He rather too loudly declaimed the words of Solomon, and laughed. "I was just on my way to make early plans for the property granted me," he added. "I'm to be your new neighbor, at some distance." He waved his arm again, in the general direction of his property.

"Not at too great a distance, I hope?" she said, her face pretty and open, expressing genuine interest.

"Not too great," he repeated. "Just as surely one you can call on for help in any need."

"Thank you, Mr. Browne." She loosened the ties on her hat. "My children have been such a help to me since their father disappeared, the older ones especially. They're a blessing. But your offer to help us is welcome. And if I can return the offer— some matter about your new house that requires my experience or a woman's touch. . . ." She wiped her forehead again, and her coarse, dirty gloves left a stain of soil on her face.

"Have you a few moments to join me now?" Browne asked. "Perhaps you could begin by giving me your opinion of where I plan to situate the house." He smiled to encourage her. "It is merely a quarter hour or so walk," he said, looking off in the general direction. "I have meant to speak with you in any event. Can the children look after one another a short time?"

"Well," she began, somewhat confused by the invitation, "they have done so before." She came through the small gate and stood beside Browne, looking up at him. She adjusted the hat sheltering her face from the sun, squinted into the sunlight, and drew out a cloth to wipe her face again. "If you really think I can be of some help."

"Certainly you can."

"Then let me go in a moment to clean off my face and these hands; they get dirty right through gloves." She removed the gloves and held up two hands to the sun. The hands fascinated him; they were delicate hands, yet coarsened and dirtied by work. He stood speechless as she turned to enter the house. Suddenly it occurred to him how recovered, how lively and energetic she seemed. How ridiculous he must appear, standing momentarily incapacitated beside the fence that protected Elizabeth Higgins' herbs and vegetables from roaming hogs, cattle, and chickens. Somehow her absent husband seemed to have been prescient concerning the danger his family might still face.

He shook himself like a man waking up, and walked around to the other side of the house, where young Jared was splitting and piling wood. But on coming around the corner he was disconcerted again, for no reason other than his state of mind, to see Elizabeth Higgins standing there talking to her children about her plans to walk out with himself.

He managed to say hello again, and to compliment the boy on the growing woodpile. The children were all gathering around their mother. Each one had some piece of work—stitching, early summer vegetables to wash, small wood to be gathered for summer cooking. The oldest girl, Jerusha, as fair as her mother, held the half-asleep baby. Goody Higgins had changed her apron and cap. She now looked clean and fresh, thoroughly in command, a compassionate captain giving final instructions to her attentive troops.

Silent, the man and woman walked along the green bridle path toward the site of Browne's property. Birds and squirrels were thick in the trees. In the sunny spaces where plants and bushes flowered bright orioles chattered and whistled. Sunlight glistened off the stirring foliage. The warm air carried the brackish and swampish odors of the ebbing river.

"It has been so long since we've seen you," Elizabeth Higgins finally said.

"I heard how well you were all doing and thought it best not to trouble you."

"Trouble us? Your company is no trouble to us, Mr. Browne. You encourage us."

"I was also away during most of May, up in the country. And I haven't given up my investigations of your husband's fate. I've been drawn away in my pursuit. But I must confess that I have nothing new."

"Again, I thank you, who came here a stranger, after all. May I be of any help?"

"Not just now. The time will come. My feeling is that I'm approaching something now. But it is too soon to speak of it."

"I don't know how it is, but I believe it's your coming here that has put an end to so many of our afflictions."

"It isn't me alone."

"No," she interrupted, "you mustn't bother with such modesty. Not with me. Let's be frank as to our thoughts. Too much lies hidden otherwise."

Browne glanced at her, but realized her words were innocent and honest. He could not help feeling dishonest himself, however. He could be satisfied, at least, that her immediate torments had ceased. She and her children were all taking care of one another, and surviving. He had not been a complete failure, perhaps, not a total sham. He might not be utterly unworthy of her faith.

"Your land is the rise above the river you spoke of before?" she asked.

"Yes, exactly so."

"And you say the land is conveyed already?"

"I received seizin last week. Mr. Cole performed the honors, turf and twig."

"It is such a property to have," she said. "He must value you highly. Are you pleased?"

"Very. I need not intrude much on the commons, being here. Though I'm bound to keep up my share of the fences."

"As all must," she said.

She then spoke of the enormous run of fish that spring, and of the wild flowers they noticed spreading in the sunny spaces. He said little until they reached the gradually rising interval overlooking the river.

"Mr. Cole says there was an Indian village and planting ground here long ago," Browne said. "And here I plan to build and plant."

They left the path and climbed the gradual incline through knee-high meadow.

"They seem to have always taken the most beautiful prospects," she said as they reached the top of the swelling meadow and looked southeastward out over the placid tidal river. It was perhaps thirty yards from shore to shore at this point up from the bay.

"Indeed," Browne said, thinking of what his future life might be in such a place. He bent over, plucked a fat strawberry, and tasted it. Finding the berry ripe he plucked one for her.

"The story is that this had been an old cornfield, and then they planted it over, or allowed to flourish, their grass-berries, as they call them." He stopped to eat more.

"Or heart-berries," she said, "which is more pretty, don't you think?" She bent to pluck a few more and ate them. "Strawberry Hill, this is called, I remember now. We used to gather berries here. And it is far enough away from the settlement that no one built here from town at first."

"Mr. Cole says that it had been put aside some years ago in case more planting ground should be required," Browne said. He held three fat berries in the palm of his hand. The berries were between one and two inches about. Elizabeth Higgins chose one, her hands and mouth already red with juice. Browne popped the other two into his mouth.

"Strawberry Hill," he said, chewing lightly. "I like that." He looked at his own red palm.

"You will build here?" she asked.

"A little farther down toward the river," he said, pointing, "to gain some protection against winter winds."

"Perfect," she answered. "I would say just off toward the southern edge of the meadow there, where that great shade tree would be pleasant in summer. And you'd turn the house to be square with the sun at noon?"

"Certainly. Just so."

"It can mean so much in this country, come winter. It's a perfect spot, Mr. Browne. Quite beautiful!"

Browne smiled and spread his arms wide. In full voice he began to recite toward the horizon:

> Ye have been fresh and green,
>   Ye have been fill'd with flowers;
> And ye the Walks have been
>   Where Maids have spent their houres.
>
> You have beheld, how they
>   With Wicker Arks did come

> To kisse, and bear away
>   The richer Couslips home.
>
> Y'ave heard them sweetly sing,
>   And seen them in a Round:
> Each Virgin, like a Spring,
>   With Hony-succles crown'd.

Their eyes were drawn again to the river by a passing cargo boat, large and flat, that steered along in the ebbing current by men wielding poles. Cattle stirred and murmured in their pen, bundles of wood and fur lay upon the deck.

Field and saltmarsh rose greenly from the muddy river bank. Beyond the farther easterly shore groves of trees were scattered like islands in a meadow-green sea. Farther still on the horizon rose a final, wooded hill between them and the unseen Atlantic.

"I had thought of a two-story house," Browne said. "Perhaps even a third, garret or corn loft. A shingle roof and plaster walls, rather than flush siding or wooden shingles."

"White walls would add to the beauty here," she said. "Chimney at either end?"

"Central. And a second range of rooms under a shed roof in the back. Nothing exceptional, but commodious. Sufficient for a future. My carpenter is traditional and insists on an oak-timbered frame. He's indentured to Mr. Cole, one John Steele. You know him?"

"Jared worked with him once. I've seen him. He is said to be the best."

"It's the sawyers that are costly, nearly seven shillings a day."

"You'll have a beautiful view and warmth if you arrange the windows properly to the southeast," she said. "My husband always builds that way. And the good high, steep roof is best, of course. Let's go down to the house site then, shall we? See the prospect. There is nothing so pleasant as a good prospect, coming and going."

They walked without speaking down the hill. "Yes," she said as they reached the site and began to look around them, "You might as well build large enough for a family, Mr. Browne. You will want to settle." She put her hands together and looked around as if she were planning and seeing the whole future of the Browne family on this spot.

"That is what Mr. Cole tells me," he said and then laughed.

"Oh, he's right. Let me begin to look around for someone likely. She should have more than common manners and style. And money?" She smiled. "Let's see," she continued, "family . . . perhaps two or three languages, music. . . . Why Mr. Browne, we shall have to send to Salem or Boston, if not London, to satisfy your requirements." They laughed.

"But my requirements are modest, Goody Higgins, as are my present circumstances." Modest and perhaps desperate, he thought. He had a flash of vision: some coarse jade from the Isles of Shoals, a dozen miles off the coast, where, as a ship's officer once told him, as many men shared a woman as a boat. The very edge of his vision awoke to a terrible debauch in some dark corner where naked men like besotted satyrs snorted and licked about the unclean, undulant body of a woman who grunted and licked back.

He forced the vision away.

"I'll think about it," she was saying. "There may even be a suitable young woman hereabouts that I can summon for your consideration." She laughed.

"I have no one in mind," he said. "As we all know maids are soon gone in this country." She nodded in agreement. "I have been too occupied since coming here for that." She did not speak, so he continued. "I simply have not had the leisure to meet unattached women. I expect to build and live alone, and to rebuild what others have squandered. Even now I am cultivating associates in the fur and lumber trades that I mean to develop between myself and certain gentlemen and merchants of London. Mr. Cole propounds the real future is in lumber products—boards, planks, shingles, masts, barrel staves, everything. Fur already promises to diminish. He sees a parade of shallow draft ships constantly plying the river in five or ten years, transporting wood above all."

"It goes well, then?" she asked, looking at him.

"Not so well as I'd like. There is the problem of avoiding as many intermediaries as possible if one is to profit by shipping. It seems I will have to return to London, toward the end of this house building now. August, September. I must go to Boston soon to book passage. But, yes, I have begun to make arrangements for trade on this side. And I plan to hire some knowledgeable men for this venture."

"Darby Shaw might advise you. I'll say a good word. He's met with success with the savages and merchants, and without even your advantages, Mr. Browne."

"None but his own skill. I have approached him. He seems agreeable to some relationship, but word from you I would much appreciate, if you wouldn't mind."

"Why shouldn't I help you?" she said and then turned toward the crown of the sloping meadow. "Wouldn't that gentle rise make a good orchard? Let's go back up to consider plantings and outbuildings."

Walking back up the slope of the hill, he said: "And I may not be alone after all, Goody Higgins. I may prevail upon my younger brother to return with me, and his wife. He is the only immediate family I have left in England. He lives on family property, where I also was living before coming to America. But since so much of my future patrimony was invested dangerously, we have been having a hard time of it. I can no longer fund the operations and upkeep of the estate, modest as it is, from America in my present circumstances. And although they have survived the civil strife without becoming embroiled with either side, their situation will be uncertain. His help could be invaluable to me, and to both our futures, here. Provided I can tighten the arrangements I have in mind in London. If not, I may need his help on the other side of the Atlantic. All that remains to be determined."

They reached an outcrop near the top of the meadow and sat down. Browne asked: "Have you seen Mr. Coffin since we last met?"

"Not at all. I'm just as pleased. I have no wish to look on his face." The breeze strengthened at the top of the hill and stirred her hair out from under her cap. She leaned forward and plucked another strawberry.

"I have spoken with him on a number of occasions and need to see him again soon. I now believe he has kept something from me."

"Be sure to place yourself in no danger. I shouldn't like to see you come to harm for my troubles."

"No. No, I think you overrate his evil intentions. I have met with nothing but kindness and reasonableness from him."

"So they say of the Devil."

"They say many things. My belief is that this man is not the source of your afflictions, but merely a principal player in the bloody drama."

She looked at him blankly. "Nevertheless, Mr. Browne. The danger is real. You had better take care to watch yourself. I would say that now both your safety and mine depend on your watchfulness."

"I will watch."

"Then I can ask no more."

She attempted to gather her hair back under her cap from the wind, but it was useless now. The breeze had been steadily increasing on the knoll. Fair weather clouds were gathering on the horizon behind them and flying rapidly over their heads in the bright sky.

The wind finally drove them from the knoll back to the pathway to her house, where the children had abandoned their tasks and were playing by the brook which ran through the yard and down into the river.

XII

〰

On another warm day that June, Richard Browne paid a fourth visit to Balthazar Coffin. Coffin greeted Browne warmly, but the older man was haggard. Browne conjectured that the gaunt face was the result of Coffin's loss and sorrow, as if his pain had only gradually worked into him during the past year. Now Coffin seemed to be the one living without sleep.

"You have been away, Mr. Browne," Coffin said. "Welcome back."

Browne explained that he had come to discuss several points that were yet unclear to him about the circumstances of Mistress Coffin's death.

"Your journey was fruitful?" Coffin asked.

"Yes. But so much remains to be uncovered."

"Ah. Ever the case, Browne. Ever the case." He shook his head and, pointing to a chair for Browne to sit in, slowly sat into another. A woman servant entered the room and asked if they would care for refreshment.

"Cider?" Coffin asked. "Claret?"

"Thank you," Browne said. "Cider would be excellent."

"Two drams of sharpest cider, Martha, please," Coffin said. As the woman left the room, Coffin added: "I'll be alone soon; Martha is leaving within the month. Then it will be just me and cook. And that old widow, Goody Hastings, grows more deaf and blind, more the crone, each day. We'll make a pretty couple." He laughed and shook his head, as if imagining two invalids hobbling about the house like damaged crows.

"To what extent did your wife know Higgins before you hired him to take her to market?" Browne asked quietly.

"I can't remember much anymore. Oh, I remember old times, way back, clear as yesterday. But yesterday itself? Or recent events? Even an hour ago? And I forget so many small things now. You'd think me eighty, rather than approaching the half-century." He laughed. "Crabwise, to be sure, but approaching." The woman entered again with two servings of cider. Coffin thanked her and added in the same breath: "I am tired, of many things. But as to your question, forgive me. Yes. Yes, she knew him. How well? That is more difficult. I am perhaps among the least to answer it. May I let it go at that for the moment? May I enlighten you further on that point later? Let's consider these other questions first that you spoke of, Mr. Browne."

"My other questions depend on your answer to my first, so we will return to it as you say. But let me ask you this, Mr. Coffin. Why did you hire Higgins? Why that man?"

"Have I not told you at a previous interview that Higgins is an able man, a skilled man? He is widely respected. There are few men anyone would hire before Higgins for river travel as much as for building a shed, or fencing, or judging the worth of planting grounds, or any multitude of things."

"There is no other reason?"

"Not in the main. I knew him, as here everyone does." He paused, waved his hand and fixed Browne with his eyes. "Kathrin knew him." He paused, then continued. "I am tired to the bones, Mr. Browne, so let me come to the point. I wish to show you something, in secret trust, something I discovered after her death." Coffin rose slowly and left the room.

While he was absent—perhaps some quarter of an hour—

Browne rose and paced nervously. He walked into the library, a room which on an earlier visit he had seen only superficially, and looked at the table covered with papers as well as writing and drawing implements. His glance passed over a flat, ornately carved, open box on the table. Within the box were delicate measuring instruments and several small round stones of a kind he had seen once before and now immediately thought of as oriental bezoar stones. He looked at Coffin's books. There must have been nearly twenty in folio and more in quarto, many bound in good leather and stoutly corded. A few in quarto seemed to have been stitched and bound, some in parchment, by their owner. He pulled a few free and discovered considerable polite reading: Virgil, Lucan, du Bartas, Jonson, and the like. But there were many more works of a speculative and investigative turn: various herbals from Dodoens, and Gerard, to Parkinson; and there were Pliny, Gesner, Clusius, Alpinus, Monardes, and Cornuti. It was, in all, a curious mixture of polarities, of the quaint and the philosophically advanced— Paracelsus the shelf neighbor of Galen, Harvey of Valentinus. He quietly discovered some of those bound in parchment to be transcribed, perhaps by students, perhaps by Coffin himself. These were shelved as bound manuscript copies of older books. There were trunks of books as well, but hearing Coffin calling to him, he did not look into these. He returned to the parlor where they had been sitting.

"Remarkable library!" Browne said upon entering. Coffin managed a smile and said: "As you know, Mr. Browne, my library is at your disposal. Perhaps some time we may discuss more pleasant topics?"

"Indeed," Browne said, but then he noticed that Coffin held a small, red, leather-bound book. As Coffin laid the book on the table and pushed it toward him, Browne noticed a gold clasp or locking device on the book.

"I have here," Coffin said, "a curious little book that may answer many of your questions. You may take it up; it is for your study."

Browne picked up the book and caressed the soft red leather. Coffin handed him the clasp key, which was strung upon a delicate necklace.

"By giving this to you, Mr. Browne, I indicate that I will have no more to say upon the matter of Mistress Coffin's death. All I know of the matter is in that book. It does not reveal all the mysterious circumstances of her tragic misfortune. But you shall learn more from it, from her, than from any other source.

"This book," he continued after a pause, "I found in a locked cabinet after I buried Kathrin. Martha and I were clearing her belongings out of the house. Such reminders weigh too heavily on my soul." He looked up at Browne carefully. "This was her private journal."

"You wish me to read this?" Browne asked.

"It will answer many questions. I trust you to keep its contents confidential. Except for confidential Court records, should you judge it new and significant evidence."

"That I can promise. Unless by your leave."

Coffin sat down slowly, indicated Browne's chair with his hand, and said, as if to himself: "She seems to have required some expression of her secret thoughts, her private experiences. Though such a tendency is not uncommon among men in our day, it is unusual in women, wouldn't you agree? And you may find an urgency and frankness that suggests something more."

He paused and looked at Browne again. As Browne was about to speak, Coffin added: "Perhaps I failed as a husband. If not in my outward duties toward her, in the ways of the heart, Mr. Browne. I think you will see quite clearly that in her eyes I did fail. And I cannot quarrel with her on that point."

"Had she never shared her private thoughts with you?"

"Were you to have asked me that two years ago, I would have answered yes. But since finding Kathrin's journal, I cannot say that she did. Oh, we shared private memories and meanings, mental sympathies and the like, as married people, even in a bad marriage, do."

"Does this journal implicate anyone in her death?"

"No more than I have told you myself. But that is for you to decide, or the Courts, should you deem this confidential evidence worthy of a Court of law, of renewed action before the bar. I hope that you will not find it so. However, I do not ask you to cross your integrity.

"For myself," Coffin continued, "I cleanse myself of further anxiousness over justice in this matter. My personal failures I will bear myself. I am no longer a man who can view his life a moderate success." He stopped to look Browne in the eye. "You hold in your hands not only her secret soul, but mine as well, in a sense. I would be in your debt if you were to treat us with tenderness. But you must do what is your duty and follow justice and conscience."

"I am honored, Mr. Coffin, by your trust and frankness with me. We shall speak again after I have studied this document."

"I think not. You're still a young man, but knowledgeable about the world and certain niceties of the law. Moreover, Mr. Browne, you are a man of understanding and education, and have none of the narrow prejudgments of those who have lived in this remote settlement. That, I take it, is the foundation of Mr. Cole's faith in you as well. You will achieve things in this New World, I am sure of it. As a partial resolution to your investigations, this little book may increase your opportunity to look after your own affairs. And, as I myself did, you too may learn useful truths from its contents.

"During the initial inquiries I showed this book to no one. I think you will soon understand why. Consider this private journal rather as a gift; learn from my own misfortunes, Mr. Browne."

"*Felix quem faciunt aliena pericula cautum!*" Browne said and smiled.

"Ah! Indeed, Mr. Browne, indeed. Fortunate is he who thus learns caution." He smiled. "Now about your trip up into the country. You met the aborigines? Would you be so kind as to amuse me with some tales? They have a certain wisdom too, do they not?"

"Yes, Mr. Coffin. But my mind is full of your astonishing gift. I fear I'm at a loss at the moment for tales of aborigines. Another time perhaps?"

"Certainly."

"My house is underway now. I'll be leaving for London at summer's end. It will take time for me to understand what you have given. May I take this with me wherever I go?"

"It is yours. I have given it to you. In confidence."

"Please accept my apologies if my earlier questions have offended you. I thank you again for your generosity and frankness whenever we have met."

"All I ask in return, my young friend, is that you press me no further on the contents of the journal after you've read it. Everything related to Kathrin is too painful for me now. I look for some release from that pain; I have long felt the need to impart these contents to another. But I can discuss it no further."

"It can be only as you choose, Mr. Coffin."

Browne soon discovered that he had indeed been tendered a gift, but he was never to thank Coffin again or to discuss it with him, nor with Coffin to follow justice, conscience, or duty. For he never again saw Balthazar Coffin. And by the time all the journal's secrets had been studied, puzzled out, and searched so that he began to understand them, he had too many entanglements and secrets of his own.

Part II

Mr. Hopkins, the governor of Hartford upon Connecticut, came to Boston, and brought his wife with him (a godly young woman, and of special parts) who was fallen into a sad infirmity, the loss of her understanding and reason, which had been growing upon her divers years, by occasion of her giving herself wholly to reading and writing, and had written many books. Her husband, being very loving and tender of her, was loath to grieve her; but he saw his error, when it was too late. For if she had attended her household affairs, and such things as belong to women, and not gone out of her way calling to meddle in such things as are proper for men, whose minds are stronger, etc., she had kept her wits, and might have improved them usefully and honorably in the place God had set her. He brought her to Boston, and left her with her brother, one Mr. Yale, a merchant, to try what means there might be had here for her. But no help could be had.

—John Winthrop, 1645

KATHRIN COFFIN HER PRIVATE JOURNAL

I, Kathrin Coffin, daughter of Deacon William Bunting of Plymouth, County Devon, undertake to record some of the dealings of the allwise God with me, in events, which I ought solemnly to remember as long as I live.

I was ever treated with the greatest tenderness by my family— my parents, brothers, sisters—from my infancy and during my continuance in my father's house. So that I passed the morning of my years in peace and contentment. My father loved all his children, and saw to the education of every one of us, taking on much of the burden himself for my and my sisters' schooling.

I was married to my first husband, Mr. Joshua Pincheon, a vintner of London, in June of my 20th year, A.D. 1640: a restless time. Our marriage was a happy one, for my husband was my constant friend. Yet because he delighted in taking upon himself the travels associated with affairs of the wine trade, we were separated more than either of us had wished. Being without the blessing of children about the third year of our marriage, I began to travel on occasion with my husband and lend my support to his traffic. I saw, as a result, other lands and was no stranger to the Atlantic Islands. Indeed, it was while stopping at the Madeiras in 1643 that my dear husband was called back to the Lord, after grievous suffering of a plaguish fever. There I buried Mr. Pincheon, and there I stopped a while longer to look after our interests. Nor was I able to leave him, but made daily visits to his grave.

There too it was that I first met Mr. Balthazar Coffin, lately of Antwerp, who eventually became my second husband. He had booked passage for America by way of the Islands and was awaiting his ship. He was a learned, vigorous, and handsome man and very comforting to me in my lonely trial. Having lived in London previously, he returned with me to that city while the lawyers settled my husband's will and estate, a project that expended six months.

I will record in few words only that we married in December of 1643, and, due to the disturbances in England and abroad, resolved to continue together my new husband's intention to remove to America.

I did earnestly look to God for His blessing upon this marriage—sensible that "Except the Lord build the house, they labor in vain that build it." As while I lived with my parents I esteemed it my happiness to be in subjection to them; so now I thought it must be a still greater benefit to be once again under the aid of a judicious and loving companion, who would rule well his own house. Just as it had been with my first husband.

But God often disappoints the purposes of his creatures and suffers mankind sorely to afflict and oppress one another; and not only those who appear as open enemies—but sometimes those who pretend to be our friends, cruelly afflict. It is happy when such treatment is overruled to promote a greater good. Job's afflictions did thus. The trials of Joseph but prepared the way for his greater exaltation. David, by being hunted and distressed by Saul, was prepared for the crown of Israel.

But I rest not yet in my deliverance, nor, I confess, in my innocence. And as I am sorely in need of some person with whom to reflect on my recent life in America, to examine it, to search it out, in order to see and perhaps to understand better the nature and failings of myself and others who share my adventure, I here take pen to paper for consolation and contemplation (even unto the yearnings, tribulations, and crosscurrents of my soul) of the events and errors of my recent days.

June 5, 1645

Having lived at Robinson's Falls better than a year, and having spent all that time settling ourselves in keeping with the laws of this place, in planting, and in building our house, Mr. C. and I were so consumed with arranging our affairs and getting our living that if our affections remained steady, they did not deepen. Beyond our joint labors and that affection, we had not sufficient opportunity to know one another more deeply than upon our marriage day. It was as if the conduct of our affairs kept us from conducting our lives as true companions, and from exploring the extent and secret of ourselves.

Indeed, my knowledge of Mr. C. has grown only since that first year at Robinson's Falls—a place as beautiful (with its fresh and salt rivers, its meads and marshes, open groves and cathedral forests) as it is unforgiving. Planning the business of one's livelihood from year to year is so exacting that there can be little tolerance for the common discords of community or breaches of law. The life of each depends upon the regulation of every other—from the granting and disposition of property, servants, and domestic animals, to the planting of fields and commons, and the management of woods, roads, trade, building, food surplus or storage. We manage better than we mismanage. This plantation is seven years old and thriving, as many others have not. The town now counts approximately three hundred souls. Every day there is talk of greater limitations on newcomers. And it seems as if our three magistrates are constantly placing some new ordinance for the administration of town affairs before our Convocations for approval. Last week it was an ordinance to keep the road open to the width of three rods.

It is in this second year of our residence in America, as I say, that Mr. C. and I have begun to apprehend the true nature of one another. He is a man of even greater ability than I had foreseen. But it is as if he pays for his ability, especially his capacity for close study and feats of memory, with humors and distractions, with fluctuations through the full range of his person. Gradually, I have become more and more impressed with the idea that Mr. C. will not lead a common life—that he will be uncommonly bad or uncommonly good.

At first each of us endeavored to adapt our ways and habits to accommodate the needs of the other. Yet as time passes we grow less accommodating. He is never idle. He contributes his share to the town's common work. He labors, as I do, to the function and fruition of our household. Much private time, however, he consumes with study; so much is thus consumed that as we approach the third year of our marriage we grow isolated from one another, even as we have only begun to know one another.

We are not without our understandings and passions. Our passions correspond and remain the single living thread of our marriage. But there is too little of that love and gentleness left, too little of those sentiments and rewards upon which marriages endure happily. Brick by brick, we have begun the wall that disjoins us.

August 22, 1645

Persons of credit, aboard London ships freed by Parliament from custom, report the sighting of two suns setting over Cape Ann on August 20. Near the horizon lay a sun more bright than the true sun, seen above it, and a small cloud between the two suns. New England abounds in prodigies and providences, the meanings of which may eventually be made known to us, but the sources and meanings of which Mr. C. would fathom as they appear or as he hears of them (for the tales of such marvels and doings pass over the countryside as quickly as sunlight shifting through wind and clouds).

September 17, 1645

This day I resolved anew for my part to enrich our marriage by gentleness and care toward my husband. I think if Mr. C. is sometimes unreasonable, I will be reasonable, and would rather suffer wrong than do wrong. Just as I hope he will kindly overlook my infirmities and failings, with which I am conscious I abound, so I feel a forgiving spirit towards him. Some caution in our every intercourse is called for, so I determined we should best live together if we might be "wise as serpents and harmless as doves." I long to obey this direction. At this moment we live in a close balance of privacy and passion, reason and unreason.

Having borne no children in two marriages, I believe myself barren. No physic has provided remedy, even Goody Warner's oils of mandrake, potion of beaver cods and wine, and divers simples. Considering the isolations and delicacy of my relations with Mr. C., perhaps the absence of children may be counted a blessing. He blames me, justly, for our childlessness, but it is not within a woman's will—fruitfulness or barrenness coming from God alone. "Am I in God's stead, who hath withheld from thee the fruit of the womb?" Even as Mr. C. retreats more into the isolation of his study, so do I become more active in our domestic and civil responsibilities. And as to the economies of barter and trade, I have begun to take on the whole of those matters myself. Therein I seem to excel, and Mr. C. is satisfied to have it so.

I have nourished a small trade in cheese and sage, and have goodwives at my door these late mornings. Some pay in spinning for me, others in pine boards, a few in tobacco or skillets or cotton wool. I have begun to look about for a maid to help me with daily chores that I might attend even more to these profitable exchanges. Mr. C. has made inquiries himself for such help, in addition to our cook, whether it be some local maid sent forth by her parents or some available redemptioner.

January 23, 1646

It was recently in this our earliest and sharpest winter yet that I learned the inconstancy of my husband. My heart has been torn with grief, my eyes with tears.

All nature is contorted, with ships frozen in the sea, horned rainbows about the sun, lights in the skies, and two or three suns at settings and risings.

His inconstancy was revealed to me thus. We had bonded a young Irish woman to serve. She had been a stranger to us, but sold for her passage to New England. I believe now she was fleeing some mischief there. I found her rude and full of vanity. Her ways to me were disagreeable. But to my grief I saw they were pleasing to Mr. C. His studies consumed him still, yet he seemed drawn from his closet more now than before. Whenever they met their whole attention seemed to be toward each other; and their impertinent conduct very aggravating to me. Conduct between them grew licentious.

I had hoped that his dark humors and distractions would eventually pass, and that he would finally return to me and regain our marriage. But now such hopes have fled. More, I feel as though my earthly joys have fled, and I mourn the loss of a second husband.

I earnestly pleaded with Mr. C. to consider the evil of his ways, to forsake the foolish and live. But he has turned a deaf ear to all my entreaties, regarding neither my sorrows nor his own ruin, confounding my speaking to him with his angry *"Grata brevitas!"*

It is only because, through the mercy of God, I have prevailed to send away this vile young woman to other labors beyond my household that he has retreated to his herbary and his library and become more regular in his ways. But my confidence in him, like my hope, is destroyed in great measure. This, however, I keep to myself. I work to put these evils from my mind as much as possible, knowing that "in the world ye shall have tribulations." Yet now I find a wife's duty most difficult. Just as he has become less and less a companion, so has he become less a husband, more a betrayer and, through all his absorption in studies, an hypocrite.

Here we have no minister—Mr. Robinson having been twice banished (the second when we joined with Massachusetts Bay in 1643)—to guide us who are troubled. Neither is there anyone I am prepared to confide in, such is the nature of my affliction. I find consolation only in prayer and in my inkhorn and pen.

May 1, 1646

The spring being earlier and more seasonable than usual, by this third month the earth had completely cast off its gloomy mantle and wrapped itself in a brighter cloak of sunlight and green. Leaves bud and sprout, birds dash everywhere, the grass in the commons and meadows has shot forth greenly into the warm air, and when town drovers pass, our herds resound with the calls of lambs and calves.

My heart does not respond as it would. My husband on a journey, I have been troubled in heart and mind. He packed some few clothes and books, explained only that he had business to conduct in Cambridge several days, and set off downriver to Strawberry Banke, and thence by sea to Boston. In the fortnight since his departure I have had signal trials of mind occasioned by exorbitant dreams.

I found myself, in one dream, alone in this plantation, my husband having abandoned me to this wilderness. No one in the town would pay me heed. Wolves prowled about my door and plundered our stock. I feared even going out to milk. I feared I would starve. I could do nothing but cry for help from my window at passersby. But all ignored me as if I cried from some other realm unknown to the world in which men and women acted and lived.

Another night I dreamt I was in a boat on the river with a boatman I knew not. I could not see his face for the black hood he wore, and he would not speak. As we traveled, the boat began slowly to sink. The stranger seemed not to notice, so I cried out and begged for help. Gradually the water filled our boat, rose above my knees and waist, pressed coldly on my chest. I woke up groaning, and thanked God. But I was troubled and could not sleep. This dream returned another night, and I awoke at precisely the same moment, in the same torment of soul.

Why, I asked, does my sleeping mind rove so over such foreign, unaccountable objects? Why must my thoughts wander in sleep at such a wild distance from everything that is real? I could not bear to consider what such things might portend. I feared perhaps the onslaught of that malignant fever which has taken so many lives in the warmth of early spring this year. But, thank God, it has not proved the cause.

Goody Sparhawk, wife to Sylvanus, met with this fever and suffered the loss of her youngest and most loved child, Deborah, nearly three. She knew the fever to be abroad, but they had remained untouched. Then last week upon entering her milking shed, she saw the sleeve and arm only of her child sticking out from the hay. She ran to fetch her husband, not being able to face it alone. Upon entering the house where he sat with his children after a day in his planting grounds, however, she saw Deborah on her father's lap by the evening fire watching the pottage warm and bubble. She and her husband ran to the shed and found nothing—no sign of such an arm or sleeve as that of their little daughter, or of anyone else. They could not fathom this sighting, but felt some relief for the moment. Within three days, however, was poor little Deborah dead from her agonies in the fever.

As I lay in bed I began to long for my husband's return, as a hungry babe longs for the breast. Might we not renew our lost companionship, and ourselves? Wolves deep in the forest called to one another. Even though I had been busy all these days and much in association with the planters of Robinson's Falls, I felt at that moment as removed from these people and from my husband, in this remote part of the world, as I had in my earlier dream.

May 15, 1646

Mr. C. returned today. He is cordial but more than ever distracted by his studies. Far from encouraging him to renew our marriage, his sojourn has served only to intensify his appetite for learning and for distance between us, only to sharpen the same melancholic disposition and prepossession.

I now wonder whether the breaking of his vows troubles him so much that he is rendered incapable of the warm relations between spouse and spouse. Or is his mind wrenched merely by constant study and increasing removal from our life together here? In either case, his disposition towards me coupled with his former behavior against our marriage sets me further from him every day. I feel a loathing, entirely foreign to my nature, of my marriage bed, so unfeeling is that rite between us now.

Not that his carnal cravings have lessened their ardor, but my secret if uncertain belief is that he would be willing to cease those relations between us. Yet if our bowels are dead to one another, there is danger in self-denial. Not only the danger of my former experience, through no instigation of my own, that carnal passions vent themselves elsewhere, which ventings are frequent enough in any case by the common testimony of mankind, and which introduce every disorder into the marriage, but there is also the danger of public disapprobation and enforcement, leveled especially against wives who deny their husbands' pleasures once marriage ceases to be marriage.

There was that action the litigious Godfrey Gibbons brought before the court. Edward and Judith Wilson being bound over to appear for "their disorderly living, upon a full hearing of the case" were bound to the treasurer in the sum of £5 apiece, "to be of good behavior each to the other during the pleasure of the court, and that the said Judith do attend her duty toward her said husband in the use of the marriage bed according to the rule of God's word, which if she refuses to do, upon complaint to the next court, the court doth order that she shall be whipped to the number of ten stripes." Everyone knows and many have repeated from the decree, in jest, or gravely.

Yet will law answer alike to every case, however distinct? Which question I believe it was brought Mistress Hutchinson so much trouble some time ago, viz., law is no rule of life to a Christian, and thereby breaking law is not in every instance sin.

June 1, 1646

What is this coldness of heart that comes to separate husband and wife? I cannot believe it to be the effluent of transgressions alone. There are many tributaries to the widening stream. If Mr. C. and I are not without smoother moments of conversation now, there remains a turbulence and a distance between shores that create an unfordable gap. I have known instances of true companionship and compatibility, as between my first husband and me, as well as instances of convenience or settlement, where man and woman still become one flesh, one mind. Yet even in such instances there are, eventually, degrees of misunderstanding and the bland acceptance of one another that arises out of sharing another being's life.

How much the weaker must be the connubial ties between those who live aloof, whose relations are all duty without love, or all passion without tenderness? And once passion dies?

I find myself still concerned for Mr. C. His connections to the life of this community grow tenuous as well. He performs that which is undeniably essential to maintain ties of duty. But his whole life begins to take on that unwholesome cast one associates with the mad. Not that he lacks wit; indeed his whole mind is sharpened, at the expense of every other passion and sentiment. Were I occupied with children might I not be so sensible of his condition? The other evening when he repaired to his library, as is his wont after a light meal, I thought that the time had come for us to subject the circumstances of our marriage to honest examination. I believed I could no longer continue with such distance between us. Why should we suffer this emptiness, like death, at the core of our lives a day longer?

I therefore went into Mr. C.'s study. He did not look at me as I entered. The floor and writing table were strewn with papers and books. His chair was turned away from the table toward the window. He sat in near darkness staring out the window whose casement was open to the summery air. It was the first such evening of the season. Unaware of the insects that had stumbled in, his face was rigid and strangely illuminated. Then it was I realized that the moon was directly above his window.

I spoke his name. He neither turned nor spoke nor made a single movement of his face or body. I stepped closer to him, leaned across the writing table, and said: "Balthazar Coffin. I must speak with you. How have we come to live apart?"

Again, he neither spoke nor turned to look at me. I stood looking at him dumbly. I was dead to him, as if his very life had taken flight to some other world. Yet he breathed, slowly and deeply, I now saw.

I became distraught and ran from the room. I wept; I then ran outside to hide in the cow shed, praying and pleading for the guidance of God's hand. The thought kept returning to me that I must somehow leave this man.

Finally a strange peace came over me and my afflicted heart came to rest. The sounds and odors of the animals, the contented stirrings of nearby fowl, the warm soft air of the moonlit evening seemed to bathe my soul in peace. And I said out loud, remembering the tribulations of others, their holy filial hearts: "If I am bereaved, I am bereaved," and, "Shall we receive good at the hand of the Lord, and shall we not receive evil?" Then I asked: "What then is man? What are all our dearest connections and creature comforts? How fading and uncertain! How unwise and unsafe it must be to set our hearts on such enjoyments." And though I longed for the overthrow of Satan's Kingdom, I was at that moment suddenly at peace with the trials set before me.

I would it had turned out otherwise, but now we live in remote quiescence in the same house. He no longer comes to our bed, but sits up and sleeps by fits. I become more and more occupied with household affairs, and with trade and village life.

Even as Mr. C. grows in his distraction, it is my duty to get our living and my delight to increase our means. In another time, I might have fled to the family and the friends of England, my homeland. But it is my lot to bear my circumstances in this less strife-torn corner of the world.

June 24, 1646

This week has been a time of infernal heat, the like of which England never knows. Even men who could no more swim than stones bathed in the river. Our animals wandered into the flood up to their bellies and shoulders when they came to drink. A goodly number of fowl have died, and four marauding cattle enclosed in the pound took ill and seem near death. Only today has relief come upon a terrible storm that might have been Doomsday's onslaught.

There are days when I am overwrought, but such feelings have no object. They are formless, and futile. I am sure I will learn to live without a husband, for so I must live though I am but in my twenty-sixth year. I have learned by my trials to judge less the excesses of my fellows, especially those in false marriages. How poorly equipped are we to persevere in this our condition of Sin. "What is man that thou shouldest visit him every morning, and try him every moment." Though I pray for perseverance, I believe I can no longer hope for the renewal of my marriage.

Yesterday at market they told of a shoemaker and a cooper's wife elsewhere on the Pascataqua. One might think us, as the ministers and magistrates of Boston have said, become a haven for lewd persons fleeing Zion. Yet this is but an instance of such widespread events throughout the colony, to say nothing of the Province of Maine. More notorious still!

A captain, known as a rake, was sent some time ago out of Boston for living up to his fame with a certain wife who was

young and comely and the most jovial of spirits. Word got about
that they were sequestered behind locked doors frequently of
mornings or afternoons while her husband, a sawyer, was away
at the saw pits. They were brought to a hearing and she maintained they prayed together. That seemed doubtful, but there
not being two witnesses to certain adultery, they paid ten stripes
for their pleasures, and their indiscretion.

July 18, 1646

In this month of our great plague of caterpillars Mr. C. announced that for the sake of certain studies and investigations
he must travel to the American tropics. Indeed, he explained,
he planned to gain passage by the return voyage of a ship
already lying and unloading at the Isles of Shoals bound for
the Indies. As he spoke of these far-off investigations, my astonishment distracted me from any comprehension of his
words. Now it seemed to me that the black worm's destruction
of our wheat and barley was the herald of Mr. C.'s final destruction of that gracile living we had created out of wilderness.
Whence come such afflictions? Many said of the caterpillars that
they fell to earth from the heavens during a great thunder-
storm. For where none were seen before suddenly, after the
torrent, the bare ground and grassy places were completely
covered with them. After the ministers and people throughout
Massachusetts and Connecticut kept a day of humiliation
against the pests, the worms vanished. Just as the devoured
tassels and withered ears, so is my green hold upon the New
World to be blasted by a husband besotted by his ambitions.

Mr. C. then said that I was to be provided for and to have
no complaint or concern. Aside from those funds he would
need to prosecute his journey, I was to be, during his temporary
absence, administratrix of his estate and all income subsequent
to his departure, which means, he reminded me, were not in-

substantial considering our combined assets from my first husband's settlement, Mr. C.'s property and currencies, and whatever modest increase in our fortunes we, and especially I, had managed so well since our arrival here. All this, he added, he had authorized at the cost of considerable effort and expense to himself, due to the lengthy process required to supervene the conventions of Massachusetts in such matters.

He advised the hiring of another servant girl, in addition to Cook, and, he added, he had hired a man, at a very reasonable rate, to see to the heaviest work and the partial maintenance of our lands and animals. The said man to spend at least half a day, three days each week, in our employ, one Goodman Higgins whom I know by reputation as a capable man of divers abilities and adventures. This news somewhat assuaged my immediate apprehensions, but I am no less troubled by the prospect of being left alone for an indefinite period without preparation and dependent for much on a man I know but on acquaintance. And how can I be certain my husband will return? Might he not meet with some accident? Or, given his melancholic ways, might he simply fail to return?

I was unable to speak at first. Mr. C. continued in the same vein: that he had given much forethought to the necessity of his travel, that he was comforted by my acuteness in the management of all our affairs, that I was indeed better suited to them than he. I found my tongue enough to express my confusion and my belief that I must indeed be nothing to him if I am so little worthy of his confidence in such extensive plans before this hour of his revelations. Should I not be consulted and prepared? Was I more than a dumb stone to receive the wormwood of abandonment for these tropical adventures, these learned fervors and vauntings? Is my usefulness and success in housewifery and trade a sign that I need no helpmeet, that my reward is to be left a lone pilgrim and stranger upon the earth?

But my protestations he would not heed. He repeated the

gist of his assurances. He added only that he would return within the year, that his work was of the utmost importance, and that he thought not so much of his personal gain as of that Elixir his discoveries might provide for his fellow man. For some time he developed these themes, without listening to me, before returning to his study.

Thus am I left in the summer of 1646. It is true I am adequately provided for in the material way. I had spoken on the eve of Mr. C.'s departure to Goodman Higgins, and discovered that he had been hired just as my husband described. Higgins further understood that he was to be at my disposal beyond certain standing directives left him for the physical maintenance of our properties. He was satisfied with the steady wage and seemed withal to be content in the details of our arrangement. I had but two days between Mr. C.'s revelations and his departure to make what preparations and adjustments I might.

But the wickedness of my husband in this sudden flight, against my protests, becomes again clear to me and renews my sorrows. In this latest of trials I can but think that "the wicked flee when no man pursueth." His loss of all husbandly sensibility is, I now fear, but the prelude to total abandonment.

I can only believe that there might be some mysterious purpose of the Lord in this my trial if He has not forsaken me. And I am reminded and comforted by the admonition: "Be still and know that I am God: I will be exalted among the heathen, I will be exalted in the earth. The Lord of hosts is with us; the God of Jacob is our refuge."

August 7, 1646

Goodman Higgins is a great benefit to me. My life and affairs here are faring well. I am in small ways engaged in the business of the town, as well as our property, and have emerged from that shroud of loneliness I wore at first. As I think on it, there is little difference between my actual circumstances now and before Mr. C.'s departure. Was I not completely abandoned already? I feel now an increasing fullness of responsibility and liberty that lightens my burden. I consult with those women with whom I have some business on a particular day and with Jared Higgins. They have proved sufficient to all questions and problems that arise thus far.

My trials have proved bearable in comparison with others'. There was a maid at Dover who, professing religion and prone to sudden distractions and speaking in tongues, gave monstrous birth to a creature reported to have horny incrustations about its head. This prodigy called her deportment suddenly into question, and she is now rumored to be a witch. She and her family have removed to Maine, to some unknown point, to avoid the investigations of elders and magistrates. Although she may discover that she must flee again to some farther and more congenial place, Rhode Island perhaps, where all—heretics and strangers—may enter with impunity.

September 24, 1646

The dryness of the daily air and coolness at night restore us. The whole town is busy with haying, harvesting, and all those first preparations against the coming winter. Goodman Higgins is so busy that I believe he finds it difficult to keep up his responsibilities in my behalf. Sometimes he brings his young son along to quicken his labors. He is a man so different from Mr. C. that one might mistake them for two separate creatures in God's creation. H. has that noticeable lack of learning and refinement of speech. Yet he seems a worthy man—industrious and indefatigable, capable of any chore, repair, or discovery. He is so full of sound advice about the house, planting fields, or barnyard that we have grown less like mistress and hireling than like true neighbors on good terms. He cares much for his family, I believe, who prosper, and seems the most practically competent and casually daring man I ever met with. He will attempt anything and explore any place or region. His adventures are famous among us.

There is a roughness and quickness about his movements too that match his devil-may-care attitude of plunging into things. This buoyancy I believe to be a large part of his success at so many undertakings, whether they be familiar or novel to him. He is never melancholic, seems ever in good humor, even if he may be angered momentarily by some recalcitrant beast or immovable object. He accomplishes each day with that cockiness I have seen in youthful soldiers or seamen, but carried, in this instance, into the maturity of manhood.

If his speech and manner can be sometimes coarse, his aspect is pleasant, his form manly and strong, his natural manner that of all lusty fellows upon the earth. He is neither tall nor stout, but about his limbs, his whole body, there is an animal sinuosity making him more subtle and stronger than one might guess from his size. His sandy hair is generally unkempt yet thick, falling like wet leaves about his face as he labors vigorously. His joy lies in productive activity, resolving some problem or task, especially if others might find the task daunting. Mr. C. could hardly have found a more able or effective man in my necessity.

October 9, 1646

This evening as I sat in the milkhouse heavily wrapped and lazily huddled against our milch cow Patience, Goodman Higgins looked around the corner and spoke: "Taste of winter in the air, Mistress Coffin!" I jumped as he spoke, dulled as I was by my fatigue, the cow's warmth, the milky squirtings of the warm teats.

I chided him for such a start. He said he had come to look

after the feed storage, as he had a moment. But he stopped
briefly yet to ask about some purchases he had heard of me
making at the fair from the merchant Steele. It seems word
spreads as quickly as I can buy and sell. I had some commodities for a good price in pipe staves, rye, and cheeses off of a
ship from London via the Indies. There was sugar, linen, woolen,
stockings, and other goods I procured through trade. Even now
the ship is about to return laden with its New World cargoes.

I explained to Higgins that I had merely met with Mr. Steele,
a man of previous acquaintance to me, at a propitious moment
in the market, several ships at once being just in, some on their
way to Boston for materials and foodstuffs in shortage in England.

He said that I seemed to frequent the right times and called
me the "closest tradesman" he knew. Then he disappeared about
his business, leaving me now fully awake to my duty to Patience.
"Not slothful in business, fervent in spirit, serving the Lord"!

October 27, 1646

All week Higgins moved cordwood, splitting off kindling,
brands, and smaller pieces, sectioning the largest logs for read-
ier burning, and generally arranging for storage the winter's
worth of wood. By next month we must begin the long labor
of gathering next year's cordwood for curing.

It becomes clearer to me all the time that without his help I
would have been put to much greater expense and difficulty,
and that Mr. C.'s foresight in hiring Higgins was the one good
turn he has done me in the last two years.

November 5, 1646

Yesterday a great tempest at the northeast. Some lost houses,
roofs, boats, etc. A ship of 100 tons laden with peas and wheat
in bulk, some hundreds of West India hides, beaver, and plate—

all valued at 5,000 pounds—and above sixty persons aboard, was among the lost.

Our losses were not great, thank the Lord. Higgins has spent the whole day, however, and I fear tomorrow, on repairs.

December 29, 1646

The last three days I have taken to my bed. We, Higgins and I, had set aside a day to shift the season's second quantity of firewood from storage to the hall and wood shed against the back of the house. We had devoted some hours to this with good progress when a storm came up out of the south and all was enveloped in rain, fog, and darkness. It was a rain that endured until day's end when it turned a mixture of rain and snow. But when the rains finally began to blow up heavily Higgins said he would need to leave me for a time to attend to his own lot and animals. His family would be needing his help. No one could say to what extremity such winds might heap. He advised me to go indoors until the worst was over. And I agreed to do so.

But upon his leaving I secured some of the sheds as best I could and decided to continue a while longer, until I should be driven indoors, stacking under good cover more of the kindling and some of the manageable chunks which I had already begun to tuck away into tight, dry corners. The storm soon grew so violent, however, that I was within little more than an hour as thoroughly fatigued, as wracked by coughing and tremors, as an unwanted infant exposed to the ravages of the tempest by her sinridden mother.

Once inside and shut away from the storm, I was unable in my feebleness to raise Cook, who had probably, as in previous storms, hidden herself under the bedclothes in her own quarters. I dragged out our great washtub, placed it before the fire, and began filling it with hot water from the two big kettles hanging on their trammels above the fire, tempering it slightly with colder water from the storage cask. I raised an enormous fire to warm me, to boil more water and, still wracked by violent shaking, quickly stripped all my wet clothing from me before the fire and wrapped myself in a woolen blanket. I could not sufficiently warm myself thus, so I adjusted the water temperature in the tub as hot as I could withstand and struggled in.

With a groan I sank into the water and found salvation. Life, it seemed at that moment, might endure and be good again. Every ligament of my body was loosened, searched, beneficently bathed by the warmth. I must have swooned or fallen asleep. For how long I do not know.

I awoke only at the sound of Higgins' voice and the pressure of his hands shaking my face. He had risked returning in the storm later to insure my own security. When he found me as I was, he later told me, he had feared my life at first, until he perceived my shallow breathing. He asked if I had met with some accident, and I slowly explained what I could recall to him. He stoked the fire and heated rum as I spoke. He had warned me, he said, to take greater care, to seek shelter. Yes, I agreed. He spread and hung my wet clothes (which I had dropped on the floor) about the fire. He replenished the tub, whose waters had somewhat cooled, with hot water. Then he offered to place the blanket beside me over the top of the tub to cover me, but I said it was not necessary now. I felt no shame, for there was no force or vitality in my body then. I had grown, however, warm at last. He handed me the hot, sugared rum.

We said nothing while he adjusted the logs in the fireplace and refilled the water pots. He roused Cook and had her place a light supper on the table board for me, and then made ready to return to his family. I thanked him, but my voice betrayed my weakness and he grew concerned again. I managed to assure him that I was restored enough to get along on my own with old Cook, Goody Hastings, though secretly I did not know how it was to be done. We agreed, once he explained his own obligations, that he should return in two days to finish the wood for me. In leaving he added only that he would have his wife look in on me tomorrow to be sure I had regained good estate of body.

After he left, I lay back in the hot water for some time. How long I cannot say. It was only after finally leaving my bath that I suddenly grew weaker and chilled again. I barely made my way to my bed, with Cook's help, fell immediately into the deepest sleep, and have lain here three days. It was Goody Higgins who kept me alive during my illness with her oat cakes, broths, decoctions of root and herb, and directions to old Cook as to the necessities of my welfare. Tomorrow I shall walk a little, thanks to her ministrations. But she does not turn a friendly countenance upon me. I rather think she performs what is a duty to another of God's suffering creatures.

January 5, 1647

Higgins himself stopped in today to see how I was getting on. I had been walking again; he asked me about my strength, which, as I assured him, I was regaining. He asked me to walk for him and to see if I could carry implements from the fireplace to the table. I was improving, but slowly, when for some reason I stumbled and he immediately caught me up. "Not well enough to be unattended yet, I think, Mistress Coffin," he said, helping me to a chair. My sensations upon this event were strange to me. I had lived so long without the caring touch of a man that a ripple of unfamiliar pleasure and sympathy for another spread through me like the stirring of fish suddenly feeding in deep pools.

He seemed not to notice. He said that he would ask his eldest daughter to attend me twice a day until my strength completely returned. I protested that there was no need, that she was too much needed by her mother. Then it was that I began to think about hiring a servant again, as Mr. C. had recommended. I mentioned this to Higgins, and he thought it a good idea, said he would look about for a prospect himself.

February 6, 1647

Today Higgins repaired a hole in the roof of the cow shed where heavy snow brought down a large hickory limb. I am sure it was a frightful labor in such snow. But he approached the task, as is his wont, undaunted by the practical difficulties.

When he entered the house, unwrapping his coat and shaking the snow from it, he said that he had managed it. He laid his coat on the hearth, stood before the fire, and took the refreshment I offered. I was offering my gratitude for this most recent assistance in my need and had fully launched into an expatiation upon all he had done these past months for me, when he looked at me a little strangely. I continued, saying how far he had surpassed his agreement with my absent husband. For a moment he looked away into the fire as I spoke rapidly, trying to express all the gratitude I felt. But he turned his face back to me, looking up from the fire through the damp fall of his hair. The odor of warm wet wool rose from his coat on the hearth between us. But now the look in his eyes arrested me. It was as if some unmistakable flash of recognition passed between us, some bond of sympathy, a momentary but certain intensity of passion. I cannot now say whether I soon spoke or whether we stayed for some interval in silence. But I felt as if I had been cast away near an island in a burning sea. I beat back and forth between that island world and the world of all my fellow creatures. I could not choose. I knew only that if he were to touch me I would be tossed upon that island with him in the violent gale.

What a mystery is the heart inflamed with desire! Are not our passions our greatest affliction and severest test? The Creator has filled our cups beyond their rims, a far greater draft than mere necessity would require. My thoughts have grown so curious now. They switch and snap in all and opposite directions. One moment we are humbled, in another we cry out that an angry God has left us in his outrage to swill and grovel like beasts until the night of utter death visits each of us alone. I do not begin to express the turbulence of my thoughts.

Now that he has gone, I cannot conceive how we shall act or speak to one another at next meeting. Sleep forsakes me once again. And wakefulness is filled with night and torment. Am I not a deserted wife, a woman stripped of her carnal life in the very morning of her second marriage? What is this man to her now whom she married in the sorrow of early widowhood and the sweet freshness of love?

In wakeful hours I recall not only so many events of my life, but I find my mind wandering over cases of adultery and brutality between man and woman. Moreover, is it not indeed evil even to be capable of evil? *malum est, posse malum!* We are so readily humbled, stricken neither more nor less than any of these other lost and troubled creatures beneath the sun. Where are we but in God's cauldron, there to be tried and wrung of every vanity and compulsion of the flesh that grips our earthbound spirit.

February 10, 1647

Returning to me today, H. revealed no hint of what had passed between us. He went about his work without so much as a questioning glance. I soon saw the wisdom of such deportment. This innocence of silence left with me the choice of our future conduct, and the time to consider wisely in my turn.

Any pursuit, I now see with a renewed clarity, of the direction begun facing one another before the fire, if it would not by some twist of precedence or circumstance cost us our lives, might at the least cost us much in the way of public humiliation and stripes. Moreover, I should never be permitted to maintain my authority over that portion of Mr. C.'s estate that he had so assiduously arranged for my management.

Was it not only three years ago that a man and woman were turned off the ladder in Boston? A young maid, on a dare, vowed to marry the next man to come down the road. She made good her vow. But the man was old and infirm, and she comely. Keeping true cost her dearly, for it was not long before she sought some lusty young fellow. These two were caught in the most shameful of circumstances. It was their misfortune to be discovered by the magistrates at just such a time as to be made an example against wantonness. If a certain leniency of law had been applied toward others, these two now were made to feel the full weight of retribution. This and other examples of wretches in similar circumstances return to me frequently now.

February 23, 1647

Might I not plead that the spiritual and material bonds of my marriage to Mr. C. had long since dissolved, by his frenzied will and action? Was it not he who abdicated all responsibilities and ties, save one last pecuniary debt, to me his wife, while I, on the other hand, had fulfilled every duty toward him, my husband? Would not the just favor my cause over Mr. C.'s, in *foro rectae rationis*?

Why should not a woman in my circumstances unwive herself?

H. speaks of journeys in the spring for the fur trade. He brought to me today one Martha, to be considered for a servant woman. He saw the need, as I did, for this addition to my household. Newly arrived, unmarried, more mature than that previous jade, she may do well enough.

March 10, 1647

There is another tale of much sorrow about a maiden lately in Boston. I first heard of it on market day, the fifth day of the week now being set aside for such, but the woeful tale is generally about. At 22 this maiden was the eldest of two daughters to a widower, one Martin, of Casco Bay. He had returned to England on some business for a time, and left his daughters, both known as modest, Godly maidens, to make their own ways. The older daughter, Mary, went to work in the house of a certain Mitten, a married man, who became much taken with her, solicited her chastity, and gained his desire of her for some months. Perhaps because she was so shamed by the circumstances of her life, or for some other reason, she removed to Boston and entered the service of Mrs. Bourne.

Discovering herself with child, this maid concealed her shame, even though finally others came to suspect her. Her mistress, however, so admired this young woman's modesty and faithful service that she would give no credit to any reports of the maid's condition, but thought them merely malicious.

But when this young woman's time came on a December night, she withdrew secretly into a back room, gave birth by herself to a woman child, and attempted to extinguish the child's life by kneeling upon its head. The child being strong, however, it recovered and began to cry, so that this Mary used some greater violence to stifle the life. What suffering and horror she passed through alone that night, one shrinks to envision.

She might have kept her dark acts hidden had not her master and mistress left for England, causing Mary to remove to another house into the service of a woman, a midwife, who had suspected her condition previously. Upon examining the young woman, her new mistress found her to have been delivered with trial, which the young woman then admitted, saying however that the child had been still-born and that she had placed the tiny corpse in the fire. But a search being made of her former house, the child's corpse was found in a chest where she had hidden it. During the trial, the jury caused her to touch the face of the corpse, and the blood came newly into it. Hence she admitted all the truth, including the further prostitution of her body with another man since coming to Boston. She was shamed and penitent, but they condemned her to death.

She complained of her heart's hardness even at her death. Likewise she prayed for pardon, then for Christ's mercy, until she was finally turned off. But hanging some time, she met not death, and she asked what they meant to do. Whereupon two men stepped up, one turning the knot of the rope backward, and she quickly died.

There is much that men and women do outside the laws and strictures of the magistrates and the teachers. I mean not only black arts but fornication, passing a babe before its time, and the curses and assaults that crowd the courts. But to kill one's own newborn with one's own hand? To bash out its brains or deny it care for months and turn like a stone against its agonies? Some have pleaded they would prevent their coming into public shame. And though that may be sufficient motivation for a few, must not there be also greater desperation for many others in this departure from all natural sentiment? Must not there be some wrenching of mind from heart to turn the bowels to such darkness? What must be our circumstances and afflictions to act thus? "Who can understand his errors? Cleanse thou me from secret faults."

Worse, who among us might not be sufficiently scourged to allow such evil to come into her that she become the instrument of affliction against the innocent of the world? Are we not all of the same nature and kept from like evils not by our own hearts, but through the pleasure of that Greater Power alone? "Also in thy skirts is found the blood of the souls of the poor innocents: I have not found it by secret search, but upon all these."

The frightful story has caused me anguish. We are tempted and fall, abandoned, moving toward life or death, passing our time upon the earth in strange joys and travails, amidst awful signs.

"Thou hast set our iniquities before thee: our secret sins in the light of thy countenance.

"Make us glad according to the days wherein thou hast afflicted us: and the years wherein we have seen evil."

March 12, 1647

H. makes final preparations to go up into the country. He speaks of a fortnight or three weeks. That is as he arranged with Mr. C. But I doubt he will return before April is out, perhaps even May. I, Martha, and Cook are prepared to manage. It is only strange to me how I fear I shall miss his quiet company as much as his help.

May 13, 1647

"Run ye to and fro through the streets of Jerusalem . . . and seek in the broad places thereof, if ye can find a man, if there be *any* that executeth judgment, that seeketh the truth; and I will pardon it."

This spring I saw again the inconstancy of a man. And am I stricken, humbled by my own failure to free myself of corruption and withstand God's trying of me?

It was mid-morning. I had been searching for Patience in the wood near my house where she likes to forage. She never ventures far nor stumbles into trouble there, being an old homebody herself and always returning punctually. But this winter, and deep into spring, there had been many wolves about, so I was apprehensive for her on that account even this late into the season.

The men had organized hunting parties with dogs and set a good reward on wolfskins. But the creatures are so prolific that their constant menace to domestic animals was hardly reduced until their worst season abated with the fish spawnings. As Mr. Surrey remarked, there is so much wolf dung about that we need not hear from colicky babes for years to come. In the bleakest time of winter, I had seen them by the house at odd hours. They arrive in divers colors—shades of sand, black, grizzled, white. Some are quite huge. These marauders have been quiet of late, but, Higgins being still away so far as I knew, about mid-morning—the first moment I had been free to look for her since missing her at milking hour—I took an axe along and stepped into the woods, calling to Patience.

The woods were cool and resinous, with hints of blossoms hidden in the sunny corners. I followed the old trail in the wood which, I knew, she often used, and which was gradually leading me around toward the river. I had nearly broken out onto its grassy margin when I heard laughter. Stopping, I determined it to be the laughter of a man and a woman. I ceased calling and moved quietly forward until the trees began to thin into the marshlands. Then I stopped again and, standing behind the thick stem of an old oak, saw the river itself and the hunter's wigwam upon an elevated stretch of bank. I now recognized my exact position upon the river. The laughter had ceased momentarily, so I stayed still, merely watching the dome of bark and matts in the sunlight. It being warm early in the season, only waterbirds and marsh blackbirds moved about in the open, yet behind me the woods were full of the movement and sound of birds.

Suddenly a man and woman, naked, ran from the wigwam to the very edge of the riverbank. I could not tell at my distance who the people were, only that the woman had flowers wreathed in her hair. By their white bodies, their voices and laughter I knew that they were English. Had it been a month later, I might have walked in the marsh hay toward them completely hidden, but at this season the grass was still low.

As I watched the couple I became consumed more by curiosity than common sense. Bending as low as I could, I hurried toward a thicket by a closer tree in one patch of the descending marsh field. Their faces had been turned away from me, and they were too preoccupied with their bodies to notice a foolish woman bettering her position to spy upon them.

Had they been caught and exposed in their pleasures, punishment would have been grievous indeed, but I had no desire to reveal the dark secrets between them. Had I known what I was about to see, I would have known even more certainly the impossibility of ever relating openly what I witnessed.

Then it was that I recognized them, as their faces kept turning toward me while they danced in circles holding one another's hands. The woman was the widow Gage, one of faultless reputation and carriage, whose husband had died in the river during a log drive the previous summer. The man, whose form I had grown almost certain I recognized, I now saw to be Jared Higgins. I was far more stricken by their identities than by coming upon them in such circumstances in the first place. I was too embarrassed to make my presence known and too afraid of being discovered to move away even as I had come. I must, moreover, confess to the strange fascination of observing these two, glorying their flesh in the sunlight, the flowers flapping in her loose hair, a girdle of herbs and leaves bouncing against her waist, her hand at intervals playfully caressing or plucking his taut instrument like the string of a lute.

It would be impossible for me to write, even here, all that I witnessed between them. For their practices grew more beastly, turning their bodies into a Boggards. Had ever such a lewd and wanton woman hidden behind so chaste and godly an exterior? Is it not awful to contemplate the mysterious chasm between a man or woman's appearances in the world and the passion roiling beneath. "If thou, Lord, shouldest mark iniquities, O Lord, who shall stand?" They might have been demons inventing in the course of their eternal dalliance all the carnal lusts bequeathed to humanity down the ages.

Patience I suddenly saw on the other side of the wigwam where Higgins must have tethered her after, perhaps, coming upon her himself in the wood or meadow.

When, near mid-day, these two had spent their final passions and lay by the river caressing one another, I took my secret leave. I went about my labors avoiding any more than necessary conversation with Higgins upon his return to my house as one who had been away many weeks. He came leading Patience and smiling, as if he had had great success in his trade and was bestowing upon me a gift. I was just able to keep up enough conversation to avoid his suspecting me. I could not then, nor can I now, expunge from my mind the sight of them wrapped like two great blacksnakes, as we find hereabouts, biting and wreathing about one another in their frenzied, sunlit copulations. It was as if a gate had opened upon another world that mocked my own temptations and sentiments; nay, as if all the hopes and aspirations of fragile humanity were mocked, all our small pleasures and all the ancient works of God upon the earth.

I felt, and now feel, that bleak, oppressive certainty that the Kingdom of Satan rules all, that we are all foolish creatures and dolls, and that the laughter beyond the gate is the blast of Hell. "Behold, I will make my words in thy mouth fire, and this people wood, and it shall devour them."

June 23, 1647

This is a sorrowful mid-summer's time, for an epidemical sickness has come among all—Indians, English, and it is told Dutch and French as well—that takes like a cold and light fever, but upon bleeding or using cold drink, kills some, while others inexplicably recover in a few days. Worse yet, a ship from Barbadoes and the Indies was isolated for a plague and great mortality there. Many cannot but despair.

August 20, 1647

Mr. C. returned today. His tropical sojourn has ended.

There was a clatter before the house, I looked out the front door, and there he was, dressed in light clothing, stepping down from a horse cart driven by a Negro man and full of trunks and cases. I quickly closed the door and drew my breath, trying to calm myself while he directed the man in the unloading of his impedimenta.

Later, I discovered that he had hired the man and his truck at Strawberry Banke, taken a river barge up with the tide to the landing below the falls, and ridden the cart sitting beside the truckman right up to our door.

While the truckman carried the boxes to the house, I collected myself and ran out to greet Mr. C. Immediately I saw that he was changed. Not only was I surprised at his sun-darkened flesh, his loss of fifteen or twenty pounds, his loose light clothing, but I was taken by his face and eyes, by his peaceful demeanor and speech. Here was a man who looked upon me with interest, as if two faulty years of marriage had been wiped clean. We might have just arrived in the New World. The source of this transformation I am never more likely to know than I knew at that moment.

This evening we walked about our garden, inspected every outbuilding, promised to walk to our planting fields in the morning. Whatever outrage I had stored to unleash upon his possible return he has completely disarmed. All the more so since he begs forgiveness for his inexcusable and unhusbandly behavior toward me previously. He promises to be my husband and true companion, and he asks me to take whatever days or weeks might be necessary to consider whether such a life together might be possible. At that moment, as at this, I confess I do not know what might be possible between us. My instinct tells me to think it unlikely. But it will certainly require my consideration—the implications for a lone woman are so pregnant and uncertain—and there is of course my confusion over Jared Higgins.

Our first night together, however, Mr. C. related his travels and adventures, albeit in far too much detail and number to record here. He ranged through Brazil, Barbadoes, Christophers, the Summer Islands, Grenada, St. Lucia, Guadeloupe, and so on, hiring his passage in English, Dutch, French, and Portuguese ships. He promises to tell me of six weeks spent in Spanish captivity headed into a life of slavery until an English privateer, in turn, took the Spanish ship.

He seems pleased by the state of my household and his lands. So much has passed between us since his arrival that I will stop to record only that he further demonstrated his new sympathy with my own state of mind by offering to sleep, for the indefinite future, in his own chamber, where he has stacked a princely collection of books and specimens in cases piled to the ceiling. His last words to me were: "Let us be off, now, to sleep. Think on all I have said, and will say, these coming weeks, and then in good time we shall decide how it is that we are to regulate our lives."

I go to my bed this night strangely happy, strangely sorry, asking the Lord again to guide me and forgive me. As I contemplate my transgressions and my share in fleshly corruptions to which all are prone, even the mastering desire to sleep confronts my secret kernel of fear, viz., might the slightest provocation unbalance him once again, or might this transformation be but another guise of the husband I had so painfully learned never again to trust?

October 10, 1647

As to the change in Mr. C., let me record that he has not cast off his predisposition to study. Rather, his preoccupation has somewhat abated. Of course his present need to pore over his specimens and books is substantial, and he spends hours daily closeted with these materials, pursuing his lodestar. But he now emerges from his study, and upon these occasions is more energetic than melancholic. In brief, he looks upon the world with a human eye.

He says little more of his previous behavior toward me, as if that were a subject too painful to discuss. To all appearances, I seem to have regained the man I married. Yet I cannot say whether I will ever again be capable of responding to him as my husband. Of course to the world, that is a wife's duty, but he makes my burden easier by his cordial distance, allowing me to determine the nature of our relations. Lately, after evening tasks, we have been spending a late supper and evening in conversation. I come to treasure his exotic tales of slave traders, gigantic serpents, strange savages and practices, enormous tides and rivers, unendurable heats and rains and mists. In his turn he seems as fascinated by tales of my daily rounds and events here. He praises Higgins' tireless labors.

In this so sudden and astonishing an alteration of my circumstances and relations, I hardly know what to say of Higgins. Nor shall I until my soul is prepared, nor until I am assured to my very soul of a deeper change of heart in Mr. C.

December 18, 1647

I feel some certainty of the general improvement in the relations between us. More, that Mr. C. feels deep remorse for past behavior, that never can those relations grow as bad as they had previously grown. Yet how does a wife remove the stain of such a past? Is it this hesitancy in myself, or some remaining canker in Mr. C. that promises to hinder a life together reborn at the least in that tenderness between men and women, which might otherwise flower? For does he not seem to revert, in some degree, to that former coldness that arose between us, rising with the patient surety of a wall beneath the mason's hand?

Part III

Oh this people have sinned a great sin, and have made them gods of gold. . . . And the Lord said unto Moses, "Whosoever hath sinned against me, him will I blot out of my book . . . in the day when I visit, I will visit their sin upon them." And the Lord plagued the people, because they made the calf, which Aaron made.

—Exodus 32:31–35

XIII

≋

In the autumn of 1650 Richard Browne returned from England to Robinson's Falls. The second day after his return Browne walked from his new house, which the carpenters had finished in his absence, toward the houselot of his nearest neighbor, Elizabeth Higgins. Among the reasons for seeing her he wished to borrow some fire. As he approached her dooryard, he heard a wild screaming and hurried around the corner of her garden fence to find Elizabeth holding between her legs the hind parts of a small but meaty pig. She was just taking the pig's snout in her left hand and poising a long knife in her right over the animal's breast.

Browne stopped. The knife plunged. The animal's blood jerked onto the soil. Only when she hoisted the dead animal up above the pot of boiling water over the dooryard hearth did Elizabeth notice Browne standing just beyond her fence.

"Mr. Browne!" she called to him. "You've come back!"

"Just as I said," he called and moved closer.

"But so soon?"

"As you see. My business in England is completed."

The pig's body slid into the hot water. With a reddened rag she wiped sweat from her face.

"With success, I trust?" she said.

"As much as I might hope, amidst the discords of the motherland. We have good hap to be in New England, Goody Higgins."

"So many say." She hoisted the pig from the water by means of a rope running over a branch, swung the carcass onto a rough-hewn table, and began to rub the animal's skin vigorously with rosin.

"I have divers irons in the fire and expect trade to go well once I arrange for proper shipping. Lumber products are greatly desired in England and the Indies."

She looked up at him; he held his fire pan in the air to show her what he needed.

"May you have good fortune, Mr. Browne," she said. "Yes, I'll have young Jared get you some fire when he returns shortly."

"Thank you, Goody Higgins. I'm in no hurry. How have you kept?"

She was now stripping the hair off the pig. "We're well, thanks be to God, well enough in this time. But I cannot rest easy. Many children throughout New England have met death this year. He enters every village and house."

"Not here, I pray, has his scourge entered?" A look of pain came quickly to his face.

"No. With the Lord's blessing."

"Then have your past trials proved sufficient, and you have entered a new epoch in your life, Goody Higgins." He tried to sound pleasant.

Working diligently, she said nothing. Eventually, in her own time she spoke. "Yes. A new epoch, and without my husband still." The hair off the pig, she began to disembowel it.

"Ah!" he said, then tried to banter: "But I daresay there have been suitors by now."

She stopped her work for a moment and looked up at him. "Yes," she said, serious. "Suitors there have been. Many place Jared among the dead, others place him among the never-to-returns, the deserters." She saved the organ meats for cooking presently and put the intestines aside for sausage casings. "I have brought my cause before no court. Though there are those who offer to plead my cause as theirs."

"I doubt not that one so fair and skilled," Browne smiled and tested deeper waters, "so sure and robust in all her ways has a royal share of suitors. But you have no pressing need for such a protector and companion? You have turned toward no suitor's bait?"

"Because I fancy none now." She did not look up from her task.

"Ah!" he said again, watching her work quickly and deliberately in the cool morning air. "Has every bait been as unworthy as that?" He laughed, but it sounded false to him.

She did not laugh with him, but looked up again briefly. "It is not the bait, as you say, that interests me, but the measure of the man, Sir. More, the husband I need is my true husband, who is, I feel, alive. Merely kept from returning to me, by what devices or arts I do not know." She turned to her work, adding: "I place no blame at your door, Mr. Browne, who have made such efforts in my interest. But there's too much unsettled, too much wanting to my satisfaction."

She began to prepare the largest cuts of meat to be roasted immediately or preserved in the powdering tub. He was tempted to tell her all he knew, but he thought and saw again how much he needed now to consider carefully the whole story he had unravelled so far before speaking to anyone. All he could think to say was: "So you have not sought a widow's status yet?"

"I have not." She looked up at him. "And be left with even less than I have now? They'll take it soon enough. We cannot live on some widow's third or lesser estate, not without a new husband to replenish us." Then she smiled at him for the first time since they had begun speaking of remarriage, and said: "What sort of fool do you think me, Mr. Browne?"

He laughed, glad to be on smoother waters. "Well, yes, you

are right. Oh these magistrates, as everyone says, these robbers and destroyers of widows and the fatherless! Yet Mr. Cole would see the best done by you. The laws and practices are changing these days, and ought not your son Jared come into some of the property? Or as is the case here more frequently in these days, Enoch, the youngest son, to care for you in your dotage?"

"Oh, all such arrangements might be made, I do not doubt. Were my husband dead, and my wishes turned in that direction," she said in a tone of dismissal. "We have a new minister, finally. Just recently here among us."

"That is good news. Who is he?"

Again she did not answer for a time, being too busy in her labors.

"One Mr. Vaughan," she said. "The Reverend Nehemiah Vaughan. Highly regarded. Everyone seems to believe we have struck fortune equal to our years of waiting and past divisions. Another Cambridge man, Mr. Browne."

"I see. Most fortunate then. Have you met him?"

"Only to hear him teach, once. Mr. Cole introduced us afterward and told him of my situation and trials. I told him of all your help to me. He seemed interested in you, begged to meet you upon your return. Which we expected much later. But now, here you are. Back with us!" She had emptied the iron pot and replaced it with a spit over the smoky fire.

"I'd like to meet him. You yourself are pleased?"

"Why should I not be? Pleased enough. Our little ship of spirit so long without a rudder. Though Mr. Vaughan's a wealthy and worldly enough man. We paid dearly to gain him in the end, settled one of the largest properties on him, along with his living. He's no lady's chambermaid. They drained a hogshead of rum at his installation."

"He is a married man?"

"Yes. A gentle wife. And four children living."

"Then he is well set indeed."

They were quiet while Goody Higgins cleaned her knives and put meat and organ scraps into a bucket. She then picked up the bucket and started toward the house, at the door glancing back to say: "I'll be back in a moment." Browne finally entered her yard and walked about in the sunshine, sniffing at the remaining herbs that were drying in the autumn air. He noticed particularly a great quantity of sage remaining and recalled that before he had departed for England she had begun to grow sage to sell.

He looked about for any sign of the children, but they were apparently all five busy elsewhere with tasks she had set them. He assumed the older girls, on this day of pig killing, had been given charge of the younger while they worked. Most likely they were in the hall.

When Elizabeth Higgins returned, her apron changed, her hands and face washed, she came right up to him, took both his hands, and said: "Now let me welcome you back properly, Mr. Browne." She looked happily into his eyes. "It is good to see my neighbor again. I often thought of your adventures these past months, and I prayed for your safety."

"I can't tell you how good it seems to be here again, and to see you flourishing as you are. I have seen only Mr. Cole briefly since landing. It was he who mentioned your suitors." He smiled.

"You found me at a busy time. But now we'll tell one another our adventures."

They walked about the gardens, pens, and small outbuildings within her houselot, talking briefly about his new house and prospects. Everything they looked upon was mellowed in autumn light. She answered his inquiries about her children, her winter supplies, and her beliefs as to her missing husband. Behind the appearance of good cheer at his return, however, she seemed, Browne began to think, less than happy, perhaps lonely. She spoke, finally, with slight, understandable bitterness toward her fate. Yet at that moment she nevertheless seemed to him, aside from his family in England, the most solid, deliberate, and honest human being he had encountered in months. He felt shamed by the secrets he held from her.

He explained that whatever freedom he could salvage from his responsibilities to his new household and enterprises he would use to pursue the enigma of her husband and Balthazar Coffin.

"That may be difficult, Mr. Browne," she said, looking down at a patch of old pumpkin vines by which they had stopped. "Mr. Coffin left us, without warning. No one knows where he went."

He was, for a second, as stunned as he would have been had someone laid a pole into his stomach. She looked up at him, saying nothing.

"When?" he asked finally.

"Sometime during the thaw it was, long after you had shipped for England."

"No one knows where he is you say?"

"Not that I have heard."

"Cole never spoke of this. I must speak to him, if you'll excuse me, Goody Higgins. You know nothing more of this?"

"Nothing more, Mr. Browne. Only that he is gone from us."

XIV

~~~

"It is just as she tells you," Cole said, nodding his head comfortably. "He left us with the most secretive preparations. A strange man. Learned, but wanting probity, it would now seem."

"Has no one been to ask for him?" Browne asked. "Has he left no place to send messages, associates, any business that might arise? How can a man disappear overnight with a house full of specimens and books?"

"Nevertheless, this man has done so."

"His property has been transferred, or sold?"

"His houselot and all its meadows upon the river were sold through the court, quite some time ago now."

"He must be found."

"I would have thought you now had other pressing interests to consume your energies, Richard. Hence I did not mention this matter when we spoke briefly yesterday. I was more interested in your prospects from England, and your news, not in troubling you further at the time. It would seem he is out of harm, or doing harm, now."

"My curiosity is much aroused, however. There may never be a resolution in all these matters, now. It is Coffin who still holds the answers to many questions."

"You have learned something more, in England, Richard?"

"Not in England. But I took the opportunity of my travel to read, and reread, a most curious document. A small gift Mr.

Coffin made me near the eve of my departure and, as I now know, not long before he departed as well. Mistress Coffin's private journal. A record of certain times and episodes since her arrival here, including the period of her husband's expedition to the Indies, and elsewhere."

"A gift indeed. He must have come to trust you, Richard."

"It was as much perhaps his confessional."

"What have you learned by it?"

"There is no evidence against anyone in Mistress Coffin's death. But there is a tale of things hidden from others' eyes, an undercurrent in these lives, as is so often the case. But I can say little as yet. The diary was given me in total confidence, which I had been sworn to bear. It may be, of course, that I will open enough passages of light into these doings and relations to necessitate disclosure of all my investigations. I can say now only that I have seen the woman's version of her marriage and life here."

"An undercurrent often lies long hidden. This tale, you say, is such a one?"

"It is a dark enough tale."

"Well, I'm anxious to hear whatever results and conclusions you winnow from these investigations. How will you proceed?"

"That I must now rediscover. Coffin's departure is a sudden turn. There must, however, be those in whom he has had to confide, if only for the aid of their labor. Even if these knew not his purpose, or his ultimate destination."

"They'll be difficult to find. Coffin is a cautious man. Let me think on it. And ask a few questions. Come tomorrow, Richard, at mid-day. Come take dinner with us. Perhaps I can be of some help by then."

"I would be grateful. For the moment just allow me one question, now we are alone, over some unpleasant details—the condition of the poor woman's body when she was found in the river. I have read and heard conflicting accounts."

"Well you might, Richard. Well you might." Cole raised himself heavily out of his chair and stood facing the fire before him. He lit his pipe and filled the room with tobacco smoke. Browne watched his back. "She had been very much tormented, unfortunate creature. Hanged or strangled in some way. Her neck broken finally; tongue black, swollen, out of her mouth. All the blood seemed to have settled in her face. But if that is not enough, her privy parts were all swollen from terrible abuse. One dare not think what she suffered at the hands of her tormentor."

"Or tormentors?" Cole looked at Browne. "Do not the circumstances of the body suggest the possibility of more than one to you?" Browne asked.

"May well be. Possible, of course." He turned to face Browne completely. "If there were further evidence of divers persons, Higgins' own defense against suspicions and accusations might be corroborated. But of course specific actions against him are long since withdrawn. Is there anything in this diary you speak of to suggest further the role of two or more persons in her death?"

"Nothing. Merely an intuition from what you have told me."

"I see." He relit his waning pipe. "Well, we'll discuss this tomorrow, Richard." Cole shook his head. "Perhaps this does merit continued pursuit."

Browne returned home immediately to conduct business of his own. His correspondence would grow heavy. And there were sawyers and mast cutters to be hired, sawmill owners to see, shipping clerks to contact. For the first time in his life all his responsibilities seemed overwhelming.

His brother and sister-in-law had not returned with him to New England. They concluded that this brother would be much more useful to their Atlantic trade situated in Old England. They were optimistic about the future of the Commonwealth, despite the previous political quietism of Richard's younger brother, William. Now the squirearchy and merchants began to look upon their mercantile interests with hope again.

It seemed to the Browne brothers the best of times, in nearly a decade, to be about the enterprise of rebuilding their fortunes. They had, therefore, entered into a corporation—to nearly the limits of their remaining resources—with some half-dozen well-connected others. They expected to reap their corporate share of the bountiful forest in the vicinity of Richard Browne's residence in the New World. That vicinity was, of course, but a tiny fragment of the enormous, plunderable wilderness encompassing, in King James' grant to the New Council at Plymouth, everything roughly from present-day Philadelphia to Newfoundland. Indeed, Browne's vicinity was but a fragment even of the still lesser patent granted in turn by the Council in 1622 to Sir Ferdinando Gorges and Captain John Mason for the region known as "Laconia," which stretched from the Merrimack to the Kennebec Rivers.

The old cavalier Gorges and the younger gallant Mason shared, in separate ways, anachronistic dreams of becoming lords of vast domains. These two adventurers sent initial agents, such as the Hilton brothers (fishmongers out of London), to establish flourishing fiefdoms in the New World. But the reach of the dreamers was so disconnected from the reality of the wilderness that their failures to exploit like feudal lords their vast estates were to be redeemed only by Englishmen of lesser reach, and only in the aftermath of the struggles, deaths, and desperate persistences of early settlers. It was men like Richard Browne who came to face the challenge of shaping out of the old adventurers' domain of gargantuan dreams a manageable and profitable harvest of wood, fur, and mineral.

XV

≋

Richard Browne had not, of course, intended to invest the greater share of his time now with this case of the Coffins and Higginses. But he felt that he owed Cole some resolution, and he had, moreover, developed a personal obsession with the matter. All his waking hours seemed to be absorbed either by establishing a lumber trade or by the enigma of Mistress Coffin's death, including its aftermath or impact on Elizabeth Higgins. He took no joy in his condition, but nothing else at the moment, not even his fair new house and its beautiful site, seemed particularly real to him. The more he contemplated his circumstances, the more anxious he grew to devote himself to trade, his house and garden, his new citizenship at Robinson's Falls. He turned fanatically to the lumber trade for some days, wary of his competitors, meeting and negotiating with various men for their services and labors.

That next morning, before he dined with Cole, Browne sat at his writing table, where he had fashioned a study out of a corner of an upstairs storage room. He was pleasantly surrounded now by his books shipped from England, which included not only his beloved poets and the usual selections from years of polite reading, but his modest collection of legal tracts, mostly at this point in his life practical guides: his own three-shilling version of *The Book of The General Lawes and Libertyes*, West's *Symboleography*, Coke's *A Book of Entries*, and Dalton's *The*

Country Justice, among some few less-useful if more learned tomes.

He glanced up from time to time to look through his upstairs window at the great flocks of migratory birds flying above or feeding in the river and marshes below his house. Again his thoughts turned to a way of disposing of the Higgins-Coffin affair to his own satisfaction. Could he simply turn over all he had learned to Goody Higgins and Mr. Cole for their own disposition of the matter? Even what he had discovered of Jared Higgins? Yet who could say what was that man's condition now?

But he would soon meet with Cole, who might have further information of Coffin. He, Browne, would have to pursue any possibilities there. He tapped his writing table impatiently, stood up, and walked about the room, returning to the window from time to time. Suddenly he slapped his hand against the window casing. Any further information Cole had to contribute he would act upon. But only through November. Then he would cut any losses and move ahead completely with his own life and trade. He would by then have done his best, helped somewhat, paid any reasonable debt to Cole. (He thanked God he had no wife and children.)

He sat down at his table again and settled into his correspondence and accounts, feeling virtuous and rested. After an hour he called his new maidservant Maggie, daughter of a local widow with twelve children, and asked for a mug of fresh sweet cider which she had bought, along with provisions, of the goodwives just yesterday. He asked her if his hired man, Elias Low, had gone out yet to purchase the horse, fowl, sheep, and pigs as Browne had directed. Yes, Maggie assured him, Elias had been out about such business all morning.

He took some time arranging his papers for later attention and then went downstairs where the huge central fireplace divided two spacious rooms. There was a separate kitchen in the back as well. He left a message for Elias with Maggie in the kitchen. Then he left for his dinner appointment with Cole, who, he found, was his usual mixture of warmth and respect. While they drank strong cider, Browne entertained Mr. and Mrs. Cole with descriptions of England under the Rump parliament. Mrs. Cole, in her bright green gown and lawn sleeves, asked about the fate of certain great families. And the king had been in prison? And they had cut off his head? It was all true, Browne assured her. There was no doubt of the victors and where their interests lay. But there was considerable doubt as to how to govern, he said. She stared quietly in her astonishment while the two men turned to speak of the climate for trade.

As they rose to go to the ample table, Cole said: "I have a few ideas you might pursue, certain people who might know more about this business of Coffin's flight." They were interrupted by the business of being seated and the bustle of Mrs. Cole and a servant about the table. The board-cloth was as fine as anything Richard had seen recently in England. The large silver standing salt glittered, uncovered, at the center. Even as they were seated and the servant girl was bringing food to the table on huge pewter serving platters, Cole, sitting directly beside his wife at the head before their single large wooden trencher, began to speak of Mr. Coffin. But as they started to eat, they all grew silent until Browne finally remarked: "I had forgotten how excellent a cook your Polly is, though how I could have forgotten is beyond me." Cole and his wife, smiling, looked up from their food and Cole returned to his subject.

"I believe Coffin was known to one Dr. Sedley, recently of Salisbury. Have you heard of Sedley? No? Well, he has a certain eminence among those who practice physic and surgery, and such like. I may have heard he studied with Harvey once. Probably just a tale; you know how such things get started. Yet Sedley is your man, Richard. Begin there."

"Now I think of it, the name seems familiar," Richard said.

"He had, I believe, something to do with the London College of Physicians, some post or influence. It may be the same man."

"That's as I understand. And I believe Sedley was at Leyden and Padua before returning to London. But my speculations are not to the point. He is the man to find, in Salisbury, if I am not mistaken."

"What would such a man, if it is he, be doing in Salisbury?"

"That you must discover, Richard. Little of this makes sense to me. Thus I called on you. I do know that he and Coffin had correspondence, most likely as to his collections and the like. Might not this Dr. Sedley be here to study our rarities as well? Who can say? He arrived only within the year, apparently." Cole paused to pass the tankard to Browne.

"Let us hope," Browne said, raising the tankard in a gesture of thanks, "they were more than casual correspondents. There may be something here, Mr. Cole, thanks to your efforts."

"Let's hope so. Such a one as Coffin has few confidants. But I have some others for you. There is Goody Hussey, the old potion doctress to whom I believe he repaired on occasion for her herbal experience in this land. At least I have one or two reports of it."

"Ah," Richard said. "Where is this woman to be found?"

"Hampton. She's mad, of course. A truly mazed creature! Don't expect to get sense out of her. But perhaps you should try; who knows what path may lead out." He put his hand up to his cheek and spoke out of the side of his face in mock confidence: "Some say she's a witch. She may hang for it yet."

They finished the meal in contemplative silence. Cole had claret brought in. When they were settled with the wine, Browne asked, "What others?"

"Only two, Richard. Or maybe one." He took a large sip of his wine. "The Fletcher brothers. Jacob and Henry. Henry's a simpleton, and mute. He has a strong back and works in his way at whatever is available—lumber drives on the river, shearing, clearing planting fields, whatever. Jacob is more alert, but just as bad, ask me. Vaultneants, the pair of them! Foresworn dogs. As often under restraint or punishment as free and working." He shook his head. "Some have charged Henry capable of everything: bestiality, theft, sodomy, smiting his father, lying with a child . . . At the least both are and have been brought up as loose and disorderly persons, idle and debauched."

"Mr. Cole!" his wife, who had been growing increasingly distraught, said. "We've had quite enough."

"Yes, of course, you are right, my dear." He shrugged his shoulders and looked in mock helplessness at Browne. "Let me say only that Henry is alive today owing to his simplicity and inability to speak for himself. Some have propounded castration, others banishment, still others that he be locked away until his death. But nothing has come of such proposals. Some say Jacob restrains him, but one's as bad as the other. And more's the blame to Jacob since he's not a simpleton, merely a dizzard."

"And the connection with Coffin?" Browne asked.

"I was coming to that. I understand Coffin hired them once or twice for labor. It seems the brothers and Higgins are the only ones he ever hired, excepting the original carpenters who built his house back in . . . wasn't it forty-four, dear?"

"I believe so," Mrs. Cole said. She was shaking her head, a pained look on her face. "Mr. Browne," she said, changing the subject, "would you not come to our merriment Thursday evening next? Thomas Andros will be here with his music."

"That would be delightful, Mrs. Cole." He asked what hour but barely heard her reply. He had so little time, he felt, to conduct what other investigations he might that he pushed ahead, saying to Cole: "There are no others, then, Mr. Cole?"

"I am sorry to say no. Or none that I have been able to discover. You may of course inquire of anyone, but all seem equally in the dark on this matter. These are Coffin's recent associates."

"A small but wondrous strange collection."

"A menagerie," Cole said and laughed. "They will be difficult to question. It seems Dr. Sedley may be away on some expedition. But due back soon. The brothers Fletcher are closer by, cast in two actions to the value of about six pounds, subsequent to a hearing to be held tomorrow. You might join us then to see what you make of these two before you question them on this other matter. The widow Hussey you may handle as you wish, or not at all, ask me. She has not talked sense for ten years."

"I thank you for the information, Mr. Cole. My time, as you know, is not so free as it was. Yet I'll pursue these people you mention. I believe Mr. Coffin can be found."

"Good, Richard. All you can do is pursue him. And I understand that you are a man of many responsibilities to your family and associates now." Cole stopped and rose from the table. They all rose and Cole, excusing them from his wife for a few minutes and refilling their winecups, brought Browne aside into the next room.

"I can't but think that this private journal you spoke of may be more productive of witnesses," Cole said once they stood alone in the room. "If there was some adultery or other evil doings come to light."

"So there seems to have been, Mr. Cole. But by her own account, and everything I've seen, there is no clear cause for that woman's death, and the brutalities she suffered."

"Such is often the case, or so it seems." He mused a moment. "Ah yes, adultery is that common evil which produces a whole race of kindred evils."

"We are looking at much more than adultery here," Browne said, "from the start."

"Just so," Cole replied. "And with attendant evils. And perhaps even with things separate and darker still."

"The whole matter may be more murky now than when I began."

"Not so, Richard! Not so. You have been a tremendous help since your arrival."

"But you, Sir, seem to have guessed nearly as much as I know by all my researches."

"Well, experience must count for something," Cole said and laughed. "And I hear many things about town. Moreover, need I remind you that history is replete with the debris of those who have believed that love excuses all."

"Or rather that lust excuses all."

"People mean what they believe, and do not make such distinctions. They believe only what they believe, so to speak. What is real, the case or circumstances or even the feeling, is not the issue, is it?"

"Perhaps not," Browne answered. He thought about it. Love excuses all. Yes, so we believe by our acts. It was simply human nature again. And by the other face of the coin, hate would excuse all, or vengeance as hatred. Yet there was no use in such speculations at this point. He was thinking, as he excused himself to be returning home, that already his self-imposed deadline was disintegrating. One month! He himself could be such a fool. It would have to be, somehow, a matter of balancing several projects, not a series of deadlines.

Suppose he were able to free Higgins of suspicion in Mistress Coffin's death, at least? Would not that be a worthy service to his friend Elizabeth Higgins? And if Higgins were guilty, especially of such a terrible murder, he, Browne, would be able to lay to rest the question of Higgins' whereabouts, guilt, and true relations to his own family. The last, of course, did not bode well. Perhaps Higgins would have learned his lesson; perhaps they could be reconciled after the truth, Jared and Elizabeth. That would be in any case no longer any of his personal concern.

XVI

≋

When Richard Browne walked into the inquest concerning the Fletcher brothers—held in the hall of Cole's house—the testimony had already begun. A young woman was testifying that upon returning from a quilting party, before her parents returned from a neighbor's harvest, she found that someone had forced his way into her house.

The empty house had been ransacked, she said, but at that time she could not have said what might be missing. Searching among the debris of the keeping room with a mind to run over to her neighbor Adams, she heard a stirring from an adjacent storage room. She was so frightened that she could not run to the neighbor's house. But hearing a sort of grunting noise from the storage room, she believed one of her family to be hurt and rushed in. She stumbled upon the accused, Henry Fletcher, lying amongst her and her mother's clothes with his breeches pulled down.

What, Cole asked, was the man doing?

The young woman blushed. Cole asked her again.

"He were jiggering his yard, Sir," she blurted. Her face turned bewildered and then red. She looked suddenly at her shoes.

There was a silence in the room. The older Fletcher brother, a man of twenty-two or three, began to giggle uncontrollably.

"Silence!" Cole commanded. "Now tell us what it was you saw."

She failed to speak up, so Cole, growing impatient, insisted, his voice reverberating over the heads of the assembly.

"Well, he had a stocking in one hand, my mother's I believe." She stopped. "And his yard in t'other. Against the stocking."

Jacob Fletcher began to snicker uncontrollably again. Henry slouched, his mouth open and his eyes half closed, as if he were unaware of the proceedings. His great body was muscular but already tending toward fat. His posture on the bench was marked by utter indolence and unconcern.

"And what did he then?" Cole's voice boomed.

"He lay there till it were all finished, Sir. His eyes were closed and he did not see me till he sort of wakes up. Then he sees me watching him, too surprised to move." She suddenly looked up and around the room. "He jumps up, makes like a growling, pulled up his breeches, and run fast as he could right past me and out of the house. Fast as he could. He must've believed my family returned. That was my luck, Sir."

She completed her testimony by detailing her clothing among the pile—stockings, a shirt, petticoats, et cetera.

Then the mother testified and detailed which clothes had been hers. Later, the father listed all the articles missing from the house—two firearms, a sword, three knives, an Indian tomahawk, some foodstuff (mostly dried corn) that had been stored in an upstairs room, and a loaf of bread from the hearth.

Standing in the back of the room, Richard Browne had a momentary vision of the brothers stalking about the empty house, gratifying any impulse that might take them, seeking any loot, boasting to one another of their finds and fantasies. He saw too the simpleton lying in the pile of women's clothing.

He despaired at the prospect of talking to these two men. What possible profit to him could there be in it? Yet how could he not try?

Now two neighbors of the family, men, were making their statements. They had both joined the young woman's father and gone after the Fletchers. Both Fletchers were discovered in a wigwam they had built well into the forest beyond town. In this wigwam was a cooking pot, foodstuffs, women's clothing, and a large cache of weapons. All of the clothes and weapons had been identified through depositions now before the magistrate. The discovery of precisely the weapons and some plate missing from the maid's house, they said, suggested that the elder Fletcher had left his younger brother behind to take his pleasures in the ladies' clothing while he made off with his booty.

A succession of witnesses followed, each one revealing similar facts. Browne left well before the testimony ended.

Early the following day Cole led Browne into the reconstructed barn that served as a town pound and jail. Shackled in their corner, the Fletchers assumed Richard Browne to be some high magistrate to take their statements or direct their removal elsewhere, perhaps the county jail. It was only after realizing that Browne wanted to question them about an entirely different matter that Jacob began to talk.

Yes, he said, they had on a few occasions worked for Mr. Coffin. The pay was good. What business, Jacob wanted to know, had Mr. Browne with Coffin and the brothers?

"We are trying to find Mr. Coffin," Browne said.

"We?"

"Mr. Cole and I."

"Well we don't know because we wasn't never told where he's going," Jacob said.

"Never told you? When?"

"Before he moved, I mean."

"Moved?" Browne asked. He was surprised, but saw they knew something after all. Yet he did not relish dragging every hidden detail from simpletons and rogues. The odors of unwashed men, of confined animals and offal, nauseated him.

"Come, Fletcher!" Cole said. "If you speak to us, and the truth, we may find you some mercy in your present troubles. You know you are both in for many stripes at the very least. Had this simpleton touched the daughter he would be in for a hanging. Better you were in England, ask me, for blinding and castration. We just might make an example of you as it is." He stared at Fletcher in disgust. "Now, what services had you performed for Coffin relative to his removal?"

"We'd done a job for him long time ago that was the last one."

"When?"

"Two years ago, wasn't it?" He looked down at his brother, who had remained slouched in his corner. Henry said nothing and gave no indication of having followed the questioning. "Maybe last year?"

"What kind of job?" Browne asked.

"Some shipping. And finding some people."

"Who? What shipping?"

"It were just toting lots of old boxes to a ship bound for Salisbury, Gloucester, and Boston."

"What people?"

"Oh, just some people owed him money. Not from around here, Sir. He paid us well not to give no names, and promised to curse us if we ever told a soul. He would too, that one. So we haven't." He swelled out his chest like a bad actor. "And we won't. Not if they torture us even!" He looked back at the straw-covered floor. "It's just collecting money owed, like I say. And nothing to do with where he might of gone to." He paused to look at Browne. "You might ask Black Ned, the Negro truck-man. He finds boats for anyone wants goods or persons shipped upriver. Or other parts. Mr. Coffin's hired him out."

"And you have," Cole interrupted, speaking slowly, "on your souls, no knowledge of his whereabouts?"

"None, hope to die, Sir. That's all the truth, just as I told.

You'll get us mercy, Sir, like you promised?" He jerked his brother up to stand beside him.

Cole looked at them in disgust. "Mercy?" he said. "What business have such long-shanked rogues with mercy? Count yourselves lucky if you are not hanged as the issue of this." He glanced again at Browne, then back to the brothers, nodding particularly toward Henry. "See that this offal eats his waterlily roots each day. As to mercy, we shall see, according to your current merit, whether you be hanged or no." He motioned Browne to leave with him. As they turned, Jacob called after them: "We'd be most thankful, Sirs. Hire us out sometime, and see if we don't do a job for you!"

Browne looked at Cole as they left. "Henry, the dumb one," he said, "*non compos mentis?*"

"I should think not, Richard. He is neither a natural fool, nor a lunatic. And as for his memory, well there is hardly a question of his gaining or losing it." He shook his head and murmured: "Bots that crawl on the beast's tail."

"'The ravens,'" Browne quoted, "'shall pick out the eyes of such in the valley.'"

"Aye to that, Richard. In time, in time."

A week later, after attending strictly to his own affairs, Browne went to Strawberry Banke after the truckman Black Ned. Cole's point about expecting little help from Goody Hussey seemed reasonable. But he had no luck in the port town. Ned was shipping with men who had hired him to move their goods and families to Gloucester. Some expected he might be back in about three days. So Browne decided to book a passage for Salisbury.

He discovered, however, that his bad luck held. Dr. Sedley had not returned from his own expedition deep inland. No, Sedley's housekeeper said, she could not say when he might return, but she certainly hoped before winter set in. Yes, she had heard Dr. Sedley speak of Balthazar Coffin, and met Mr.

Coffin once or twice, come to that, and she believed there had been some talk of Mr. Coffin's moving to Salisbury, but she would not know if such a thing came to pass. Yes, Mr. Browne might leave his name and residence. Sedley being absent some months, she explained, she had heard no more of Coffin or anyone else from the doctor.

Nor was there any further sign of Black Ned when Browne stopped at Strawberry Banke on his return. While he waited for the upriver boat, he grew angry with himself over time wasted. Never in his life had he so well known the value of time. He resolved that for a fortnight he would have absolutely nothing more to do with Coffin. But two hours into his trip upriver on the incoming tide he recalled Goody Hussey. The thought of her, of what she might know, nagged him, and he began to feel that somehow she would change his luck by knowing something, despite Cole's admonitions to the contrary. His own vacillations and uncertainties confused him. Watching herons constantly rise up with slow wing beats into the trees ahead of the boat, like truths escaping the truth seeker, he suddenly decided to try Goody Hussey.

And thus it was that he found himself, the very next day, at the center of the village where she lived, asking how he might find her cottage.

The cottage he sought, Browne was told in the village, was situated on a small peninsula of high ground that reached out into the salt marshes. It was necessary, he discovered, to travel from the village center a half mile through the wood to gain access to the old woman's spit of dry land. Suspicious of a stranger asking for Goody Hussey, townspeople reluctantly indicated the hay road leading through the wood to the marsh.

From Cole, Browne had learned that the old lady's son had discovered and claimed that elevated mead in the great marshes more than ten years before, shortly after their arrival among the earliest settlers. The son had died of a fever five years ago while working on a privateer after Spanish loot in the West Indies. The town left to the lone woman only that cottage. That portion of the hay marsh her son claimed, his back pay, and his few valuables, the selectmen had brought into the town coffers. The old widow lived on the charity of one or two of the more comfortable families in town as well as by her skill at physic and midwifery. But as her eccentricities seemed to grow with age, she was called in these days as a last but often effective resort only in the most terrible crises of illness and birth.

Word was that she had grown more familiar with the Indians than with her white neighbors. She might be seen collecting her wild roots, herbs, and mushrooms at any time of day in the fields or woods. She was on such a mission the very day Browne trod along the hay road in search of her cottage, and a rough voice called out to him: "You seem lost, Sir."

He turned quickly to see behind him an old woman standing in an open ferny space where her figure caught a rare shaft of sunlight that made her white hair and cap glow above her dark clothing. She leaned upon her walking stick and held an Indian basket in her other hand. She moved toward him, entering the shadows of the great trees.

"I may be!" he said. "You gave me a start!" He composed himself with a laugh. "I've come to speak with Goody Hussey. Might you be the same?"

"That I might, young man." She looked him over. "Who be you?"

"Richard Browne, of Robinson's Falls."

"And what business have you with Goody Hussey?"

"I am trying to find Balthazar Coffin. I understand that she knew him."

"She may know him. But he lives where you come from, Sir. Why come you here?"

"He has removed. Yet I have important business with him.

Some business we had entered together, but left unfinished. His manner of departure left no one certain of his destination."

"So that's why I haven't seen him these months." She turned and motioned Browne to follow her.

He followed, saying: "I had hoped you would have some word of him, Goody Hussey. Yet I see you yourself are taken unawares by my news."

"That I am, Sir." She kept walking in her slow way into the woods. The trees were enormous, gray-green with moss, and well spaced, retaining the look of an Indian game grove. The high, dense canopy of leaves parted at rare intervals to let in a flash of blue or a blaze of sunlight.

Browne began to feel a sense of frustration and waste kindling in him again. Yet he felt strangely vulnerable too, and his mind began to move toward his immediate situation. He was not a man given to excesses of superstition. He knew—by the common and ancient testimony of humanity—that the dead at times returned to the living. But he did not see in every old crone a witch, nor in every animal a familiar, nor in every rarity a sign from the Darkness or the Light. He increasingly believed that nature, for the most part, could be classified and understood. He knew Aristotle, Lucretius, Von Gesner, and even a recent production of Sir Thomas Browne entitled *Pseudodoxia Epidemica*. Still, he could not shake his momentary apprehensions.

"Here we are, Sir," she was finally saying as she pointed her stick at a large outcropping of ledge. "Some call it the pulpit. I find this lower section makes a fine seat for old bones. Now . . . do sit, Sir. Tell me something of this business between you and Mr. Coffin."

He saw no point in reticence before this old woman. He suspected she might know more than she yet showed. If he could not find Coffin he would have to stop. The thought of stopping filled him with desperation, however. He would see this through, then get on with his own work. He began by explaining how he had come to Robinson's Falls under Cole's dispensation to help relieve Goody Higgins' tribulations, perhaps even by answering questions left in the aftermath of Mistress Coffin's murder.

"A foul business that!" she interjected.

He nodded his head and returned to his explanation. He felt that were he to stop he would not be able to continue. So he spoke quickly, letting it all tumble out, saying finally that Coffin had given him a private journal whereby he had a glimpse into the lives of the Coffins. As a result he had begun to feel that he was making headway into strange, interlocking events when, upon his return from England, he had discovered Mr. Coffin's abrupt departure. Only Coffin, he believed, could offer the necessary resolution to these affairs, the fulfillment of his, Browne's, duty toward Mr. Cole, his neighbor Goody Higgins, and even Coffin. He did not speak of his large personal curiosity, which was also a goad to him.

Goody Hussey listened. When he had finished she said: "I'm sorry I cannot help you. You saw that already. You have no sign of Coffin's destination?"

"Only that Black Ned might have helped in the move."

"Ah!" She thought for a moment. "Then that is the path to follow."

"Have you heard of a Dr. Sedley? A colleague of Mr. Coffin's?"

"Mr. Coffin spoke of him once or twice as a knowledgeable, much honored man."

"I thought he might know something of Coffin, but he is up in the country on researches of his own."

"Another path, Mr. Browne!"

"Indeed, Goody Hussey, if obscure at present. But I have a feeling about these Fletcher brothers. They say nothing, yet I believe they know something useful to me."

"Oh, the Fletcher brothers!" she said and paused. "You may have something there, Sir. Do you see the mark of their hands in this?" From her seat she looked over and up at him with a deep, inquiring eye. He could see clearly now that she was old, and not well. Her skin was an unhealthy white; he could discern no teeth in her black mouth, but then she barely opened her mouth to speak. Yet despite what people said, her mental vitality seemed intact.

"I know only that they have had dealings with Coffin in the past," he said, "and that they shipped some materials for him at one time, probably about the time he left."

"And you do not believe their ignorance?"

"Just so."

"Well, that's the way with those two. You may have something there, Mr. Browne." She stopped, shifted in her seat, seemed to ponder a moment or two the implications of introducing the Fletchers into Browne's quest. She chuckled to herself.

"You know them?"

"Oh yes. They purchase some decoction, plant, or essence of me from time to time. Infrequently. I don't ask people many questions, having my living to get. I'll trade for whatever people need, or believe they need. If I have it."

"And the Fletchers?"

"Those two are fond of things that make them drunk, or lustful, or see things they wouldn't otherwise see in the dullness of their base senses."

"But these are crooked fragments of humanity, Goody Hussey. . . ."

"That may be, but an old woman has to live, hasn't she? I don't lead them to their ways. Nor do my sweets cause them to act in any way. It is their own will that bends them."

"But, Goody Hussey, in their wild anarchy of drink . . ."

"Sir. My truck with these brothers is scarce. Nothing I pass in itself causes men to do evil, in spite of what some may say of me. Fools and gossips! Would you, like the rest of them, have an old woman starve to death, if you don't hang her first?"

"Please don't misunderstand me. I apologize if my words seemed to say so. The truth is I have come for your help, if that be possible, good woman."

"I know nothing of Coffin's departure. I am not privy to it, Sir."

"I understand. But might you not help me now with the Fletchers?"

"How so?"

"They lie. I am certain of it. They are refractory."

"And I am to find the truth?"

"Perhaps your influence upon them. Get them to speak . . ."

"Bah! Dullards and jades, Sir. Base carnal matter. What talk of influence?"

"Perhaps they fear you, Goody Hussey? Many do."

She laughed outright. "Many will burn in Hell!" She laughed again. "They see in me whatever they want to see." She shot Browne a look. "You do not fear me?"

"I am no more afraid than any man who is honest with you, and in God's protection. But the Fletchers; they may fear your disapprobation if you question them sharply with me and Mr. Cole."

"No, Sir. I have no business with Cole or the Fletchers."

"Might we not in some way frighten them into the truth. They fear not the laws of God or man."

"Tell me what I owe to Cole or Goody Higgins, or to yourself, that I should be troubled in this affair."

"Nothing, I own. Can finding truth not be its own reward? But as I've told you, Mr. Coffin as well sought resolution to his wife's terrible death. Perchance I may discover such a resolution as well, resolve his own torment and doubt." She seemed unimpressed. "And I would of course pay you honestly for any trouble to you, in British currency. Perhaps we could represent your own displeasure to them, or interest, or something."

"English currency?" She slid another look at him.

"As you wish."

She raised herself by her stick and shuffled about for a few moments. Browne watched her. "I don't know," she finally said. "We might try a decoction."

"Decoction?" he said. It was as if Browne had caught a glimpse of the exit to a maze he had wandered in for nearly two years.

"To give them violent fits and bring them to the invisible world."

"Until they beg for relief?"

"And exchange relief—which I can offer them—for information."

"Excellent!" Browne said. "But no one must know our method."

"Just so!" She turned to look him in the eye. "Say nothing of my cause in this. I will introduce myself as needs be."

"What of this decoction? Something that would make them see what is not with them in their cells? Nightmares? Convulsions?"

"Something to make them see. I tell no one, Mr. Browne, what to believe or disbelieve. I am no Zealot. No Opinionist. We have enough of those about." She waved her arm and smiled.

Browne rose from his seat and, about to leave, promised to pay for her labors. "Balthazar Coffin may ultimately be the benefactor here as well," he said. "We shall tell him whatever I discover after he has set me on the right path, which he can hardly fail to do now that I have read the diary." She said nothing, so he continued. "One last thing, Goody Hussey. We will need access to the Fletchers." She nodded her head in agreement and continued to look directly at Browne, leaning toward him. "Cole must know therefore something of our plan."

She looked down a moment without speaking. "You ask me

to place myself in danger, Mr. Browne." He made as if to protest, but she went on. "But I am old now and it hardly matters. You will pay me well, in pounds, for my trouble."

"Anything within reason, good woman."

"If you must, tell Cole. But swear him to secrecy as a protection to both of us, and out of respect for our acts in his behalf."

Browne agreed. Since the old woman did not move from her spot, he said goodbye. As he walked back the way he had come, he felt that he would make progress now. But he could not, for the life of him, give one clear reason why he should feel that way.

XVII

A month later the Fletcher brothers talked. Cole had them brought before Richard Browne on a gray, damp morning in late November. Jacob was thin, colorless, and sickly, but his eyes retained the alertness of a harried animal. The younger Fletcher had lost some of his fleshy bulk, and much sleep, but his level of awareness seemed about the same—a heavy-lidded sensibility awake only to the possibilities of corporeal gratification or pain. The brothers had been dressed in rough homespun clothing, reminding Browne of boyish and neglected street ruffians from London who had been scrubbed and dressed against their surly wills.

Browne explained immediately that if they were prepared to cooperate, Goody Hussey, having heard of their torments, had agreed to help relieve them. But they must swear by their sinful souls to behave themselves and aid Mr. Browne in his search for Mr. Coffin. Both brothers seemed to understand yet neither had any knowledge of Coffin's removal. In fact, Jacob protested, they had not seen Coffin since just before his wife's death. And only then, Jacob explained, to be sent on some errand they could not accomplish, for the people they were to see were not where they were supposed to be.

Jacob spoke earnestly enough, but Browne did not believe him. He threatened to return the prisoners to their shackles, and thence to their whippings and exiles, the sentence resulting from their jury trial.

Jacob begged that they be saved first by Goody Hussey's ministrations, whatever else might be done to them. Even Henry became extremely agitated by Browne's displeasure.

Jacob continued to insist so earnestly that they knew nothing of Coffin's departure that Browne slowly began to believe him. They were so certain of their innocence on this particular point. It may be, Browne thought while Jacob pleaded, the one honest moment of his life.

So Browne tried another approach. What was this errand they were unable to accomplish?

The brothers looked at one another as if their boat were about to plunge over the brink of a deadly waterfall.

"He wanted us to waylay Mistress Coffin and Higgins as they came along the bay in Higgins' canoe."

"His own wife? Come, man, to what purpose?"

"Teach her a lesson, Sir."

"What lesson?"

"That she had not got away with it. He would not be a cuckold, Sir, by the blood of Christ. He knew and could punish. And Higgins, he would never lie with woman again. No one could cross Mr. Coffin in a confidence and get away."

"You were hired to kill Higgins?"

"No, Sir. Just cut off his cods. He showed us how he wanted it done, so as not to infect with death and to stop bleeding. Just how to sear the open flesh with a hot blade."

"And Mistress Coffin?"

"Oh, only to scare her proper, Sir. Rob and abandon her on Bailey's Island, where he could search and deliver her himself. Teach her the wages of sin. He were too proud a man, Sir, to be wearing her horns!"

"He paid you for this?"

"Yes, Sir. And would bring no charges against us if all went well."

"And you carried out his orders?"

"No, Sir! We was paid, but we couldn't find them. So never done the deed. They never came where they must go, where we laid for them. No Sir. So we told him we never see them, and he were right angry with us. But when his wife was disappeared, he came miserable at heart. So we heard, for we didn't go back. Seems he blamed himself, then Higgins, then any he could think of."

"He believed you?"

"Yes, Sir. And why shouldn't he? It were truth. Why would we come back later to him if not? He knew."

"You will swear upon your souls, before God and man, to the veracity of this tale?"

The brothers glanced at one another again. "Yes," Jacob said. "And may we be rewarded!"

"Tell me, Fletcher, why should a man like Coffin hire two such gross lumps of flesh for such a business?"

"He knew us, Sir. We did other work for him, beforetimes. He swore us to secrecy. On our lives. We wouldn't cross him, no Sir. Not a man like Mr. Coffin."

"You kept your oath?"

"Oh yes, Sir. You see my brother, he can't speak, so it's all on me. Just as he knew, Sir. And by the wounds of God I weren't about to go against *his* will."

Browne had pen and paper brought in, drafted their depositions, which they marked, had their marks witnessed, and then left to find Cole to review the document. Cole, however, was suspicious of the testimony. Still, he allowed Browne a free hand in discovering whatever he might. He believed Browne the only one with the knowledge, now, and the tenacity to discover some degree of truth in the whole matter. He had trusted him as long as he had known him, and Browne's father before him.

Browne did not know whether he believed the brothers. Up to a point he did. He found his perspective on Coffin changing. Browne saw that even if he should find Coffin, the man would not necessarily resolve his questions. Yet could there be any loss in confronting Coffin with the depositions and the hidden life revealed in his wife's journal? And having it out? He was learned and proud, but wouldn't even his vain mask slip before these bitter facts? And how better to test the brothers' version of events? If they had been hired for such violence, then the field would seem to be narrowed to Higgins and the brothers. Moreover, if Coffin had believed Higgins guilty, then the brothers' deposition could well be fundamentally true.

There was little more Browne could do for now, so he returned to his own affairs until he had word of Black Ned, and until spring would make travel to Salisbury convenient again. The Fletchers received their twenty stripes "well laid on" and were interned once again pending further interrogation. For the moment they were relieved of Goody Hussey's grip.

It was early December, just before the river froze, when Browne's man returned from the Banke with word of Black Ned. Once again Browne hurried downriver to the port town.

But all Ned could tell him was that five or six months ago he had shipped crates downriver for Coffin and booked his passage on a ship destined for several stops down to New Haven and back. That, Ned emphasized, was his only business with Mr. Coffin. He asked no questions of those who hired him.

So Browne spent the winter of 1650–51 attending to his personal responsibilities. The only definite plan he made regarding the Coffin affair was to engage Darby Shaw again for a journey, come spring, back into the Indian country to contact Jared Higgins once more. He expected, also, that he would first visit

Dr. Sedley's residence in Salisbury. But that spring, just as he was making more definite plans for his journey to Salisbury, a letter from Sedley arrived, dated April 14, 1651.

SIR—

I received the message you left with my housekeeper during your October visit. Please forgive this delay in my response. I had been on an expedition into the interior, fully expecting to return by early December, but *dis aliter visum!* On our return journey we encountered the most debilitating temperatures and snowfall. We lost several men, and straggled home during that brief February thaw. I have been so engaged with my responsibilities to the families of the deceased and so weighed with my own recuperation that it is only at this very moment I find myself able to respond to your inquiries.

Indeed, my friend and colleague Mr. Coffin came to Salisbury last summer in a highly agitated state of mind. He at first took his lodging at a common inn, his diet being provided in large part at the ordinary. I was to tell no one of his removal to Salisbury, and had not. But as you shall see from the enclosed, there is no longer need for silence. Mr. Coffin is dead.

There was a long wasting, but finally, it seems, he took his own life. Some violent poison of his own concoction, apparently. In my opinion he must have been close to death in any event, due to the dissolution of his body and the distraction of his once fine intelligence. His intelligence was matched by uncommon persistence. I expect we will find yet the greatest discoveries by him, equal, say, to the Peruvian Bark of the Jesuits. *Quis melior quam literatus?* Though his manner was grave and aloof, it was the gravity of the learned: *E cuius ore nil temere excidit.* He was a man now, however, in strange torment. I am given to understand that he could neither eat, sleep, study, nor converse with others toward the very end.

I myself witnessed only the beginnings of these disintegrations before departing for the interior. I was of course deeply concerned for him. He had been, formerly, a man of prodigious capacity for mental labor, a capacity matched by his aspiration to find the key to unlock, in a manner of speaking, the barriers between the vegetal and rational divisions of the soul. I considered him, moreover, one of the most knowledgeable men as to physic and the plant life of the Americas, especially regarding the surgical rarities of the New World. I was in much pain to see my friend so stricken, as if he had suddenly grown very aged before his time. Yet I was facing an expedition that had been years in the planning and that had cost me and my benefactors dearly. There was simply no delaying our departure once the time grew propitious. Mr. Coffin understood this, of course.

His own ambition to discover the quintessential or sovereign anodyne caused his deep interest in my own investigations. We were long engaged in complementary researches into the nature and properties of New World vegetables. My own investigations here among the savages are producing discoveries of potent physic. I count it, and Mr. Coffin confirmed my belief, a serious detriment to *both* Englands that there is no comprehensive catalogue by physical description and by properties of the plant life, and especially the medicinal plant life, of New England, notwithstanding Parkinson's *Theatricum Botanicum*. That is my central project. Need anyone be reminded, moreover, of the gross, even tragic, error some have fallen into by application of the English names of European plants to plants found in the Americas?

Indeed, Mr. Browne, by the time my epistle is before you, I will be in transit to London where it has been arranged for me to present certain of my more curious discoveries. I therefore enclose a fair copy of the note Mr. Coffin left upon his death. As to the sum of currency connected in that note to your name, you may apply to the County Court of Probate the Clerk. At the request of

his new wife and widow, I have made arrangements for
the disbursement of that sum to you. All other affairs
Mr. Coffin alludes to I have, with his wife who is administratrix of his estate, seen to through the local magistrates.

Forgive me, I need explain that he was married again
very shortly after his arrival here to a woman widowed of
some nearly ten years. He was sufficiently capable of orderly carriage at that time, and though she knew of his
troubles, seemed much taken with him, and desirous of
restoring the health of so extraordinary a man. But the
issue of her efforts, as you now see, was failure. I think
no one, not even she, saw the degree of his distraction
nor the depth of his illness. "His heart died within him,
and he became as a stone." This good woman, by the by,
had the administration of her former husband's estate, as
well as the bulk of Mr. Coffin's. Hence there has been no
contesting of what he particularly left to you. The poor
woman left us immediately, I am told, removing far off
to Hartford, or the vicinity thereof.

Again, please accept my apologies for my absence
when you called and for the further delay in responding
to you.

Thus taking leave, I commend you to God.

JEREMIAH SEDLEY

Attached to Sedley's letter were several documents, including
Coffin's last note, dated simply December 1650.

I, Balthazar Coffin, who can no longer support the
burdens and afflictions of my life, do hereby enclose a
copy of my will and testament for the benefit of my wife
Mary, the London Philosophical Society, and Mr. Richard
Browne, that he may have resources to complete his inquiries and for recompense of his labors thus far.

Would that I might have left a just portion of my estate to my former wife, Kathrin, but she departed this

life before me, in no small part owing to the very infec-
tions of my own mind that still weigh upon me.

Once I had thought to regain my marriage after long
absence from this land. But ultimately I discovered, on
the contrary, that my previous lofty ambitions and pre-
possessions had irreparably lacerated those tender
threads that make of man and wife one true flesh.

Why it is that only after great shock, or illness, or violence we begin to see our lives and persons for what they
are, only the gods can say. How far I have transgressed
from humility, justice, and love—nay, from every manly
virtue—I dare not speak. *A recta conscientia transversum
unguem non oportet quenquam in omni sua vita discedere.*
I know now that there is no arrogance or meanness I
have not practiced, no *vinum daemonum* I have not
sipped.

Although I have left certain useful books to the London Philosophical Society, as well as the detailed history
of my investigations of the earth and the heavens, in
twenty-four journal volumes, I have burned the unfinished manuscript of my treatise on the history of magic,
as I now believe it more likely to cause greater harm
than good. Likewise, I have dispatched to the flames
those of my philosophical tracts in which I have dabbled
over the years. I now understand them to be riddled with
human folly, to the history of which I once aspired to
contribute as one more of the *Cymini sectores. Quos vult
perdere Deus, dementat prius.*

—BALTHAZAR COFFIN

"Sic ego componi versus in ossa velim," Browne murmured as he
put down the letters and lifted a fair copy of the will, which
Sedley had also enclosed. But what shocked Browne most, what
opened upon new corridors of darkness and suggested new
interconnections, was a note, painstakingly scrawled, that fell
out among these other papers.

SIR

Your wife has not been true. She has taken your absence as leave to satisfy her carnal lusts. Watch her close,
and see if she does not prove false. These be appearances only, Sir, as you may soon see.

And how should I know but that it is my own husband
turned her paramour. I intend soon to make him true.
For he belongs not to her, but is my own, only this once
strayed.

> Yours faithfully
> ELIZABETH HIGGINS

In the will itself, Browne found that he was named for the
sum of £450. He was staggered by it. His first thought was that
the man must have gone truly mad. Then, as he thought about
it further, Coffin's whole scheme in taking his own life and
leaving such a will began to make a certain kind of penitential
sense. Furthermore, his own labors might have benefited Coffin's understanding of events, and he was probably expected to
continue helping Goody Higgins whom, perhaps, Coffin had
tormented (or at least he might have been unfair to her). He
would visit Cole for advice. He felt that he must tell someone
of this sum left to him. Would it not seem somehow unclean if
anyone were to discover later that he had taken it quietly, as if
it were an act worthy of hiding?

"You have responsibilities to yourself, your family, and your
associates," Cole advised. "You've lost much time better spent
developing your forest trade." He seemed almost jolly as he sat
before his fire smoking his pipe at the end of day. "And in this
country especially must a man have his helpmeet." He smiled
at Browne. "Few men improve themselves in this wilderness,
Richard, without a good wife. Quite the contrary!" He took a
long draw on the pipe. "Your instinct to get on with it seems

right to me, Richard. Pursue the present course of your investigations to their end as quickly as you can. You have done the
job well, as well as anyone could hope or expect in these strange
entanglements. Yes, that legacy is an exorbitancy, but consider
it genuinely tendered and, on your part, earned."

"Were I to collect the sum, I could not in good conscience
do less than share it equally with Goody Higgins. And I suspect
that any other arrangement would raise her suspicions and war-
rant complicated explanations."

"Ah, yes! I see. You may be right. Very good, Richard. But
say nothing to anyone of this or there will be talk of collecting
from her for the town coffers. The poor woman, with those
children, will be needing help. You are right there. She may
marry again, but there seems some pain in her that prevents
it. And in any event, should she not be given something now,
she'll end up on the poorlists anyway, collecting from *us*."

"She would receive some relief from her condition, would
she not, if her husband were declared dead?"

"Yes. Some. At least she would know just where she stands.
But then too if we could prove desertion, her circumstances
might become settled."

"Not necessarily to her advantage, I imagine."

"True. Not necessarily to any advantage under current practices." He relit his pipe, drew deeply, looking steadily at Browne.

"Then I should help."

"Indeed, Richard."

"I find much relief in your advice, Mr. Cole."

"Ah!' he said, the smoke rising between their faces. "You've
done well, ferreted out certain of our vermin. We may never
know all that has happened. But think too of the relief you've
brought Goody Higgins. Jared Higgins, guilty or not, is gone
from us forever, as near as I can fathom. Coffin's role, his
instigations, you yourself have said we've discovered in this diary. Or so it seems. I'm anxious for you to tell me more of it

some day. And in any case, whatever his guilt, he is dead now. I doubt we shall uncover sufficient evidence to turn off the ladder whatever rogue squeezed the life from that poor woman." He pulled on his pipe. "And those Fletchers are to be sent from our shores as soon as you deem them useless to any further inquiry."

XVIII

≈≈≈

"You say you have no reason to suspect my husband's where-abouts?" Elizabeth Higgins asked Browne.

"I have none," he answered. He loathed lying to her, but there was more truth in this now than in some of the things he had told her. After more than a year in the wilderness, what might not have befallen Jared Higgins? He might be with the savages still, or he might not. He might have left for England, the Indies, or one of the southern colonies. Might he as possibly be dead by now, a white man living as he had? He tried an explanation: "I have only the sense that I have not hunted for him sufficiently. Darby Shaw has agreed to guide me once again."

"No," she said. "It is hopeless." She looked at the floor. "I'm sure of it now, these two years. The loss of my husband is but one of my torments that began since Mr. Coffin hired him. That past is gone now." She looked up at him. "With much thanks to you, Mr. Browne."

"You credit me with too much, Goody Higgins. Now I merely want to see this final matter through, as I believe it's all I can do."

She rose and walked to the open doorway, where she stood looking out. He rose from his rude chair, which Higgins had made immediately after building his house, and stood three feet behind her.

"I don't want you to waste your time," she said. "Why not stay here and attend your trade?"

"It's a matter of curiosity at this point. Don't feel in any way responsible yourself. I'm being more selfish than you think."

"Curiosity?" She turned toward him.

"Yes. A hard taskmaster."

"Why so curious?"

"Once one enters a maze, one desires the secret of it. Even if one knows he will not live long enough or maintain the strength of purpose to emerge."

"You sacrifice much for curiosity."

He pulled a purse out of the large pocket he had worn over his shoulder and set the purse on the nearby table.

"You must accept this. It is half of the legacy I told you Mr. Coffin left to us both upon his death. I don't know whether it is merely guilt money or not. But it's left to you, as to me, so you might as well take it."

She stared at the purse, seeming for an instant both angry and pleased. When she looked directly at him, her pale eyes searched his as if to test his truthfulness.

Browne turned away, and she again looked at the purse on the table. He said nothing but began to pace, his hands folded behind him, his eyes on the floor, his mind reasoning with itself. Certainly he owed her nothing, and Coffin had left the complete sum to himself. He had been through all such reasonings before. One hundred and twelve pounds was a lot of money. It was a gift that would change her life entirely.

He had been forced to retain better than half himself, well over £300. He had been growing troubled lately by the discovery that men from Massachusetts—Hutchinson, Broughton, Hull, others—were buying up timberland and sawmills of the Piscataqua watershed to insure a flow of timber products in their own trade. In his first surprise at Coffin's legacy and his impulse toward generosity he had briefly forgotten how worrisome such competitors had become. In his reasonings, he had convinced himself that Elizabeth would refuse any sum unless she believed the legacy left to both of them. Therefore, he had, before traveling to the probate clerk, paid her a visit to smooth the way, telling her of Coffin's death and of an as yet uncertain sum that had been left to them equally. There had never been a question in Browne's mind of giving Elizabeth Higgins a substantial gift, but, he told himself, he had to concoct this further untruth to make her *accept* his gift. The more than £330 that he had kept he used to purchase nearby sawmills and timberland ahead of his competitors to the south. It seemed an obvious solution. He simply could not afford to lose timberland— the very lifeblood of his accelerating trade.

Finally, she stepped over to the table briefly, opened the purse and looked in, then after a little start returned to the doorway, looked out, and finally turned toward him.

"One hundred and twelve pounds," he said.

"One day, I don't remember when, it became clear to me that I won't see him, Jared, again," she said. "I was sure of his death. Like someone diverting water from a mill. The wheel simply stopped. There would be no more water. And that was that."

Browne walked back to his chair, leaning on it rather than sitting. He watched her as she rubbed her chin with a finger and turned back to look out the doorway. If Higgins were only dead, he thought, it would all be much more simple. He would have no journey before him. Cole might simply dispose of the Fletcher brothers according to their sentence. He would be able to return to his trade. And why might they not then become more than neighbors? He wanted to protect her from further torment. Her life had been plain, even humble. But she had none of that coarseness he had found so often in those of her station. Yes, she was without learning. But she was quick, and capable of learning, and she was wise in womanly craft. And she was so alive with her fair skin and hair, the very abundant hair he had once seen for himself and which even now strayed from her cap as if nothing were equal to containing it. What, come to think of it, had he before him as things now stood? Years of living and laboring in the wilderness alone?

She turned to look at him, still silent. And suddenly he saw himself a fool, a fool and a liar. Who was this Jared Higgins to him that he should keep his oath of secrecy now? He would have to tell her eventually. Yes, he would tell her when he got back, whatever he found. And that would be the end of it. He would be completely his own again, without ties or interests other than his own. There would be no more oaths sworn to.

She came over to him now and began to speak about the legacy. She stood close and he caught a scent of her and felt the rough tongue of desire lick his loins. He felt his own throat swell and ache pleasurably, and he had to turn away from her that he might not be discovered with the beast whimpering and mocking at his feet.

He felt a certain terror that he was about to express his feelings to her, which feelings he told himself were the result merely of physical deprivation. He would have to count in years the time since he had felt the touch of a woman who loved him. He would count in many months the time since he had felt the touch of any woman at all. He told himself that he was feeling only the *contre-coup* of celibacy—those assertions of the baser mechanisms. It was all at its most simple level hydraulic, pressure and release, he told himself.

"It will be a shame to have you away so long," she was saying now. "We shall miss you, Mr. Browne, our neighbor who never stays."

"This shall be my last absence for some time, I believe," he said. "I must tread other paths very soon. Whatever I discover this time out."

"You'll not find him, Mr. Browne. He is dead. Or as far re-moved as one dead. I know that now; I have felt it."

The beast had departed. "I'm not so certain."

"He is dead to me," she said. "But God go with you, Richard Browne."

XIX

By the time he had returned from his second journey to contact Higgins, Richard Browne had half decided to let the truth about Higgins rest. At this point he saw little choice but to hide the truth from those who knew of his recent expedition and say that the man was dead. Walking to see Mr. Cole, Browne recalled his questions to Shaw as they had paddled homewards from their unproductive interview with Higgins, who had been more immovable than ever.

"Do you believe him?" Browne had called back over his shoulder as they ran downstream.

"Why should I not?" Shaw answered.

"And should I? His resistance to his loved ones due to his new family, his tale of woe?"

"You have nothing else, Mr. Browne, and you never will. Don't expect the Fletchers to be your measure of truth."

"But Higgins, after all he's been through? This White Indian?"

"He's as good as his word, ask me. He has chosen. He has taken his leave of me. Neither of us will ever see the man again, you can be sure. You might sooner find the tormented soul of Balthazar Coffin."

"But I cannot rest for this man's family!"

"You had better rest, Mr. Browne. You had better, than squander yourself. Anything more here is impossible now. Better to say we found he is dead. Then the poor woman can get on with it. I'll back you. And he's as like as dead."

"I cannot," Browne said. "Not yet."

Shaw had said no more about it in the following days as they negotiated their canoe toward the seaport at Newbury.

Yet now he found himself once again before Cole distorting some of the truth while revealing some of what he had hidden previously.

Higgins, a White Indian, he lied, was dead. The essence of Mistress Coffin's journal, however, he now uncovered for Cole. And they had the Fletcher testimony. That testimony lent possibility to a version of events something like what Browne now secretly knew as Higgins' story. Even without the benefit of that story, Jonathan Cole was fitting the pieces together. But Cole was greatly troubled by the direction the truth seemed to be taking, and by the number of these discoveries Browne had hidden from him for so long.

"You knew the nature of Balthazar Coffin from the journal, corroborated by these criminal Fletchers, and you said nothing? I had come to believe they were lying to save their skins, to be honest, Richard. Am I some tattling schoolboy or gossiping crone?"

Cole's mood smouldered. Browne quietly reminded Cole of the many delicate dimensions of his researches. "I have always told you the truth I was sure of, nothing I was either unsure of, or that would make you responsible for the jeopardy of another."

"But this man's whereabouts? Kept from me and, worse, from his long-suffering wife? This fool of an Englishman-become-savage!"

"I determined her in danger from such knowledge. And I was sworn to secrecy. Any breach might have destroyed all possibility of the trust necessary between us if I was to nourish the chance of Higgins' return. Mr. Coffin has never seemed to me a man to take chances with. Higgins too was in grave danger, it seemed to me, might there be any possibility—however far-flung—of Coffin's discovering his position. Each time any person is told such information, the information is tenfold more likely to come out, somehow, despite the good intentions of everyone. Anyone might be in danger with such knowledge and such a man as Mr. Coffin appears now to have been."

"No matter. No matter. Who am I? Someone you cannot trust? You disappoint me, Richard. No, don't interrupt me. I could have helped you more. We could have restrained this dangerous man, whatever he was up to. Exactly what, is not so certain, and never will be now."

"I endeavored to keep as many souls from harm as I could, Sir. I was uncertain of his powers myself. If I have let you down, I tender my deepest apologies and regrets. . . ."

"From now on let me worry about keeping harm from myself or another soul. Keeping information from me does more harm than good, and it reduces our chance of progress towards some resolution." He looked sharply at Browne: "Take as your motto with me, from the Apostle Paul, that you can do nothing against the Truth."

"As you say, Sir," Browne said. He felt crushed between Cole's reaction and his new lie. He was tempted for a moment to throw it all over and tell Cole everything. But he feared further outrage, hesitated a moment, then decided to persevere. "What," he asked, "would you advise, as to telling Goody Higgins?"

Cole got up, started pacing about the room, and ordered two brandies of his new servant girl.

"I am conscious of all I owe you, of all you have done on my behalf," Browne said. "I have never, I hope, wanted gratitude on that score, nor affection for you as a friend and advisor."

"I know that, Richard. I know all that. Let me think on Goody Higgins. Let me think."

The brandy arrived.

Richard Browne could no longer contain the truth about his disposition of Coffin's legacy. Cole looked surprised at first, but as Browne explained his reasoning, Cole began to nod his head in understanding. The two men agreed that £112 was generous, and that in the battle over trade one must be at least as ruthless as one's competitors.

"The Fletchers are what trouble me now," Cole said. "They must be gone tomorrow. We'll no more with them." Cole slammed his fist on the table. "There's little else we can do under law, as things are left now. As to their hands in this affair, and their degree of innocence, we have only their own testimony. Nothing else is likely to come. But they must be sent into exile, according to their sentence." His fist hit the table again. "They are a blight on the land, on the community."

Browne nodded assent. "The Lord shall reward the doer of evil, according to his wickedness."

"And you have said nothing, not a word, to Goody Higgins as yet?" Cole asked.

"She does not yet even know I have returned."

"Good. Now, what to do. She had better know," Cole said. "Tell her he is dead, I suppose, eh?"

"I believe so. That was my thought, Mr. Cole."

Cole drank the residue of brandy straight off.

"She can decide what to do from here," Browne said, "once we tell her. All for the best, even though it will cause her pain."

"It will," Cole agreed, "but it will also relieve other kinds of pain." Cole pondered a moment, licked a spot of brandy from his lips. "Young Elderidge has been around, trying to court her," he continued. "Now he'll leap in after her. A few others have had their eyes on her, if I'm not mistaken." He paused as if tallying up the would-be suitors, their names, their positions. "Not that I blame them." He smiled. "She is no mere snout-fair young thing. But she's come to be like a daughter to me, a daughter who married less than she might have, but a daughter whose difficulties I cannot neglect. Whether she follows my wishes, or not. You see what I mean, Richard?"

"Yes."

"How about you?"

"Me?"

"Yes. Your interest in her. Don't be the blockhead."

"Sorry. I've thought about it . . . her. Her housewifery, her delightful person. With some book learning a fit consort. I must admit I have found myself increasingly drawn to her. But I could not expose such feelings even while I sought the woman's husband."

Cole laughed. He seemed assuaged now. "'A just reward for her high housewifery,'" he quoted. "She may not be from your people, of course," he said musingly, "but she's all the woman any man could hope for or deserve."

"I quite agree."

"Then hadn't you better discover whatever her feelings for you are?"

"I suppose I could test the waters, after I have borne the news, and appropriate time for sorrow has elapsed. . . ."

"And you'll let Elderidge, or some other beat you at a man's game?" Cole laughed. He was happy to be joking with Richard again, man-to-man, in their private moment, as if they were putting all secrets and lies behind them.

But Richard Browne was uncomfortable, his misery increasing every moment. He thought of running away, confessing his errors, begging forgiveness, returning to England, suicide, shooting Higgins himself. None of the possibilities was satisfactory. He merely stood up to leave. "I'll speak to her now," he said. "Get the awful news behind us."

"Good."

"Then we shall see."

"No. Court her, Richard. As if your life depended on it. Make that your first business. We'll see she gets a widow's third, at least. He left no will, I suppose, the blackguard, skulking in the suburbs of Hell. She'll need time for mourning, yes. But she's a quick and resilient woman who has long prepared herself for this, expects it." He looked at Browne, who was in the act of leaving. "Mind you, Richard, don't let the others get there ahead of you. No hesitant blockhead will win such a woman." He winked and laughed. Browne finished his brandy and left. At the end, he told himself, they had become simply two men in frolic company.

So it happened that Browne eventually lied again to Elizabeth Higgins that her husband was indeed—just as she had expected—dead. Shaw came along to confirm the story, the two men grimly walking together to her house, dead to the beauties of field and meadow—the drooping blue flowers of flax, the violet of flower-de-luce, the deepest greens of grains and grasses about to ripen into yellows and browns.

She took the news calmly. "Do you know how it happened?" she asked.

"Some sort of hunting accident, it seems, Elizabeth," Shaw offered. He too was uncomfortable, but believed this course the best. "He had completely gone over to them, as far as we can tell. He was an Indian. He had taken the name White Robin."

"And here am I," she said, folding her hands on the table and looking at the table top. "I knew it was so."

"Can we do anything?" Shaw asked.

Browne, after delivering the news, was speechless. He felt as if he were in a dream, helpless to change the course of events. For a moment he thought he might weep, as one might in such a dream until waking.

"Not just now, thank you," she said. "May I be alone for a day or two? To think what I will do."

Browne found his tongue. "Do nothing immediately, Goody

Higgins. At least until your mourning has passed. Let me, let us, help in any way we can. These matters need maturation; they need to be properly considered." Then he was suddenly silent again, holding back an unfamiliar anger with himself. Surely, however, as Shaw had said, they were laying the foundation on which she might build a solid life for herself and her children.

Or, he wondered, was he a mere hypocrite making excuses for himself. Yet both men had sworn to secrecy for the woman's sake. He was buffeted by desires he had not even admitted to himself. Were our lives so saturated with sensuality? Must we human beings always be so blown about by the storms in our flesh, like ships at bad anchorage? Was it all some jest played on humanity? No. Nothing in God's world was in jest. Blasphemy. How lucky he never entered the ministry. How much more suitable the law in such a world. And even in the law he had foundered.

How many escaped these hungers? Very few. Despite all our pretensions. Damnation to the miscreants and election to the few, the very few. That was the way of the world. And he not even a Calvinist, merely a wayward Anglican adrift in the New World.

The two men left her. Never again did they speak to one another about their journey or Jared Higgins. Browne lost himself in his work for three months. He avoided Elizabeth Higgins, who had gone into an official period of mourning. The suitors, he knew, drew ever closer about her and waited, as inevitable as the tides. But he could make himself forget nothing of what he had done, and he could not say whether he had done the right thing. He fought himself to ignore it all, and that was the best that he could do.

Finally, three months later he paid her a visit. She was appropriately dressed. She seemed to him more than ever a woman of integrity, humility, and energy. He realized how much he had missed seeing her.

"They have begun leaving their little gifts and names, as if we were in Boston," she said and let out a small laugh.

He tried to enter her mood. "I would add my own, but being a simple neighbor, I have none to bring."

She looked at him curiously and smiled. "Suitors must be fools," she said. "They ignore my sorry condition. One day I am married, the next a widow. Thenceforward when I open my door, men enter. I look out my window, more men. If I go to my garden to gather herbs and flowers, I find men blooming in the late summer winds. There are days I dare not enter my pantry. Have we all gone mad, Mr. Browne?"

"I fear we may have, Goody Higgins. Why not choose one?"

"Oh, I cannot! These fools who leave their verses and prayers, their gift sermons and trinkets?"

"I suppose it is all so much impertinency."

"Worse. I do not know these men, but as names on town lists, or mere acquaintances—a few—as speakers at meetings and taverns. Or tradesmen, woodsmen, soldiers. My children do not even daunt certain widowers with broods of their own. One spoke of doubling the size of his house.

"I have sat before the fire evenings, my children gathered about me, and I ask: 'My dears, what shall become of us?' "

"Have you any thoughts of what shall become of you?"

"Nothing that seems possible. I had thought of opening a tavern, if Mr. Cole would help me through the regulations and approvals."

"Surely with all these men offering themselves, you have better prospects before you."

"Better? Perhaps. But I cannot see it so. And in that matter I have no advisors. I am still too unsettled to know my mind. And I will not be hurried about like a leaf in November winds."

She quickly rose from the settle and walked to the table, upon which sat a small cake.

"It may be difficult to remain rooted here, however."

"Yes, but I've managed. I have nearly determined to winter here, once again. Not because I wish to."

"Because you are too uncertain to decide your future?"

"Just so." She handed him a piece of her cake.

"Then winter will allow proper time to consider."

"If I am allowed privacy." She sat down again, crossing her legs, and leaned forward to eat a piece of her cake.

"I'll stand before your door with my sword." He laughed.

"Some such protection might be best," she said and smiled.

Even if it be, Browne thought, this avuncular neighbor Browne?

"Well, Goody Higgins," he said, "you may call on me at any time or in any pass. Though I fear I cannot turn men's affections or desires, even with my sword. One might as well try to turn the rivers from the seas."

She smiled again. There were awkward silences and pleasantries, and he saw that he was himself becoming a nuisance. So he made ready to leave and left a gift of his own, making her promise to read it and tell no one. He had examined his motives in this instance too. Had he merely wished to discredit the "dead" husband, to look the better in the widow's eyes? (He had such an advantage here over the suitors.) Or was he an apostle of the truth, just now? After hours of internal debate, he thought that she had better know the truth in the private journal at least. She deserved to know, and Mistress Coffin deserved whatever exoneration was due her. As he departed, he reaffirmed his wish to help her in any need.

As autumn turned into winter, Richard Browne and Elizabeth Higgins saw nothing of one another. Neither wished to impose upon the other. And when he took the time to think about it,

Browne realized that it would be best to allow her suitors opportunity to pass before her without interference, to allow her
time to assess her own condition and future. To be honest with
himself, further, he saw that he had been hesitating like a shy
schoolboy as he became more and more aware of her attractions. His impulses toward her had begun to feel like violations
of his protective friendship.

By January, however, she again called on him, arriving alone
and bundled beyond recognition against the drifting snow and
high winds. She began by explaining that least of all did she
wish to become a neighbor who visits only in need, but it was
he she had learned to trust.

He welcomed her and begged her to speak her mind.

"You may think me foolish," she said, unwrapping herself.
"I don't want the thing to start again."

He asked her to explain.

"I awake in the night and feel him standing there."

"Him?"

"I know he is dead. . . ."

"Your husband?"

"No. Mr. Coffin."

"You are overwrought. I can see that." He tried to make his
voice very calm. "All that is done with. Don't punish yourself."

"Please do not believe I would come to you were I not sure.
I sleep, dream, wake, and he is there. I feel him."

"Feel him?"

"Watching me."

"Where?"

"In the room, standing below my bed. Like a shadow."

Browne considered this new turn. Had she lost her reason
wintering alone with her children? Such things happened. She
had always seemed to him competent and completely connected
to the earth, yet she was prone to visions. And here she was
again claiming to be the object of dark intent.

"How often?" he asked.

"Three times."

"Three?"

"I believe so. He is *there*. I believe he wants my life." He heard a touch of anger in her voice. "It is like hunger."

The only way, he decided, was to treat this thing as real and see where she led him. How could he refuse her appeal?

"You are able to sleep, you say?" He waited until she nodded. "Are you eating?"

"Yes," she said. "But it is in sleep that he comes. He does no harm to me, but he will if he finds the power. That is his desire."

"If you like I will watch. I'll come tonight? Tell no one."

"On the Sabbath. He comes only then, the night following Lord's Day. I cannot say why only then."

"Well, I shall come to you next Sabbath then, to watch for you. Unless you prefer Mr. Vaughan in this instance."

"I have come to you."

"I'll come then, Sabbath night."

She looked relieved. Finally she said: "You attend now. I've seen you."

"There are few who escape Mr. Vaughan's teaching. Now that we have our minister, the old strictures are enforced. It would be foolish of me to keep Sabbath quietly within the confines of my house and garden, as beforetime."

"Come at the close of Lord's Day, then," she said. "We will have a light supper. I find myself in your debt again, as seems my fate."

"Don't speak of it," he said and smiled. "Haven't we traveled this road together before?" He wanted to say something about taking responsibility for one's fate but he knew she would not believe it.

"Why must the road be so dark and endless?" she said.

"Life, as Mr. Vaughan says, is much in darkness."

"And might not even the Lord dwell in the darkness, as Solomon says," she added. "And as Moses before him found: 'Unto the thick darkness where God was'?"

"But let's give one another strength as we travel," he said. "Banish this shadow, whatever it be."

She was about to leave when she turned to him again and, with a curious look, said: "It has been so long I had almost forgotten. Forgive me." He said nothing and she went on immediately. "It was widow Gage then." It was simply a statement. "I knew it was somebody."

"Yes," he said.

"There was a time of difficulty between us," she said. "We had grown dependent on each other, as husbands and wives do. There was that foundation of some deeper understanding or love . . . something lasting and as certain as the warmth of the other's body as he sleeps beside you night after night." She looked directly into Browne's eyes. "But suddenly I just knew it. I put it to him—that I knew, that it must cease, that I would not live with a man who betrayed me."

"And he admitted . . . to something?"

She turned away. "To nothing! He feigned ignorance. His denial, now that I felt sure, drove me into a passion. That he could lie about this betrayal.

"Together we got through it finally, made our accommodations toward one another again, out of necessity. In all his troubles after Mistress Coffin's death, he needed me. I took pity. It all might have destroyed him. I believed he had returned to me. I will admit even that much of my old feeling for him returned. He seemed resourceful. He had said before that he had severed this other relation, and I believed him."

"He never blamed you?"

"He never placed blame upon me by his tongue. His deeper feelings were perhaps otherwise. And there may be something in that, some fault of my own I mean." There was a weariness, a defeat, in her voice that he had not heard since their first meeting.

"But you reacted vehemently. At the moment of discovering the betrayal."

"Yes. I sent my letter out of anger, the anger of that moment, as you say. I wished to expose him, if he would not admit the truth to me himself. If he should both betray and lie."

"Expose him to embarrassment or punishment?"

"I cannot say. Not now. Both? At the time it was perhaps both."

"And you never knew for certain the issue of this missive?"

"I never knew." She was facing Browne once again. "But I see now how it is connected to all our torments thereafter, in some dark manner I know not."

"In our unruly passions we mortals make many errors. It ever has been and ever will be so."

"So it must be. You shall have her journal back when you come, Mr. Browne. Thank you for helping me see."

XX

～～

So it was that he came to her at the closing of the next Sabbath in the cold calm that followed a snowstorm. As he approached her house, Browne looked up and saw stars blowing
ragged clouds free of the evening sky. There was a half-moon.
The air felt unusually dry and sharp, making his cheeks numb
and his nose sting. He thought of her fresh from observing the
Lord's Day, saw her again making her way in the snow with the
children and all of them in the new meeting house at the sound-
ing of the great trumpet shell in the sharp morning air, the
rows of benches, the few high pews among which Mr. Cole had
been seated, the ministerial sonorities booming off the sound-
ing board as the Reverend Vaughan stood at the scaffold above
the deacons' pews, the people rising, singing, praying in the
cold, the musketry slam-and-rattle of the seats coming down
again, the tithing-man watching over the restless boys, the few
Indians and Africans in the loft looking over the lengthy proceedings as if from Heaven. How this woman would be reso-
nant, he thought, with her day of obedience, song, and prayer.
How the strictures and meditations of the day would tremble
to the surface of her flesh like a lamp of holy oil flickering deep
within, or like a spirit wavering on the verge of this world and
the next.

As soon as the children finished their supper, Elizabeth dis-
missed them from the board to complete certain chores before

bedtime: Jared to shell corn—brought down out of winter stores —against the fire-peel, the girls to attend a large kettle of yarn, to knit, or to card while watching Enoch, the youngest. She and Browne slowly ate their pottage. In the parlor all of the beds had been ranged around the hearth, forming their winter re- doubt. They could hear the children working and laughing. Browne said that Jared, who had yet to carry in extra firewood, must be a great comfort to her, being nearly a man now. She agreed that were it not for her oldest son she would have grown mad by now, but he was still a boy, a boy in a man's body. And like all boy-men, she said, he will be off soon to some girl- woman.

After everyone had gone to bed, Browne again found himself waking before the kitchen hearth. He fed the fire, sipped hot cider, sat, stood, paced, and thought all the while of so many things he had not taken the time to think of lately. By midnight his mind had turned to the lies between them, and he could not shake himself free of them no matter what else he tried to think about. It was, he realized with a grim sorrow, too late to turn back to the more complex truth before this woman and Mr. Cole.

Looked at with a certain distance, what could the truth mat- ter anyway? Jared Higgins was as good as dead to them all. He was dead to the life they were all living at Robinson's Falls, and alive only in his other life. These two lives would never intersect. Higgins had no choice, nor any other will, but to remain what he had become.

But then, he thought, how can one be certain of such things? For the first time it struck Browne that he should not remain at Robinson's Falls. If he would keep from any further em- broilments or betrayals or lies, he must leave.

Yet how could he? How abandon everything he had worked to build right here, everything he had come to enjoy—his house and grounds, the high promise of his labors in the forest trade, his friend Elizabeth Higgins, Mr. Cole? He could not at the moment trace backwards how he had come to take so many risks, or even whether he had been aware of risks while he had acted. Had he built his entire new life here over a dangerous void?

As the night passed he began to feel ill with fatigue. Now he would have to spend the next day sleeping. He sat and dozed before the fire. But he moved in and out of consciousness. He was aware that the sleepers in the other room were quiet, and felt that they were alone in the house. He had felt strange presences before, he knew what that was, but he felt nothing now. There was nothing. Was she playing him like some poppet? Using his ties to her for some purpose of her own? He dozed off again. The fire ebbed. He started awake. Nothing.

He got up and replenished his fire. How much time had passed? Dawn must be close. He found he had absolutely no idea. He sat down and dozed again. Then, shortly it seemed, he was awake. There was wind outside, but nothing else. Finally, he faintly heard her and came to full consciousness.

She was catching her breath. Had she forgotten about his being in the house during her sleep? He rose quietly so as not to startle her. "No," he heard her say. Then there was a tremulous whimper. He reached for his Bible and moved slowly, quietly toward the other room. He heard nothing, not even her breathing, as he moved.

She was sitting up in bed. At first she seemed awake. As he moved toward her silently, watching her, her eyes were open but, he believed, unseeing. She began to breathe heavily again, her chest rising and falling, the smallest tremulous whimper again escaping from someplace as deep as her soul. The children were all undisturbed. He moved right up to her and saw her shaking as she sat. He touched her very carefully on the shoulder, and she turned to look at him, seeming fully awake now. But she was still not speaking. He could feel her woolen shift clinging to her with sweat. Her face glistened in the low light of fire coals. She shook her head sharply twice, still unable to speak, then closed her eyes and bowed her head. Her body relaxed now, her innermost trembling ceased. Gently he stroked her hair, as a man might calm his dog after a chase or a fight. But he felt that tenderness a man feels for a woman.

She raised her head and looked at him again, fully conscious now. "Thank God you are here," she finally said.

"You are safe, Elizabeth," he whispered. "What happened?" The smell of the wool and bed linen wet with her perspiration seemed profoundly intimate to him.

"He spoke to me, in a dream; his mouth was bloody. Then I woke and felt him here again. Then you came and it was your hand on me."

He sat on the bed beside her, and she began to weep.

"What did he say?"

"I don't know. It was not our language."

Browne put his arm around her shoulder and pressed her against him. He saw and heard nothing unusual in the room. The room was gradually turning gray with first light. Her damp body had collapsed against his like that of an injured child after the first shock of pain had passed. She wept quietly. Whatever it is, he thought, it is real to her. She might have just run a mile in July from some raging beast.

They sat together quiet on the bed. His lips near her ear, he tried to comfort her by whispering: "'The Lord is thy keeper: the Lord is thy Shade upon thy right hand. The sun shall not smite thee by day, nor the moon by night.'" Then her voice softly joined his to the end of the psalm: "'The Lord shall preserve you from all evil: he shall preserve thy soul. The Lord shall preserve thy going out, and thy coming in, from this time forth and even for evermore.'"

She grew still. Eventually she fell asleep against the hollow of his chest, her body beginning to dry in the cool room. He covered her legs with the bedclothes and held her a little longer. Then he laid her back into the featherbed, hearing the soft crunching. He got up, stoked their fire quietly, and returned to his chair in the other room.

He began to wonder if there were something he did not know in all this. Fundamentally, she must not be well. But such dreams every seventh day? And what might he do? Spend every Sabbath night like this, indefinitely? There would be scandal in two or three weeks at the least.

He looked into the fire, reduced now to red and black coals in the shape of disintegrating logs. He knew he should rise, stir the coals, stoke his own fire, but he was too tired. He pulled his blanket more tightly around him. His legs resting on logs he should have set into the fire, he dozed sprawling in the chair and slipped into deep sleep.

When the family arose in the morning they did not wake him. He might have been some sickly elderly uncle asleep in his chair before the hearth as they went about their business. He did not awake until noon, but just as he was coming up out of the nothingness of deep sleep, he began to dream.

He was bathed in May sunlight, and then realized that he stood in a flowering orchard. Orioles sang in the trees and the buzzing and flipping sounds of bees and hummingbirds seemed magnified, as if his sense of hearing were tuned to a most unnatural degree. Then he heard a woman singing a ballad he recognized.

> In this merry Maying time,
> Now comes in the Summer prime.
> Countrey Damsels fresh and gay,
> Walke abroade to gather May:
>
> In an evening make a match,
> In a morning bowes to fatch.

Well is she that first of all,
Can her lover soonest call,

Meeting him without the towne,
Where he gives his Love a gowne.
 Tib was in a gowne of gray,
 Tom he had her at a bay.

Hand in hand they take their way,
Catching many a rundelay,
 Greeting her with a smile,
 Kissing her at every stile.

Then he leades her to the Spring
Where the Primrose reigneth king.
 Upon a bed of Violets blew,
 Downe he throwes his Lover true.

She puts finger in the eye,
And checkes him for his qualitie.
 She bids him to her mothers house,
 To Cakes & Creame & Country souce.

He must tell her all his mind,
But she will sigh and stay behind.
 Such a countrey play as this,
 The maids of our town cannot miss. . . .

The woman came out from the cover of the far trees and
began to walk in his direction. It was Elizabeth Higgins. As she
walked past him—unaware of him, still singing—he hid behind
a tree full of flowers.

Thou at the first I liked well,
Cakes and Creame do make me swell.
 This pretty maiden waxeth big:
 See what 'tis to play the Rig.

Up she deckes her white and cleene,
To trace the medowes fresh and green:

Or to the good towne she will wend
Where she points to meet her friend.

Her gowne was tuckt above the knee,
Her milkwhite smock that you may see.
Thus her amorus Love and she,
Sports from eight a clocke till three:

All the while the Cuckow sings,
Towards the evening home she flings,
And brings with her an Oaken bow,
With a Country Cake or two.

Straight she tels a solemne tale,
How she heard the Nightengale,
And how ech medow greenly springs:
But yet not how the Cuckow sings. . . .

Then he noticed a man emerging from the trees at the other
end of the orchard. She drew closer to this man, who now
stepped fully into the light, and Browne realized that the man
was Balthazar Coffin. She was not the least surprised or afraid.
Indeed, they spoke pleasantly to one another as old friends. He
stopped and she moved very close to him as they spoke. He
smiled; he folded his hands behind him.

Later, he drew out one hand and gave her a little red book,
which Browne recognized as Kathrin Coffin's journal. As she
took the book with one hand, she reached her other hand into
his codpiece, which Browne suddenly realized had become gro-
tesquely enlarged, as if belonging to some buffoon in a rustic
morality play.

Thus the Robin and the Thrush,
Musicke make in every bush.
While they charme their prety notes,
Young men hurle up maidens cotes.

But 'cause I will do them no wrong,
Here I end my Maying song,

And wish my friends take heed in time.
How they spend their Summers prime.

Browne began to panic, but just as he fought to catch his breath, he awoke to Elizabeth Higgins shaking him. Startled, nauseous with fatigue, he looked up at her.

"You cried out," she said, and smiled at him. "Would you like to lie down? You need sleep, Mr. Browne. It is just past mid-day."

Half awake, he continued to stare at her. For a moment he believed in his dream, that she had been Coffin's lover, that he had tormented her in outrage at Jared Higgins' trespasses against him. Gradually he grew more awake, the dream receded, and he was increasingly able to separate her from the figures in his dream. He struggled to stand up, stretched, and began to gather his things that he might leave.

"No, thank you, Goody Higgins. I have much to do myself today and cannot afford to sleep away the afternoon as well."

"If you say so," she said. "How can I thank you for being with us?"

"We need to think more of what to do now. But please thank me no further. It is enough to help you through this." He waved his arm toward the other room. "I must be off." He was fully awake but confused and tired.

She stopped him a moment and pulled the red book from under her shawl, as if it had been in some pocket hanging out of sight. He gave a start, but then becalmed himself and took the offered book.

As he stepped out into the dooryard, he bent and scooped up a handful of snow to press against his face. The snow and the walk home braced him, made him clear and alert finally. He forced the previous night and his dream completely out of his thoughts.

Closeted in his study, he worked all afternoon on correspondence, accounts, legal documents of sale and agreement. But an hour or so after darkness had returned, he grew tired of working in the bad light and sat back to rest his eyes. Then the details of his dream returned to him. He could face it as a dream. But he could not avoid the feeling that the dream had significance. What it signified he could not begin to say. "We have dreamed a dream, and there is no interpreter of it. . . . Do not interpretations belong to God?"

He heard Cole's voice again telling him from some previous discussion of the law: "Richard, fornication and adultery, taken together, are the most common crimes in these colonies. Any magistrate will tell you the same. And though I have not studied it, I believe there are as many 'early' babies—six, seven, eight months—as there are babies born to a woman's full time. Now, why is that, Richard?"

He could not recall his response. And he believed he had even less of an answer now than he must have had then. He had heard the litany of lusts, of wives and daughters and their paramours—others' husbands, lads, servants, and of course the transient seamen, soldiers, and Indians, and even some of the ministers, one or two notorious for aging lecherously. There are good people, of course, he thought. But were some gods to look down on all the lusty antics and falsehoods of mankind, they would surely laugh. However tragic the issue of such goings on to men, women, and children in their individual lives, the gods—he saw them as Olympians at the moment—are laughing. Is not comedy the best approach? The bright lines of Jonson occurred to him:

> 'Tis no sinne, loves fruit to steale,
> But the sweet theft to reveale:
> To be taken, to be seene,
> These have crimes accounted beene.

But then his mood changed again and the lines did not reflect a feeling of bitterness, a strange cynicism and even anger. Why was he feeling this way?

There was more at stake here than merely being caught, perhaps, he thought, trying to account for this bitterness at the human sexual comedy. It was the not infrequent tragic issue of our hidden indiscretions that bothered him at the moment. The tragic face of the same mask. "If I find in Sodom fifty righteous within the city, then will I spare all the place for their sakes."

Could so much of peoples' lives remain hidden from him? Had everyone at Robinson's Falls and its environs shown him only so much as they had wanted him to see? Had he been both the poppet in their drama and the hoodwinked groundling? The truth, he told himself, is always difficult to know. But is it impossible to know? In its completeness, perhaps. Yet truth can be approached, grasped in part, through trial and labor.

His dream of Elizabeth and Balthazar ran smack up against everything he had seen, known, and believed of her; against every feeling, impression, witness. Could so much of the nature of her person and her life have remained hidden from him? Is that what his dream signified?

Impossible. There were limits even to comedy; restraints, boundaries between the real and unreal, even if one granted with the common consent that the boundaries between the natural and supernatural were unclear and, at times, fordable.

But just as he was discounting the thought of Elizabeth Higgins' duplicity and adultery, and feeling comfortable and on stable ground again, another terrible thought came to him. Coffin had, in the dream, handed her the journal, with that strange, self-satisfied smile on his face. What possibility might that signify? Might he not have fabricated the entire journal himself? Another string to jerk the unwary poppet? Or the two of them together? No. In his mind now he acquitted Elizabeth Higgins of the worst. But Balthazar Coffin was surely another matter. His guilt might be great, as the legacy left to himself hinted. But then, he thought, what would be the purpose in concocting such a journal? What benefit to Coffin? He could not dwell on the possible reasons and benefits. He was becoming frightened and confused. His mind turned instead to the various problems with the testimony of others that he had seen, even the original depositions of, for example, Shaw.

He stood up from his chair and paced about, trying to force his mind off of everything associated with the death of Mistress Coffin. He was so confused and so terrified at the thought of having uncovered nothing real that he could not bear it any longer. He did not know what to think. He could see no way of proceeding further.

He noticed that he was perspiring. Was he being driven mad himself? Had he long since entered her nightmare to be swallowed by it?

He told himself that he could not continue. Things seemed to be moving beyond his power to contain them. He must turn her over to the Reverend Vaughan; this was more properly within his province.

He ran downstairs, bundled himself in heavy clothes, and went out into the night. It was still clear and frigid in the aftermath of the previous day's big, fast-moving storm. He tried to force his mind back to his own work while he walked where the snow had been trampled. But somehow the voice in him kept leading him elsewhere, and he began to ask himself if Kathrin Coffin was not the completely innocent victim of some conspiracy against her, with her own husband the archconspirator. Might she not be a woman murdered by her husband and his agents for no plausible reason from the surface of their lives?

Yet how might such a theory undermine the innocence of Goody Higgins! He had nothing against her, no. And was it not her children who had suffered and died, her family broken, peace disrupted, her heart torn? He was for the moment comforted by this thought. At the moment, indeed, Elizabeth Higgins and Mr. Cole seemed the only solid people in the New

World. Yet, he finally had to ask himself, do we not bring on so much of our suffering ourselves? Is it not in our natures to cross our own best interests? To bring on so much of our own suffering, to say nothing of the suffering we cause others. Again and again our worst natures cross our best.

He felt suddenly so helpless that he began to weep. He stopped, leaned his arms and face against a tree and wept out of his confusion, his fatigue, his sorrow for everyone, for all the harshness and loss and pain caused by our worst, and truest, nature. All these defects he pictured as a host of infant souls, the souls of all the secret children that had been murdered at their very births.

All that was clear to him now was that he had not uncovered what was real. He had succeeded only in finding Jared Higgins, and that had ended in a lie. His own. He and Higgins ended as liars together. One crossed oneself, again and again. Worst overwhelmed best.

He returned home, poured a cup of fine brandy from a bottle his brother had given him as a parting gift, and drank until he was drowsy and forgetful enough to fall asleep. He awoke early, in darkness, his mind racing and heart pounding from the brandy, and rose to look out the window. The stars were still clear and strong. His mind seemed cleared. His trade was what mattered. He must cultivate his own plot. He returned to bed, able to think only about his prospects for trade. To relent was to fail at trade. Just at dawn he fell asleep again.

All that day he worked, convinced that the decision to tend to his own work was the right one. No longer would he torment himself over the true or false nature of Goody Higgins. He would be neighbor, friend, and parallel life. There was too much unsettled, and impractical, to follow Cole's advice about courting her. Their lives lay in other directions. And it was best, fitting, wholly more proper that she turn to the Reverend Mr.

Vaughan in her present strait. By the end of the day he knew he should tell her as much.

He entered her yard in the dark, seeing the dim light from a small window. Unsure of just how he would explain his thoughts to her, he hesitated. He moved toward the window, not entirely aware that he was doing so. When he reached the window, he looked in. Elizabeth Higgins and her children were gathered around the fireplace, each busy in some domestic chore. Suddenly he realized what he was doing and felt like a fool. But as he turned away to retrace his steps home his feelings of foolishness turned to relief. Indeed, he began to feel emptied of the doubt and confusion that had troubled him since spending the night watching and waking for her.

He would have to speak to her soon, he thought, about Mr. Vaughan. But he would not disturb her this night.

XXI

Browne knew he had to see Elizabeth Higgins, but it was very easy at the moment to busy himself in other matters. So it was that she again arrived at his door. She had brought him fresh bread and wanted to thank him again. She could not explain it, she said, but she was feeling much better, much less fearful now. And she hoped her fears would trouble him no further. She had seen some footprints about her dooryard and window; these alone troubled her. Did he know what they might mean?

For Richard Browne it was one of those moments when you suddenly step outside your situation, knowing that the moment will pass, yet forced to savor the intensity of your embarrassment. He explained, as close to the truth as he was able, that he had gone to see her two evenings ago in a troubled state of mind, troubled by dreams and forebodings of his own. In his confusion, he said, he found it difficult to knock on her door. He began to think better of it, his visit, just then, and turned to go home when he was drawn by the light in her window. To be sure they were all right since his waking with them, he merely glanced in at the window to set his own mind at ease.

He apologized. "There it is, that explains the footprints. They are the marks of an indecisive fool."

She looked at him a moment and then laughed. He was startled. Then he laughed with her. *"Misce stultitiam Consiliis brevem —Dulce est desipere in loco,"* he quoted, and then translated, "For once, be unwise; there is a time when it is sweet to play the fool."

She laughed again. "Now I have the explanation," she said, "I am pleased you take such an interest in us, Mr. Browne." He smiled but looked down in his lingering embarrassment, unable to hold her eye. "But what was it you wanted to speak to me about?"

"Several things," he said. "Most of which I think better now ought to be left unsaid. But I did want to say that I believe myself unfit for the role I had come to play, as your protector and advisor in these new torments. I was going to suggest that the Reverend Mr. Vaughan might be far more effective in your present distress, as he is your minister and more suitable for handling these troublesome apparitions."

She looked at him quietly, enlarging his sense of embarrassment again. Then she said: "I was coming to the same belief myself. Not your being unfit, Mr. Browne, but that I have lain my broken life at your door so often I no longer have any right to ask you to indulge me."

"I did not mean . . ."

"No, Mr. Browne," she cut him off pleasantly. "You see I agree. I feel this way myself, I say."

"When I find a song bird that has blown up against my window or door, I try to help the unfortunate creature. But if I believe that things have gone beyond my capacity to help or heal, I seek another who may be more gifted and knowledgeable, or possess the necessary physic. I can do no less for you."

"Yet no neighbor should become a burden."

"And so you have not! I have taken up your cause of my own will, please do not forget, not as a mere duty. Every step I have taken is of my own choosing, out of my affections for you and your children, and for Mr. Cole, and then out of my own curiosity. You have never been to me a burden. Yet I find the larger matters in all that I've pursued in your behalf and in my curi-

osity have defeated me. I've grown less certain and more confused. Shed too little light. If what little I have been able to
accomplish has offered some relief to you, and your children,
that must be sufficient for me now."

"You too quickly shrink the result of what you have done.
But I'm pleased by your honesty."

He felt all his resistance to her, all his faith in returning to
his own life completely, beginning to melt and flow toward her.
But she quickly added: "I shall ask Mr. Vaughan whether he
will help me, as my own heart told me to do."

"He knows of your past tribulations."

"Yes. And of your aid." She turned away from him and gathered some needlework. "I've not told him yet anything of recent
trouble."

"Then speak to him," Browne said, hoping his voice did not
plead too much. "Can we not arrange for the three of us to
discuss these apparitions next Sabbath evening? After delivering his sermon again, of course, to his family. We may draw
him from his final hours in his study before his deserved rest.
At that time we can determine who will watch with you that
night."

"If you think that best, but please don't trouble yourself, Mr.
Browne. I can turn to him myself."

"He will be wanting my experience of this," Browne said,
"and I would see you safe in good hands, Goody Higgins. I am
not the proper Shepherd in this matter."

So it happened that the Reverend Nehemiah Vaughan agreed
to champion Elizabeth Higgins in these recent bouts with whatever had begun to accost her. And so it was that these three—
Browne, Elizabeth Higgins, and the Reverend Vaughan—came
together in her house at the close of the next Lord's Day.

At previous encounters Browne and Vaughan had found certain common interests and understandings. But Browne did not

possess the temperament of faith and fervor that would have put the two men on more intimate terms. Short, grave, and intense, the Reverend Vaughan, a man just into his forties, was a model of the "hard study" ministers of his day. He was considered one of the colonial frontier's greatest Hebricians, and fluent also in Greek, Latin, Arabic, and Syriac. Beyond that Browne knew him as a man who strove after righteousness by his preaching, his labors, and his example of keeping the beast in him tied with a short tether. And if Browne was not himself a covenanted member of the church, he was unlike Elizabeth Higgins in that neither he nor anyone else—above all Mr. Vaughan —would have expected Browne to become a member.

Had not the Reverend Vaughan reproached Richard Browne and all his kind in his sermons? More than once Vaughan preached that merchants had charged planters unfair prices to cover their risks. Browne had to agree that there had been a degree of such practices, but not so much as Vaughan made out.

His mind jumped to a day long ago; he had been sitting about the fire in a tavern with a group of merchants. Pipes in hand, aglow from their cordials, they spoke of the impracticality of John Cotton's old principles of commercial ethics. That pious gentleman had thought it meet in 1639 to protest against such time-worn practices as taking advantage of another's ignorance or necessity for one's personal gain, recouping one's losses by raising prices, or selling as dearly and buying as cheaply as the market would bear. Cotton had witnessed extortion, usury, the overpricing of "foreign commodities," and the host of ancient excesses, and he thought they might be stopped in this new Canaan by appeal to conscience and to law. But Browne clearly saw in his mind the hearty, laughing merchants, himself included, ridiculing such unworldliness.

Yes, Browne had to admit, even he had raised prices to cover his own risks when he had tried diversifying his trade. In conversation on such matters, Mr. Vaughan once told Browne: "When the Lord stirred the spirits of his people to come over into this wilderness, it was not for worldly wealth, or a better livelihood here for the outward man. It was to further the reformation of religion according to God's word." Browne then responded that the Reverend did not understand the background of settlement among the Piscataqua planters. But Mr. Vaughan was not to be convinced so easily.

Nearly from his first acquaintance of Elizabeth Higgins, on the other hand, Mr. Vaughan had designed that she would eventually be accepted into membership in his church. Not for her social status, certainly, but for what he recognized in her of those tremblings in the soul that rose out of her depth and which he hoped to nurture and channel. She had, or so the minister seemed to believe, that ripeness of spirit which sensed and reflected in those bound to the earth the supernal presences and conflicts. If he could but tutor, develop, direct such a gift as hers, he would, he intimated, have a presence of spirit in his parish that few could claim to equal. He would know, of course, that mere ecstacy and vision were never enough, were in themselves no sign of salvation, were indeed as like as not to arouse contention and unholy excesses in the communities where they manifest.

During the meeting at the Higginses' house, Mr. Vaughan spoke to his auditors of the "breathing of Elizabeth's soul after Christ," of her soul's struggles against dark powers, and of her overcoming threats and temptations and trials. Looking directly into her eyes, his body compressed with assurance and the force of his rapid speech, he assured her that he believed she would be accepted into church membership, if she but desired it, at the next membership hearings. There was no substantial doubt, in his mind, that she would "give good satisfaction" in both private and public testimony.

She promised to consider such an honor, although, as she

said, she harbored doubts as to her worthiness. She agreed that throughout her trials her own salvation had been much on her mind. And she admitted that she hoped earnestly to come fully into the bosom of Christ before, as the minister put it, the trap-door of death dropped beneath her.

"The Lord is at your elbow," Mr. Vaughan told her. "He is in this world among us every moment. We have but to turn to Him."

"I would turn," she said. She looked down at the table top.

"Then you shall," he said, his eyes shining. "This life has eternal consequences. That, good woman, is the deepest truth confronting every man, woman, and child. To learn righteous-ness—*that* is the great trial of each life."

Browne asked what the minister proposed in her immediate extremity.

"I wake late into the night at my lucubrations, Mr. Browne," he replied immediately. "Surely I can find such excellent em-ployment here while I see Goody Higgins through whatever passage this night after Sabbath might bring."

Browne realized that the transition had been made, and with little effort on his part. He himself was no longer prepared to meet such adversaries as she continually placed before him, nor had he been comfortable with the nature of her growing de-pendency. As he said his good evening, he left them before the fire, the minister already opening biblical texts to her.

During the rest of that winter Browne tried, and largely suc-ceeded, to forget the Coffins and Higginses, and all the rela-tions of events and people that had absorbed him so much. He was gladly immersed in his own work. And it was only during an odd moment of respite—enjoying a cup of sack, noting the lush winter reds of late afternoon sunlight drifting over his bookcloset, sliding into sleep in the night—that he found he was not as comfortable as he thought he should be by Elizabeth Higgins' growing independence from him and, so far as he knew, her growing dependence upon the Reverend Vaughan.

When the spring of 1652 had fully arrived, he realized that he had seen her only twice, and briefly, since he had left her before the fire with the minister. She was about to be elected into the small circle of actual church membership. But he also concluded, to his discomfort whenever he thought about it, that her fastings and readings, her sessions with Mr. Vaughan, her complete entering of the church's circle of protection, led to "the estrangement," as he began to put it to himself, between them.

Moreover, she had begun to speak of the minister as a kind of personal savior, as one who had exorcised evil presences from her life and substituted the joy of Christian covenant, community, and spirit. Of all such things and changes she had spoken happily, even, it seemed to Browne, distractedly. She was becoming for him a kind of lovely figure diminishing in a dream. Had he himself become too distracted by his own work?

What finally forced him to confront himself on the matter was a three-week sojourn that spring to Strawberry Banke and the Isles of Shoals. To conclude a certain large shipment of wood products to England in the best possible way, to diversify the products of his trade on a more solid foundation, and to extend his company's partnership to fishmongers of London, he found it necessary to oversee the handling and transfer of certain commodities himself.

It was while staying on the islands some ten miles offshore from the Banke that, in a number of idle moments, he had the opportunity to examine his recent life and his true desires. As he thought about Elizabeth Higgins he discovered a sense of urgency and loss.

From his room at an inn on the islands, while watching a

ship take on its cargo, he sat at a tiny table by the window one afternoon near the mid-point of his island sojourn writing to Elizabeth.

As he sought the best way to put things, the words of a song revelers had been singing in their cups at the tavern two nights ago kept ringing through his mind.

> A batchelour I have beene long,
>   and had no minde to marry,
> But now I find it did me wrong
>   that I so long did tarry;
> Therefore I will a wooing ride,
>   there's many married younger,
> Where shall I goe to seeke a Bride?
>   Ile lye alone no longer.
>
> So many sinnes are incident
>   unto a single life,
> That I all danger to prevent
>   with speed will seeke a Wife;
> If I with Women chance to drinke
>   I'me call'd a Mutton-monger,
> But now Ile stop their mouthes I thinke
>   And lye alone no longer.
>
> O Fate send me a handsome Lasse
>   that I can fancy well,
> For Portion Ile not greatly passe,
>   though Money beares the bell.
> Love now adayes with Gold is bought
>   but I'me no Money-monger,
> Give me a Wife, though shee's worth nought
>   Ile lye alone no longer.
>
> Yet if she chance to proove a Slut,
>   a Scold, or else a Whore,
> That could not chuse but be a cut,
>   and vexe me very sore.

A Slut would make me loath my meate
　　were I halfe dead with hunger,
But I must leave this fond conceate,
　　And lye alone no longer.

5 June 1652,
Smuttynose Island

MY DEAR GOODY HIGGINS,

You may, or may not, know by now that I have removed myself temporarily to the Isles of Shoals to oversee some shipping. I endeavor to establish some
importing of goods such as wine and cloth, etc., through
a certain fishmonger in trade for dunfish and others.
The opportunity arose quite by chance through my
brother's watchful eye. And he believed it essential that I
give the matter my immediate attention as a lively prospect.

This is a rocky, windy, and bawdy sort of place that
has given me time and cause to think about my own circumstances and about our neighborly relations, which of
late neither of us has sufficiently cultivated, for divers
private reasons.

From my lodging in the Rose and Sun Chamber, I sur-
vey a half dozen ships at anchor about these bright and
raucous isles. I have a prospect as well from another
window of the brick meetinghouse of this island and a
number of fine houses tucked in about it, also the court-
house. This Smuttynose Island looks a prosperous place
perched atop the main. Indeed, there are men of modest
fortune here, one would think more so than ashore, although some few as I understand it have recently removed to the more comfortable mainland while retaining
their holdings here.

As the ships unload and load, come and go, and as the
sea gulls call and argue in the passing days, I have often
time to ponder and examine myself and my ways. These

same sea gulls, by the by, have begun their annual nesting, I believe, and have turned most boisterous and ill-humored, to the point of attacking the unwary intruder. Just as we human beings, so with God's creatures. For they are sometimes known for their playfulness and spirit, yet at other times they turn morose and ill-tempered and even lash out at whatever they unjustly imagine might in some manner harm them.

So have I seen with the fishermen here whose drying racks surround us. Just at the moment the fishing is prodigious, and the fishermen and their bawds grow daily more exuberant and joyous. Yet nearly a fortnight earlier, upon my arrival, the catch was slim and there were arguments and fights and accusations breaking out continuously.

I am most happy that you have found, through Mr. Vaughan, relief from your afflictions, that unholy visions have turned holy. But there is a great deal on my mind now that I need to say to you with all the directness and honesty I can summon. I set these thoughts down here for fear that I might not speak them as I have resolved to do once I stand again before you. You see, I intend to give these thoughts a degree of irrevocability from which I, however timorous in speaking them before you, now must address when we next meet.

For you see I have not written to relate such descriptions of the turmoils and delights of these seaborne rocks which I temporarily inhabit, but rather to tell you that I can no longer pretend the indifference of mere proximity or even friendship toward you. Perhaps the wild and open beauty of this place loosens my tongue, or pen rather; perhaps my removal from the habits and routines of our lives on land makes me bold, as if I had regained some lost element of my manhood here. I cannot say.

In brief, I would be more than a good neighbor and protector. I would be your constant companion. It has become clearer and clearer to me that I cannot continue

indefinitely to live alone, to deny the common affections
of humanity, to flee responsibility for others who are
dearer to me than any other woman and her children.
"Love makes me write, what shame forbids to speak."

I now have prospects and income enough to make us
comfortable. Yet I suffer the greatest apprehensions that
I may have delayed for too long, that some one of your
suitors might through his persistence and attractions
have won you, or at least captured your affections sufficiently to insure the future bond between you. Nor am I
comforted by the thought that your liberation from these
darker apparitions and your joy in Christian fellowship
might have turned you from me, your friend and neighbor, to an irrevocable degree. I hope, I pray, it is not so.

When I return I will come to you that I might speak
my true feelings openly, and that you, after due consideration, might answer mine with your own, whatever they
may in truth be. Until then, God keep you, dear woman.

I remain your faithful neighbor,
RICHARD BROWNE

XXII

≈

When he returned to Robinson's Falls, satisfied with his work but tired and anxious over Elizabeth Higgins' reaction to his admissions, he found that she herself was away visiting relatives who had just moved to Strawberry Banke. He did not know who these people were. His maidservant, who had accepted the message and a note, had no further information.

He opened the note, noticing first that it was brief and written in an unfamiliar hand, understanding that she found writing onerous.

MR. BROWNE,
    The children and I are to the Banke for a fortnight. Thus we shall not be able to speak to one another when you return. You might foretell how your letter surprised me. For some time I have thought your feelings for me honest. And mine are warmest towards you. And we both know how much I am in your debt. But do we not also know that men and women cannot live together only by such feelings?
    I cannot say to you what I feel. I do not want to offend such a dear friend. But as I look at my mourning gown, and as I see the kind of man you are, I cannot foresee a life of constant companionship, as you say, even though you speak so readily of it.
    You also speak of suitors, but I have no interest in them. And how would that Christian fellowship under

Mr. Vaughan turn me from another? Christ turns not from others, only from Evil, but turns in love to all His children.

I can say no more until we meet, my dear friend. Let me commend you to the protection of the Almighty.

E.H.

Had he become now just another in the line of suitors competing to win her skill, her labor, and her flesh? None of them, he told himself, could know her even as he did—and she him—nor feel such pangs of tenderness. But of course by now her own feelings toward the Reverend Mr. Vaughan had grown in ways he could not know or understand, perhaps did not even wish to imagine. Had she, perhaps, been incapable of natural warmth toward a man, as the poet said: "Doth carry / June in her eyes, in her heart January"?

And what of Higgins? Wouldn't he, Browne, have to expose the true history of Jared Higgins? Only then might she be able to obtain a bill of divorce from Higgins on grounds of desertion.

When she returned, she did not let him know. He discovered it by the way and he felt certain now that she could not face him, so that he himself began to grow ashamed and hesitant again. He doubted that he would ever regain the courage he had found ten miles out at sea to tell her the truths he had discovered, to claim her back from across the gulf that had opened between them.

It came only by chance that Richard and Elizabeth met, just as by the time it happened, they both knew it would be only chance. As late summer approached, Browne was walking in the wood near the settlement along a well-trodden path, as he sometimes did when he felt as though he needed a change of scene to think. The air had turned clear overnight, cool enough for such an outing, and he felt invigorated.

He had turned to retrace his way and had been heading for

some minutes back toward the point where the path opened upon the settlement when he heard women's voices below him where the stream ran. He stopped and peered downward into the wood, but had to leave the path and descend some twenty feet to see who it was. The woods were open here, but the terrain rolling in its descent, so that he began to recognize the voices before he could see who spoke. His impressions were confirmed when soon before him, just on the opposite bank of the stream, were Elizabeth and her oldest daughter, Jerusha, and son Jared. They all held baskets and wore sacks for collecting wild mushrooms, herbs, and berries. They had not noticed him yet, and he stopped, hesitating between making himself known and quietly returning to the path above. But realizing he might be seen anyway, he called out to them in as friendly a voice as he could raise.

"Mr. Browne!" Elizabeth called out, smiling. "We had been just wondering if we might bring you some of our wild harvest later this day or tomorrow." Her children smiled and confirmed her.

"It has been a long time," Browne said. "I had not even known when you returned. But here we are now, finally." He smiled, spread his arms, looked about the wood. Her laughter seemed a little embarrassed. Jared and Jerusha returned to their work as Elizabeth began to walk toward him. He took a few more steps toward her and added: "Come walk with me a moment, just over here."

She selected a great tree trunk and tucked her basket and bag within one of its rooty folds. She began to ford the stream on exposed flat rocks. He hurried to give her a hand and she accepted his help warmly.

"And how come you here, Mr. Browne?" she asked.

"Exercise only, good for clearing the mind when there is much weighing upon it." They began to walk along a slight ridge that ran roughly parallel to the stream. "Good for one's humors."

"I see," she said. "You are troubled in mind?"

"Were you really intending to pay me a visit, with your harvest?"

"We had spoken of it. I believe we will, yes," she said and looked at him as they walked. He avoided her eyes.

"It has been so long, Goody Higgins," he said, as if preliminary to some other point, but he stopped.

"On both our parts," she said.

"Everything would have been simpler, as before, had I not written to you. I made a fool of myself?"

"I was," she said, "taken unawares, of the strength of your feelings I mean." She paused and turned her head to glance at him. "There should continue such feelings of friendship between us, even tenderness, as you say, but I had not thought of marriage, Mr. Browne."

"Then I fear I am more than once unwise," he said. "Mr. Cole advised me to court you as if my life depended upon it."

"Would he meddle in privy matters?"

"He meant it only in the most helpful spirit."

"He sees no differences between us? He thinks such a match—" She stopped as if searching for a word.

"Appropriate?" he offered.

"Yes." She looked at him, but he avoided her eyes a while longer as they walked slowly through the big trees.

"He sees nothing real or substantial against it, not here, in New England." Browne spread his arms out toward the whole forest and the settlement. "There need be few such considerations here. Here the world, and everyone in it, is new!"

"Nonsense," she said. "We bring our stations with us, as laborers their indentures."

"That is not so clear in these parts, as you well know. But

put all such thoughts aside. We are speaking of one another, not of others."

She ignored the direction his speech was taking. "And you expect to stay in New England?" she asked. "I had thought you'd be returning to your home in Mother England at some later time."

"I have no intention to do so now, certainly not for a long time." He stopped and turned toward her, looking directly into her face. "You have considered my letter, no doubt?"

"Yes."

"And has there been any issue of your considerations?"

"As to marriage? I am sorry that I have not responded, as I should have. You threw me into such confusion. And then I had to visit my cousins. Everything at once. I didn't know how to answer you. Or it seemed I could not." She looked at him, almost defiantly. "So I have not."

"I thought you had, more or less, run away from me," he said. "I too became confused, frightened by what I had done."

"I'm sorry. I owed you honesty."

"No. I have not been honest either, from the best of motives of course, as most who are dishonest will tell you." He found, however, that now he had started, he could not continue.

"Oh?" she said to prompt him.

"No. This is not the place to tell you everything. May I come to you, some time convenient for you, and explain these things? There is so much to explain. Perhaps if we face it together. . . ."

"What is it you have found, Mr. Browne?"

"It must wait until we may talk calmly and honestly to one another, and when you are in a more comfortable place than this wood."

"Then let's return now and be true with one another." She turned back toward her children and he followed. She remained pleasant but efficient. They walked together, all carrying their harvest, to her house. She looked after all her children immediately and set them about cleaning and preparing what they had gathered for cooking and storage. Then she returned to Browne, who had been mentally rehearsing a hundred ways to tell her, and they sat down opposite one another. She looked directly at him.

"Well?" she said, a trace of a smile on her mouth, her eyes intent. Then he began. He briefly reviewed the contents of Kathrin Coffin's journal, and from there told her everything he now knew, and had heard. She asked an occasional question, or rose to walk about the room and then sit down again several times. He told her about Goody Hussey's help with the Fletchers, about the bungled conspiracy with the Fletchers in the face of Coffin's vengeance, Coffin's death letter, and, finally, her husband's continued but separate life as an Indian. Before he had finished she was weeping, but he went on, even stopping to explain why each secret, and even the lies about her husband, were necessary at the time, or seemed to be terribly necessary, part of the oaths he had sworn, the protection he and Shaw had ringed about her. What he still could not bring himself to tell her, only, was the full amount Coffin had left to them, or rather to *him,* in his last will. He could not admit to her that she had not received the half he had promised and intended.

It was some time before she spoke to him, but he waited, feeling as if he himself had ended all his hope forever. And once she stopped weeping and seemed to gather herself again, he had to tell her his final doubts about the murder of Kathrin Coffin. For although Jared Higgins had told him and Shaw a tale that incriminated others, he could not decide from one moment to the next whether to believe it or dismiss it. Only the truth of her husband's life did he know first hand. Everything else was based on sometimes conflicting testimony, and on the journal and letters of others. He could not himself say at this point how much he now believed, how much had been concocted and staged for him, or for them, just as, he now explained, the Fletchers and Jared Higgins had once supposedly staged a violent, bungled tragedy to fool Mr. Coffin.

"It may not be worthy of credit," Browne said, "but I have written out the full account, in his own words, of your husband's version of the events leading to Mistress Coffin's death. Shaw and I have witnessed this secret document, but I will send a copy over to you tomorrow morning. You may judge then yourself of its truth or falsity.

"At this very moment," he added, "I am inclined to believe, in outline, the general pressure of the events I have told you, and let smaller inconsistencies fall by the wayside."

"Mr. Cole knows all of this?" she finally asked.

"Some. Some more than you did. But not all you know now. And neither has he seen the document of Higgins' secret tale. I do not yet judge it worthy of his notice."

"And will you tell him?"

"I must. But I have not been able to. Perhaps now I can. That he too may judge for himself. Yet if I do I can no longer live here. I don't believe he would forgive me what further secrets I have kept from him, what further lies I have told. Whatever my reasons, or reasonings. I could not now, in conscience, remain here as so much his beneficiary, so much in his debt. Nor, I'm sure, would he wish me to so remain. Do you see?"

Yes, she said, she saw.

Then she thanked him for being honest with her finally. She thanked him for trying his best to protect her from the worst until now, but she wished he hadn't. She thanked him again for all he had done for her and felt for her. But she asked him to leave her. She wanted to be with her children. She wanted to consider what she would do now and what, in all this long, terrible dream she had been living since Mistress Coffin's death, was real.

Part IV

How long halt ye between two opinions?
If the Lord be God, follow him: but if Baal,
    then *follow him.*
And the people answered him not a word.

—I Kings 18:21

XXIII

≈

The gathering about the grave of Elizabeth Browne at Point of Graves was impressive. Among the dignitaries and guests were Colonel Waldron (President of the new Province of New Hampshire), prosperous merchants and their ladies, the Reverend Nehemiah Vaughan from Robinson's Falls, six of Elizabeth's surviving, grown children—Jared, Jerusha, Sara, Enoch, Aaron, and Apphia—and numerous grandchildren. Near the front of this group, looking into his wife's grave as the simple farewell progressed, stood Richard Browne in his black bombazine suit, a man well into his sixties, gray, stooped in sorrow yet plainly still strong. The day was windy and clear with a brilliance that only a great river, as it opens to the sea, can impart to the light. Browne squinted at the gravestone.

HERE LYES BURIED THE BODY
OF ELIZABETH BROWNE
WIFE TO RICHARD BROWNE
DIED MAY 14 1682
ON Ye DAY OF HER 66TH YEAR

Had she chosen death, as the date would suggest, or had there been a terrible coincidence? There were hard feelings now against the Indians. Many placed the blame there. So had Richard Browne upon first hearing that his wife's body had been pulled from the river. But he no longer placed the blame elsewhere. For some time her mind had been unsettled—perhaps in more torment than he had realized—so that she had seemed unaware of this world. And there were bodily ills. She had long complained of occasional weakness in the heart and bowels, ever since a difficult pregnancy and birth with their youngest child, Apphia. In her later years these afflictions seemed to grow more frequent and agonizing.

Yet the strong spark of her life had never really flagged until, as he now supposed, she walked into the Piscataqua River. Of course no one would believe it of a woman so steadfast in her observances of the Lord. Even the Reverend Vaughan—normally a very pragmatic man—blamed an undefined group of wandering Indians whom she must have had the misfortune to encounter on one of her meditative walks.

Mr. Vaughan did not pray or actively officiate in the port town's lingering absence of a minister, shunning in the old tradition any hint of ritualism even regarding the dead, but he attended, a grave old man, a stern reminder, as some might say, of earlier times and political ties. Neither could he, Vaughan, admit the possibility of self-murder, a crime against church and country. Grounds to refuse Christian burial. Who among one's friends and one's neighbors would suggest such a thing?

No, Browne thought, and what matter would her secret be to the public mind? There was for Browne irony enough in either death. Here was a tragic quirk of Fate that humbled: a good woman who with her whole family survived the Indian wars of Metacom's Rebellion only to meet a violent death by her own hand (or even the hands of savages). His sense of Fate's cunning might have increased, however, had he known that his wife met her death in the uneasy lull between King Philip's War and that long series of more bloody Indian wars—if more profitable to these gay merchants—beginning with King William's War in 1689. For it would take nearly a century for the colonists to defeat what they had aroused of outrage in the local tribes and of commercial competitiveness in the French.

He held in his hand the large silver brooch that was his wife's favorite, and usually her only, ornament. And just as his mind began to unloose a horde of memories and old associations from the nearly thirty years of their marriage, his daughter by Elizabeth, Apphia, placed her gentle arm through his and spoke.

"Come, Father," he heard her saying now. "We must return with the others to the house." Her eyes were also wet, but she managed to smile as he looked at her. Her dimple as she smiled reminded him of Apphia the child, even as he began to walk with the grown woman, to see her again near the age of two walking uncertainly about the house clutching some object. Was it a doll? He saw again her childish, natural ringlets jiggling brightly on the back of her head, heard her high sweet voice talking some private nonsense to imagined auditors.

It was as if her coming not long after the miserable death of another baby girl, somehow to redress an imbalance of pain and ugliness in the world, caused Apphia to be an extraordinarily beautiful child. And in the first years of Apphia's life he had struggled to keep a distance from her, for he had not known until the death of his first daughter the pain of watching one's own very young children die. He had not known how he could ever bear it again, however common a thing it had once seemed to him before he had children of his own. But then the childbearing stopped suddenly and there were only Aaron and Apphia for his own offspring.

Of course he knew death was the price of life, and he was enough of an Anglican to gather some relief from the thought of the heavenly peace of the souls he had loved, now that the suffering of each one's passage was over. Yet just at the moment he was in that state of meaningless emptiness which facing a loved one's burial brings. He walked on Apphia's arm like a partially animated corpse.

Once the duties of putting one's dead to rest were completed, the mourning rings and gloves appropriately distributed, Browne went directly to bed. He lay awake in the daylight and well into the night praying for strength, weeping from time to time, and hoping to live long enough to enjoy his grandchildren as they grew. How one held on to life against any pain, he thought. How one sought to squeeze every possible moment out of life when one might better be seeking to join that gathering of beloved spirits too tired or beaten or blasted to remain bound to the earth!

The next day at home he tried to begin attending to his commercial interests, but his heart was not ready. Neither could he read nor write his correspondence, nor eat, nor even walk in his garden.

He was merely sitting dumbly at his writing table, staring at nothing in particular, feeling vaguely nauseous, vaguely stiff-jointed, vaguely pained about the chest, when his son Aaron and daughter Apphia entered his study.

He smiled at them, his first smile in days, and stood up stiffly to embrace them both at once.

"I feel," he said, holding them, "as if I have lost some part of myself." He began to weep again and turned away toward a window overlooking the street to collect himself. Below, people bustled about their daily rounds. "That's a strange sensation to me," he finally added, "that sense of bodily loss and pain that endures. One would have expected it to be more a longing or aching of the soul. But something vital has been cut from me and now the pain of the wound has come into itself." He turned as if to be sure they understood him. "It is, you see, a physical pain I speak of, more definite than that pain I suffer in my thoughts."

"Yes, Father," Apphia said.

"You can talk to us, Father," Aaron added. "We can help with this burden."

"Father, we wish to learn more ourselves," Apphia said.

"More?" her father asked.

"About her. About both of you," she said.

"Who knows her better than you two?" he asked.

"We knew her, yes of course, Father, but there was so much of her life we did not know," she added.

"She loved us," Aaron added, "and we her. But Apphia means we knew her not as her other children, in the earlier days."

"Neither of you ever told us what happened to Mother's first husband," Apphia added, "even when we asked. We know little of her people in England, even though Aaron has traveled to Old England with you." Apphia stopped and looked at her father as he sat down again at his table. "Something happened, long ago, Father. Can you finally tell us what it was?"

Richard Browne motioned for his children to be seated. He said nothing for some minutes, only looked down at the papers before him. When he began to speak his voice was so soft they could hardly hear his words: "I suppose you should know some of these matters now." He looked up at his children. "It seems, no it is, another life. It is not our life, our life in this town." He waved his arm about as if to indicate the street, the small and great houses, the port itself, and all the ships and earnest people of trade.

"Your mother," he continued, "was a strong woman. When we first met she suffered great distress and impoverishment, which you shall never or fully understand. Nor will I, to be honest." He shifted in his seat, leaned back to look at his patient children, and began to tell what he knew of the death of Mistress Coffin, of the small success and larger failures of his efforts on Elizabeth Higgins' and Jonathan Cole's behalf.

He spoke for more than an hour, and when he had finished

his children were silent, expecting him to continue. But Browne could say no more.

"And so you had to keep a portion of the truth from Mr. Cole?" Aaron asked finally to stop the silence.

"For a time," his father answered. "He learned part of the truth—Jared Higgins deserted his wife and family for a life of savagery—as magistrate in the court that granted your mother's divorce on like grounds. Your mother wouldn't have it any other way. I told him in deposition all I knew of Jared Higgins, and then later I told him privately what I knew of the entire matter. And of course made many excuses for myself for having divulged only partial truths previously.

"What Higgins did to his wife and family was an evil thing," Browne added. "He seems to have believed his reasons sufficient, the curses laid against him by whatever powers formidable enough, to excuse his behavior. But he had betrayed his wife from the first. Yet I don't know that any of us was free of a share of foolishness and lies.

"Naturally, Mr. Cole would have little of my self-justifications and there grew an irreparable rift between us. Finally, there seemed to your mother and me little else we could do but remove to the Banke, the most reasonable place considering my trade, her cousins, so forth. Even the Reverend Vaughan at first looked upon me as a pariah.

"Just prior to our removal to the Banke and our marriage, I met, at his request, with Mr. Vaughan." Browne looked up; his eyes wandered about the room. "To tell you the truth, I had nearly forgotten it after all these years. When I came to him he was no longer cordial, as he had remained even in our disagreements, even when I more or less turned your mother over to his more appropriate care. The Reverend Vaughan had come to take a sort of proprietary interest in her it seems. He spoke to me of her gifts, a woman of visions and utterances; he went on in that vein. She had become one of his visible saints, under his care. As Mr. Vaughan spoke with vehemence of his concern for her, I began to believe he had come to see her as a gift—to himself, perhaps his congregation. A sort of holy vessel. For so he had transformed her visions. A vessel easily damaged once out of the hands of its protector. Or perhaps a vessel for evil, in the wrong hands.

"You see my conceit? She was like the beautiful, magical vessel of some exotic tale. One did not own the vessel; one was granted her for a time. And her gifts were yours only so long as you needed them. I believe now that is how he came to view her then.

"Of course to marry such a woman and take her to a place without a minister of its own again, well, you see how that placed me, in his regard, beyond the pale. But we were married in town here shortly after I had removed my entire household. We joined our households here. What more could I do? I could not face my old benefactor continually as I must had I stayed on. Had I dissembled to gain this woman? One might interpret events that way. Though I've searched the matter in my own heart and do not believe so. Yet does one truly understand one's own motives?"

"And Mother," Apphia asked, "did she not also charge your dissembling against you?"

"She did, to be sure, and justly," he answered. "I did not give up, however. Too much had been lost already. And I continued to offer my help in worldly matters. I've never understood exactly how she worked it out in her own mind—she was never able to explain it herself, so far as I know—yet she eventually came to accept my position. We had traveled a long and dangerous road together. I suppose that counted for something. And how explain the way love grows between two people, even in the most improbable of circumstances?

"She confessed to me, after we had been married some years, that as far back as the time we discovered Mr. Coffin's death she, your mother, had begun to think of me as more than a neighbor or protector. She confessed that my concern and kindness toward her had led her, in those nights when she had difficulty falling asleep, to little half-dreaming fancies about strengthening relations between us. By day, she said, she saw such fancies as preposterous. Yet these innocent dreamings continued harmlessly, fluttering back to her, as she put it, like bright silver birds.

"Something more than dependency had been growing between us in the inexplicable ways it does between men and women. There was, well, a capacity within your mother's nature. How explain it? Say simply that she forgave me."

"Out of love," Apphia said, smiling.

"If so, I did not know it at the time." He looked at each of his and Elizabeth's children again. "She grasped, somehow, the complexities and delicacies of my position, of that world I had entered and which had entangled me. I believe her love and forgiveness blossomed only from the ground of that understanding, clearer than my own, however she attained it. And I can say, dear children, that the love between us, once planted, lasted to the end with a strength I have seldom seen in husbands and wives. I am more proud and lucky in that than in anything else in my life. Love that surmounts the differences, the vices, the pettiness, and the vanities of men and women is the rarest gift. There is more explanation in such a gift than in anything else I can say to you."

"You have been fortunate, Father," Aaron said. He sat up straighter in his chair.

"Yes," Browne answered. He did not wish to recall all that he had lost any further. He stood up and paced about the room as his children sat watching him. He said only, in the course of perhaps five minutes, that he saw no savage's hand in her death now, that he accepted the fact that his wife, in a state of extreme distraction and illness, had taken her own life.

His children said nothing.

Browne moved to his bookcase, scanned the volumes a moment, and took down a relatively slim red book with a golden clasp.

"You might as well know as much as I," he said. From the book he pulled out several sheets of yellowed paper and handed one to his son, who began to read, silently sharing it with his sister.

Apphia looked up, confused.

"That note," Browne explained, "fell out among certain of Mr. Coffin's papers sent to me over thirty years ago by Dr. Sedley. Coffin, Sedley, and I are the only ones who have seen it. And the author, of course."

"So it was Mother who alerted Mr. Coffin, by this accusation?" Apphia asked.

Browne nodded his head and was about to speak when she continued.

"Mother always knew things," Apphia said.

"She had a sense, like a steeple attracting lightning," Browne said.

They were all silent again. Apphia and Aaron reworked the patterns of events they had just been told. Apphia spoke first: "A misunderstanding?"

"Yes. As to Mistress Coffin's acts."

"And Mother, she discovered this, her misunderstanding?" Apphia asked.

"Yes," Browne said.

"How could she have borne the truth, Father?" Apphia asked.

"At first, somehow she managed to. Now I see that she might have carried it all these years. That it might not have been bearable, after all."

"It must have eaten at her," Aaron said, to no one in particular. He shifted in his chair, slowly crossing his legs.

"Lately the bite sharpened, I believe," Browne said. "I was not sufficiently aware of it, being too enveloped in my own business.

"But I happened across Mistress Coffin's journal again a month or two ago, among volumes I had not consulted in years. Not having read it since our marriage, I was drawn to the journal. So I placed it upon some papers on the table here, intending to return to it at my first opportunity. Perhaps she saw it there, even read it, even came across her letter of accusation again. And this too," Browne said, handing to Aaron his old fair copy of Balthazar Coffin's will.

Aaron read the will aloud, slowly. Then he asked: "Hadn't you said half of Mr. Coffin's legacy to Mother?"

"Yes," Browne answered. He looked away from his children, his body seeming to sink against his chair.

"But £112, Father?" Aaron said.

"Yes, that's correct, Aaron. I had told her that amounted to half, so she'd take something, you see." Now he rose from his chair suddenly and walked to the window.

"It became a commercial decision, finally," he said. He explained about the growing competition for timberland and sawmills just at that time.

"So mother received but a quarter of the sum," Aaron said.

"Yes," Browne said without turning from the window.

"And you told her of this, later I mean?" Apphia asked.

"I did not," Browne said. No one spoke, so he added: "I never found the courage to tell her."

"But she would have understood, Father," Apphia said. "She would have forgiven, as before. And is not marriage a kind of truth? Isn't it honesty between partners, or nothing?"

Looking at his father's silent back, Aaron said: "Sometimes it is necessary to be untrue, for greater good. In rare cases, mind you, but sometimes necessary. Why need mother know? The money was left to Father, after all. Her quarter portion was a gift, a generosity. The amount, as Father said, was determined by pressing matters of trade."

"But to live with such untruth between you, all those years?" Apphia asked.

Aaron made a motion with his hand to quiet her, but Apphia seemed not to notice him and pressed on: "Is not a lie a broken stone in the foundation of marriage?"

She looked up at her father's back and suddenly blushed. Her hand rose to her mouth.

"If it is difficult to discover truth," Browne said without turning, "it is even harder to live truth."

Neither Apphia nor Aaron responded.

Browne turned toward his children. "No, Apphia is right," he said. "I did your mother wrong, God help me. I can only hope she never discovered my lack of honesty in this instance, but of course it is possible, even likely, that she did. We'll never be certain." He pointed to the journal and the papers now tucked back within it. He looked each of his children in the eye in turn. "I should have been more alive to her inmost heart."

"The Indian wars have caused her great distress," Aaron put in immediately. "She suffered in her heart under God's scourge of our people."

"That's true, also," Browne said. "Perhaps too many things came to press upon her. She was distraught as well by the drought and terrible winter. She seems to have seen some rebuke from God in it all."

The room was silent again. Browne lowered his head like a man fatigued beyond restoration.

"Yet I cannot see," Aaron finally said, "that Mother would ever grow so separate from her God that she would capitulate to such diabolical temptation, such apostasy, as to take her own life. That is unthinkable, Father."

"Yes," Browne said, "what you say is true, Aaron. Yet everything is possible to a distracted and melancholic mind."

No one knew what to say next, but silence grew intolerable. Aaron finally spoke against the Indians, in the manner common to the time.

Browne too found that he had become capable of mouthing the same phrases and sentiments. Everywhere now white people spoke of Indians this way.

"'Oh, daughter of Babylon,'" Browne said, "'who art to be destroyed: happy shall be he that rewarded thee, as thou hast served us. Happy shall he be that taketh and dasheth thy little ones against the stones.'"

Outside Richard Browne's window the daylight was taking on an evening hue now and the clatter from the wharves and markets was subsiding. He felt thankful, for some reason he could not name and did not care to pursue, that day was done. There was also a feeling of relief that had come from speaking to his children. They were silent as he looked out over a few rooftops to the masts of ships in their berths, some of which would be unloading and loading into the night. There were ships at port that he had built or bought. The thought comforted him at the moment. Then without speaking he turned, went to a cabinet, and removed a bottle of claret. He began to pour a substantial draft into a bowl. He sipped from the bowl and passed it to his children, who stood up and sipped from the bowl in turn. When Aaron passed the bowl back to his father, the old man raised the bowl slightly and toasted his wife, Elizabeth. He then added that they must continue their lives and labors together, drawing now greater strength from one another.

Browne found that for the first time in a week he felt the need to eat. He invited his children to dine, but having business and families of their own, they declined.

"Of course," he said. Then he pointed to the red, leather-bound journal and the papers tied and enfolded beside it. "I have kept among these papers a secret deposition signed by

Shaw and myself many years ago—against the possibility its contents might become useful in any proceedings against the Fletchers, prior to their banishment, or in any necessity to protect your mother's interests."

His children said nothing. He merely looked at them and continued.

"It is the story White Robin—Higgins—told us during our second journey to the interior. His narrative of the events leading to the death of Mistress Coffin."

"You credit such a narrative, Father?" Aaron asked.

"Not at the time, particularly. Shaw seemed to. I knew not what to make of it."

"It is written, you say. May we read it?" Aaron asked.

"I wrote it from memory immediately upon our return from the interior, read it to Shaw, and we rewrote it together as close to our recollections as we could manage. We tried to recapture the precise story, in Higgins' own words, just as it was put to us. I think it is a good enough approximation." He looked at each of them in turn. "You can see the condition of the manuscript. I will read it to you."

"But now, Father?" Apphia asked.

"No. You both have your own affairs pressing now. Tomorrow. If you'll both come to dine."

As they gathered downstairs for leavetaking, Aaron raised a troublesome point relating to trade. It seemed that Edward Randolph, New England Customs Collector, had momentarily invigorated certain duties and restrictions against the exchange and importation, through Barbadoes, of selected European, as opposed to British, goods.

"I don't wish to garnish continually favors of officials nor take chances with the law unless you yourself agree, Father, that we need more such compromises now," Aaron explained.

"I'll have a word with the Cutts and William Vaughn," Browne said. "We'll see which way the winds of law are blowing and what is necessary. Come by tomorrow and sup with me. I'm not sure but we'll have to retreat on the French and Spanish trade, at least for now. Goods crowding the market these times anyway, though there's always a market for French grain and liquor."

"What the Lords of Trade don't appreciate, Father, is that the whole of New England profits by such trade, strengthens, grows, reflects greater glory on Mother England and all her dominions."

"Oh, I believe they understand that, Aaron," his father said. "But they'll not have us clearing the largest cut. Nor will the London merchants, come to that, despite all of our ties there. It is the King's revenue *and* Cheapside's they begrudge us."

"But they all profit enormously from our labors," Aaron began to protest.

"Of course. Of course." Browne waved his hand and smiled. "No, it is simply our assertion of any independence and our profit by what they call this 'smuggling trade' they deplore. And if the courts were not our own, even Randolph would have cooked us long ago." He laughed. "It's a good fight, Aaron. Their duties depress our profit enough to score us too. We give and we get."

"Surely Cranfield in Barbados can be counted on?" Aaron asked as he began to move out into the street.

"I have no reason to believe otherwise," Browne answered quietly, looking up and down the street. "He owes me a turn or two nevertheless. What's here now?"

"Clearing rum, molasses, divers wines. I shall bring the lists by when I come."

"You are exporting next month?"

"Deales and pipe staves. The fish looks doubtful at the moment, something of a pricing war on. But the mast ships are contracted directly for England, with Sir William Warren."

"Good," Browne said. "Keep to Sir William, and the mast

trade, Aaron; *that* is where the largest return and greatest security lie. I believe Sir William and some few others will control the entire trade before long. And I'm not alone in that belief. Yes, keep with Sir William."

"I shall indeed, Father."

"And Blathwayt," Browne added. "Without the support of Whitehall, without the favor of the Lords of Trade, one piles his fortune upon thin ice. Only fools say otherwise and try to cheat these men of influence out of any profit by our activities. The fools must lose every time, Aaron. They always have."

The son and father smiled knowingly at one another.

"Excepting the case of Africoes, Father," Aaron said after a moment of thought. "There is no getting around the Royal African Company, their lock on all legal trade."

"Of course," Browne said, "but that is a separate trade, and we are but dabblers yet. Mark my words, some day the whole of the British trade in Negroes will be opened to all comers. The demand is rising fast. Until then, like so many others, we are but interlopers, careful interlopers."

Aaron smiled. "Cunning interlopers!" he added.

Then just before turning indoors Browne looked at Apphia and added: "And will you, dear daughter, join us for a light meal? Shall I tell Mrs. Hawksworth?"

"I don't see why not. I'll send Millie over later this evening to confirm, Father," she said. "Thank you."

XXIV

~~~~

Aaron arrived earlier than Apphia the next evening that he and his father might discuss commerce. But after Apphia joined them and they had sharpened their appetites with a cup of sack, it became clear to Browne that his children had returned not only to comfort him, but to satisfy their further curiosity.

As they stood before a large, newly made fire in Browne's hall, Apphia opened the subject again.

"And you believed the Fletchers, Father," Apphia asked, "and then Higgins' account of what finally took place?"

"Eventually, although no judgment has ever been ruled in the matter. And of course Mistress Coffin's journal would account for much that would fit as well. There is a thread of truth running through all three accounts. Up to a point, of course."

Browne began to explain the circumstances of their finding Higgins for the second time in the interior. "When we returned to the village by the lake, Shaw and I discovered that Jared Higgins had departed with the family into which he had married some time, perhaps a year, before. I can still recall how Shaw kept his face expressionless when the Indians were telling him this. But I kept pushing Shaw to get more information.

"One of the savages answered that Higgins had gone on the big river with the Amoskeags. He guessed he would be found where the river crosses below the pinnacle and the salmon falls.

Shaw asked were they sure Higgins was still alive, and they assured us he was, that he had produced a healthy son.

"The river being strong and the portages few, Shaw and I camped only one night in pursuit of Higgins. But we did not find him among the small Amoskeag encampment at the falls. Moreover, Shaw was unknown among these Indians. They insisted that they knew nothing about a white man among their tribe. But Shaw persisted. He explained who had directed him to their tribe. Eventually we managed to prevail. There was, you see, no 'Higgins,' only a man called White Robin who might be found with their people near the village of the Wamesit, farther down river.

"That, finally, was where we found Higgins. His tawny skin, his carriage, his ornaments and clothing, his hair, his dialect—all were those of his new people. Even his eyes seemed to have changed, their movement, their darkness, their strange serenity. To our eyes, the transformation was complete. Only the nose and a few missing teeth might have suggested an Englishman to us. In his wigwam close by the river, we came upon this white Indian's squaw and son.

"He—this White Robin—was circumspect. He chose not to speak English. Shaw had to interpret for me. Before we three sat down, White Robin sent his wife and baby out to an old woman who was cooking directly in front of the wigwam.

"Shaw began translating my words to him: 'Balthazar Coffin is dead.' White Robin responded that 'he was an evil man.' For a time, White Robin said, he thought he would return and kill Coffin. But he realized he did not know what power he would be up against, and lost his courage. Shaw then explained, at my direction, that he, Higgins, might return now to his proper wife and children. But he continually refused, saying that he had no wish to live among the English. I persisted; after all, his own wife and children! But White Robin only said: 'I have the tenderest feelings for them, but I cannot return now.' He emphasized that he was sorry events turned out as they did for his white family, but he could not change all that.

"I tried appealing to his innocence, which we could establish at the bar, but he only retorted that his innocence was clear to him. Finally he asked us to report that he was dead, then they would easily find someone to look after them. I'm afraid I only made matters worse at that point by accusing him of bigamy, adultery, forcing his wife to scorn God's laws, whatnot. White Robin repeated that he lived by the laws of his gods. He said that once he was a false man, but now he had become a true man, or as Shaw translated it, 'a man'. He said that no truth nor cozening would move him from his life. 'The life of the English is dead to me,' he told us.

"You see, he had cut himself off from all natural affections of a true Englishman. I believed it was now that he was living the false life, not formerly. He only asked us then if we were certain of Coffin's death. When I assured him we were, he grew silent. He looked at the skins on the floor, his face drained of expression. I thought that surely there must be some conflict between the Indian and the white man. No one, it seemed to me, can deny a former life, however unpalatable it might seem from the present life. I finally said as much. Then White Robin rose and looked at us strangely. He turned, said something, and left the wigwam. I asked Shaw what he had said. 'He says he needs a sweat,' Shaw replied."

"He did not tell you the story you have mentioned?" Aaron asked.

"Not until the next afternoon. Here it is," Browne said, pulling out from beneath some papers on a table a faded, fragile manuscript. "Just as we wrote it from memory upon our return. Higgins had sent word for us to meet him near the bank of the river just north of the encampment where a great tree made open space. By that time I had decided that the only chance

remaining to bring Higgins back was to tell him everything I
had discovered, including the diary. I remember now that as I
spoke, I could see the river sweeping heavily by. I believe that
it must have taken me an hour to tell the whole story, occasionally circling back to fill in a forgotten detail or incident. White
Robin listened, interested but serene. He asked a question or
two only about the Fletcher brothers.

"I remember now too that Shaw rose and walked about for
some minutes before White Robin spoke. 'The Fletchers are
those you seek,' he finally began, in English now. 'They were,
as they said, hired for Coffin's vengeance.' I asked him if it was
vengeance against himself and Mistress Coffin."

Browne looked down at the faded manuscript now and began
to read to his children the words he had written long ago.

"'I learned Coffin was suspicious of me. What led him to
believe in such falsehood I didn't know, but it was God's truth
to him. Even in his hiring me to carry his wife to market I felt
something wrong. But then Jacob Fletcher came to see me. I
was planting a late crop. He had information, he said, that
might save me. But he made it clear the information should be
worth something, so we finally agreed that he'd have my new
axe and an Indian bow of mine. I'm not sure how he knew
about the bow. He had hoped for coin, but I had none to give
him. Only if I agreed the information as important to me as
he had promised need I pay. So I didn't see how it could not
be. And of course it was.

"'We had worked together at times. And I knew him for a
local tosspot and rakehell. He said first that he did not like the
job he had been hired to do by this strange man Coffin. The
more he thought, he said, the more he saw we might design to
benefit us both, act out a sort of stage play for Coffin's plaudits.
Then he told the details of his covenant with Coffin.

"'The game he had got up to was this: they would capture
and bind us as planned. Yet I was to know the playbook as it

played, not the woman. Too dangerous for appearances of the truth. They would filch whatever she had, knock her about, leave her on the island to be "rescued" as arranged. "Coffin is to rescue a cuckold and his lady!" Jacob said and laughed. I would now bear the weight of their attack, but short of death or mutilation. I was to make my escape while they were busy with her.'" Browne looked up at his children, ceasing to read for the moment the words of White Robin.

"I remember accusing him," Browne said, "of lying in deposition to the court. But his only response was that he withheld certain of the truth to save himself, and others, from the vengeance of the law. He said that he was 'a false man' in those times." Browne then looked back down at his manuscript and began reading White Robin's words again.

"'From Coffin's own thirst for revenge, from his arts, his ways, our playacting began to seem an escape. Short of immediate flight alone—or with my confused family deep into the wilds of Maine or some faraway place—I saw no other way out. I confess I hoped that being his victims in our spectacle might slake his desires against us. How else appease, I thought, that awful serpent in his heart? He would not have listened to truth. Was this plan not worth a trial? Of course, I knew I would have to make ready to escape his reach should our performance fail to entertain and satisfy him.

"'So we went ahead with it. Mistress Coffin alone unaware of what we had staged. I disappeared as planned. While she was at market, Jacob Fletcher connived to meet her after she sought me and offered his services, as he was returning himself and as I had told him that I had to return home for a mishap befalling one of my children. He said I had asked for his help in returning her, and so on in such vein until she finally got into the canoe with him. She knew who he was; her husband had once or twice hired this man who, if his reputation were smirched, worked well when you hired him.

"'By the time they reached Bailey's Island, I had been bound to an oak tree, dirtied and beaten somewhat, stripped to my breeches, my mouth tied, my clothes strewn about. You see? Henry Fletcher sat below me whetting his knives by the fire.

"'But even then I began to regret my part in the drama as soon as I saw her face. And they seemed to use her with more force than necessary from the first. You see, as soon as she saw my condition she began to resist. They were hard on her, and when she began to scream for help they tied a rope around her throat, with a slipping knot, and gave her pressure until she ceased. They searched her, taking whatever valuables they found, including the corn and some coin in her purse. They removed her clothing and searched her nakedness. Henry piled her clothes aside carefully. Jacob began to threaten her with what would soon befall us, while Henry acted dumb shows of our waiting agonies.

"'Jacob stripped my breeches off while Henry continued with Mistress Coffin. I knew they had begun too much to relish their roles. I began to see that they had counted this woman a portion of their booty. We all moved on a knife edge between the true and the staged. At any moment their lusts might spill over, making the show grow real. I almost broke free of my loose bonds to fight, but then I thought better of it—a naked man defenseless against their double weapons.

"'That is what happened, at the bottom of it. It all went wrong. The final turn came just as Jacob was flourishing before me his heated knives, and Henry ran over to motion that he needed help with the woman. This we had planned. When they turned from me to attend to the struggling woman, I was to flee. But somehow she had loosened the rope and found strength enough to begin screaming again. They became very busy with her. Henry pulled the small canoe up on the land and turned it over. Jacob dragged her by the rope to the canoe, her screams stopped, while she clutched at the rope to relieve its choking.

They pulled her over the canoe on her stomach, tied the end of her rope to a sapling, and then bound each foot to separate trees, so that she lay over the canoe wide before them.

"'Then it was that Henry started in on her, with less mercy than a butcher's cur toward an ox cheek. He removed his breeches and started to come at her on hands and knees, even though Jacob was calling to him: "Not yet you goddamn fool." But there was no stopping him; it had all gone wrong. He had come right up to her, grunting in her loins like a calf at the salt. She had been made so helpless by her bonds that she could neither move nor utter a sound now. Her free arms were pulling against the rope to relieve the crush at her throat enough to stay alive.

"'Henry grabbed his inflamed yard and slammed into her, and then Jacob ceased his complaint and began to laugh as he watched the two of them. It was just as Jacob began to remove his clothes that I finished undoing my own bonds, certain by now that everything had gone awry. As they busied themselves upon her, fore and aft, I ran, grabbing my breeches on my way, and jumped into the water. I swam to the western shore like a demon.

"'On shore I saw that neither brother had stopped his pleasures of her to pursue me. I was supposed to have escaped, after all. I'm sure they were not worrying whether anyone had thrown out the playbook. I pulled on my wet breeches, and fled barefoot overland to my house.'" Here Browne paused briefly again in his reading. When he looked up his eyes looked distant and glazed.

"I recall somehow," Browne said to his children, "exactly how he looked just then as he told his story. He briefly shifted his position and then began to slide a strand of beadwork through his thumb and forefinger." When Browne failed to continue his reading, his son prompted him: "Father? Go on, please." Browne seemed to return to the present, shook his head, and looked down at his manuscript. He began reading again.

"'The upshot is that when they found the poor woman's sorely beaten body in the river, I could neither eat, nor sleep, nor think. I prepared to flee, fearing to tell anyone, even my wife, of my role. Who shall believe me now? I resolved to take their lives, those Fletchers, but before I could make ready, there were hearings. I came under close watch, had to shift as much blame as possible. Then the Fletchers had not, it was said, returned to the town. They managed earlier to get the half part of payment out of Coffin, who was desperate for his vengeance, and by what they took from her purse. When Coffin saw that I had returned whole, he took recourse of the law against me. Under questioning, I began to hint that his own hand was in this and that his wife, as he still believed, was an adulteress. Then he gave up on my punishment by the Courts.

"'The missing brothers drew scant suspicion. They were believed to be hunting in Maine, using the house of an uncle in Casco Bay as their base. Once suspicion turned from me, I tried to find them, but their trail had turned cold and their distance, by then, too great. It was when I returned from Maine that I discovered what was amiss in my own family. For then it was our own torments began. It was later, after the Fletchers had drifted back into town, and I finally fled, that Mr. Cole—seeing the sufferings of my family—settled with you, Mr. Browne, to look into it.'"

Browne looked up at his children. "There," he said. "That is all."

"All?" Apphia asked.

"All that was written," Browne said. "I remember some things now, of course. Much of it came back to me as I was reading to you. I remember that when White Robin stopped speaking there was only the sound of distant birds and of the river thrusting beside us. I felt as if I had awakened from an evil dream. I thought I would be ill. I saw again and again Elizabeth Higgins' sealed note to Balthazar Coffin drop out onto my table from among the papers Dr. Sedley had sent. I looked at Shaw, who gave no indication of his belief or disbelief in his old friend's story. The story had felt absolutely true to me as it was told, but in the crush of emotion afterwards I wondered.

"I also recall standing up and trying to shake off a sensation of dizziness, and walked around before I spoke again. I think I said to White Robin: 'That, however, is all in the past, as dead to us here today as that poor woman, and now her husband. You cannot now act as if your life, your children, your wife back at Robinson's Falls are a story or a dream. You're still responsible for them. No one, least of all I, will bring action against you again in this bloody matter. The Fletchers may have to answer. I can procure agreements with Mr. Cole to keep you clear of any retribution, especially if you testify. I can secure all this and return in two months for you.'

"'The Fletchers have their punishment coming,' White Robin said to me. 'What more can it matter now?' How could he have known that they were to be sent into exile before any action would be initiated against them again? At the time I explained that it was for his wife, his family, that I pleaded. But he only answered that his family was here, meaning the Indian camp. Then he asked Shaw and me to leave him. In desperation I tried to get Shaw to agree to bring Higgins' wife and son to see him, but Shaw, correctly no doubt, said simply that he, Higgins, would not be found again. Indeed, he had already, Shaw said, made his farewell to Shaw in the dialect. We left the next morning."

"When you consider," Aaron said after a silence, "that Mother suddenly faced not only an adulterous and deserting husband, but one who had likely joined with these ruffians in a conspiracy leading to the torment and death of that poor woman. . . ."

"Oh, Aaron. He had *become* a savage," Apphia said, her face still astonished by the news. "And continued bigamous, or rather adulterous, relations there in the wilderness!"

The energy of Apphia's outburst silenced her brother and father momentarily. The two men looked at her kindly.

"Yes," Browne finally offered, "what we all know now has carried you about as far as it has carried me. Once she faced all these events and doings, you see, your mother awakened, so to speak. At the least her husband had violated her truly as much as if he had beaten her without cause, denied her himself, or failed to care for his family in any of the common ways. And I too was in the process of making arrangements to leave for the Port. My fortunes were increasing comfortably during this time. There was further the prospect of combining our legacies. Your mother finally thought better of striking out alone."

"Surely your charm and position must have prevailed with her," Aaron said and clapped his father lightly on the shoulder.

Browne found his heart lightened by the wine and bright evening fire. "As to my charm," he said, "I cannot attest. But my situation improved daily, that is true enough.

"And one has to know when to move on to other things, especially since one always has responsibilities to others. That, finally, is what we, your mother and I, tried to do. It took time, of course. But for the past twenty years I have given those events and inquiries little thought. That lack of any complete resolution in the case of the Coffins and the Higginses is a fact we soon learned to live with and, as I say, put out of our minds.

"Even now, the principals, the places, the events recede into uncertain historical record. Cole is deceased. All that remains is fragmentary." Browne paused to adjust the fire with a long iron fork. No one spoke while he did so. Aaron and Apphia merely looked at one another. Mrs. Hawksworth stuck her head into the room and announced supper. The old man straightened up, placed the fork against the hearth and added: "None of it is my affair any longer. This is the world we live in now."

XXV

When their evening meal was over, Browne's children wished to return to their own homes, so he climbed to his study with another dram of mulled wine. He hoped to order, for an easier start the next morning, the papers he and Aaron had spread about on his writing table. But he went to his window over the street first and watched Aaron and Apphia walking towards their dwellings. He saw again how much Apphia reminded him of Elizabeth, just as Apphia's own daughter mirrored her mother. It could have been a young Elizabeth Higgins walking below out of sight. In a whisper, he recited:

> A Lillie of a Day,
> Is fairer farre, in May,
> Although it fall, and die that night;
> It was the Plant, and flowre of light.
> In small proportions, we just beauties see:
> And in short measures, life may perfect bee.

And would they not prosper, his beautiful children and grand-children? Yes, he thought, prosper they must. Aaron one day—not too far away now surely—would come into all his father's trade and, more importantly, his land. For he, Browne, had turned much profit over the years into that safest and most transferable of investments. Above all, the wealth that tied the ensuing generations together would be land. Moreover, between them Apphia and Aaron could count in their relations by marriage the wealthiest families in the region—the Champernownes, the Cutts, the Sherburns, among others distant or close. A warmth, like that of red wine reaching an empty stomach on a cold day, spread through his body as he thought how substantial would be the increase unto his children and their children for generations to come.

Apphia had been delighted when he had offered her any of her mother's most costly clothing—a silk hood and sleeves, petticoats, a few silver clasps, combs and such things as Elizabeth had accumulated over the years, some of them gifts he or her children had given her. She might as well have the best of it, he thought. He could not have any of it in the house much longer. He wondered briefly what to do with the rest, the mundane clothes and personal effects, the worst reminders of his loss, these possessions that renewed pain.

Elizabeth seldom wore the "gaudy garments," as she called them, excepting the most formal occasions and ceremonies, preferring against the time plainness of dress and demeanor. She had grown fond of quoting Zephaniah: "He will visit or send his plague among such as are clothed with strange apparel." The great picture he had had painted of her in the proper attire of a wealthy merchant's wife he knew to be false to her. And most of her plain clothes would have to be thrown out, he realized, unless charitable distribution could be arranged shortly.

He turned back to his table and stood over the papers, but he could not concentrate on them yet. There would be time enough tomorrow. The street was darkening now. He thought that he had begun to feel a degree of regeneration that day, as if his severed limbs, the open wounds, were healing over. His appetite was returning also. If the physical qualities of the pain were slowly receding, the internal or mental pain remained. This, he thought, is what it's like to be left alive. If one survives the wounds to body and soul, one slowly begins to heal, growing again like a lightning-shorn tree. One's will has nothing to do with it.

Below in the street a woman hurried home, her cloak pulled tightly about her. About the vanity of this life, he thought, Elizabeth had been no doubt correct.

> But you are lovely Leaves, where we
> May read how soon things have
> Their end, though ne'r so brave;
> And after they have shown their pride,
> Like you a while: They glide
> Into the Grave.

But if he was to live in the world, he could not change himself. No, he did not wish to shun the world.

So he was to survive after all. Then he could but continue to work for the benefit of his children and grandchildren (with whom Aaron and Apphia had promised to visit soon, at his insistence). And to work in continuing good faith for his brother's sake and for the sake of the subscribers to their company. He thought, however, that he would no longer enlarge his trade; he would leave all new ventures to Aaron. Full of days, he must now devote some thought to the other business of launching himself into that ocean of Eternity where all must go, to prepare his posture, as Elizabeth might have put it, for my Lord's coming. "For a thousand years in thy sight are but as yesterday when it is past: and as a watch in the night," he thought, and then picked forward a few further of the psalmist's lines: "We spend our years as a tale that is told . . . for it is soon cut off, and we fly away."

He glanced back at his papers but did not move to them. At the moment they only reminded him of his dead wife's other sense of what was most important. But now he was alone, and what was there to adjust the balance in his life; what would be his equipoise now?

He thought of the burgeoning town and port about him as he stood before his dark window. The place was rapidly coming into its own as a center of international trade. Settled by fishmongers, lumbermen, fur traders, and the like under the aegis of that old gallant Mason, especially, for the profit of the Laconia company, one of those early unregulated and poor communities inhabited by seekers of adventure and profit, Strawberry Banke seemed to have shone with a more lurid than divine light, and now it promised a future of trade and power second to none in New England. Each citizen and every newcomer seemed to contribute to this growth of industry and independence as a province. That gulf of independence seemed to be growing as large as the gulf between the old elegant, agrarian dreams of Captain Smith and the theocratic visions of the New England saints. A great material civilization was growing on the twin trunks of investment and the tractability of those who labored. But then, as he had often said, the whole world had changed, and was changing still.

The real New World was not America, it struck him, not British America at any rate. The life he saw around him now, materially as spiritually, was increasingly the life of England since the Restoration of Charles II, less the life of biblical utopias or even the relatively humble Christian life his wife had preferred. She was, he had to admit, not suited to this coming century, this—for all he could tell—secular millennium. He began to realize, as if for the first time, though he had been aware of it, how separate his wife had become, in her deeper life, from the very women with whom she associated: those wives of important merchants and officials, those few even who co-directed their husband's estates and adventuresome interests, those local Dame School teachers, liquor sellers, keepers of public houses, and cheese vendors.

One might say that while he had been growing more and

more a man of his time, she had been receding more and more into earlier centuries still. It mattered not that she loved, was industrious, associated with the grandest of local ladies. Her private life had been otherwise, growing less and less attached to this world. The Reverend Nehemiah Vaughan had seen to that development of her vitality. Was he putting it too strongly? Perhaps. He knew only that he had not really contemplated their lives in quite this way before, had been too much caught in the nets of commerce. There was perhaps a stroke of broad truth in it. Some final lines of Donne's "Break of Day" shot into his mind.

> Must business thee from hence remove?
> O, that's the worst disease of love,
> The poor, the foul, the false, love can
> Admit, but not the busied man.

He thought about this New Time, as he put it, and he saw that of course here too, despite the advancing disenchantment, there would be evil. Mankind succeeded, everywhere pushing ahead, establishing order and profit out of wilderness. Just as he himself had done. And if all is tenuous before God, none, it seemed, thought his particular life to be as fragile as it is. The trick all must play on themselves. Each little order created amidst the gigantic wild. A world rife with violence—war, persecution, pestilence, famine, pride, greed. Men speaking evil of good, good of evil. Works of mankind a righteous God might scourge with terrible swiftness. Generation upon generation, each with renewed expectations and will. Yet each doomed to the same excoriating round.

Suddenly he recalled reading in some exotica about an ancient slave revolt in the East. The name of the black rebels returned to him like a concrete fact that he had seen for himself, the Zanj. Was it about the seventh century? They had revolted against their masters, whose cruelties were explicitly in violation of the Koran. They had created a great community of fugitive slaves; for more than a decade they were invincible. But they turned their power upon their oppressors and upon others, seizing cities, killing Arab men and enslaving, in turn, the women and children. What horrors must have occurred under the sun in those times for such women and children, the slaves of the Zanj! "And all their wealth, and all their little ones, and their wives they took captive, and spoiled even all that was in the house."

A train of brutal images swam before him and he shook his head rapidly to throw them off.

Still, he thought, if evil is palpable, so is mystery: the invisible made visible, spirit shot into matter, the dark and wonderful intricacy in the ways of Providence, the mysterious presence of the rebellious, secret self. Who would be ever without guilt? Maleficence and malefactors might change, as the shapes always change, but as Elizabeth knew there was no escaping it, whether in the shapes of yesterday or today, in others or in oneself. Moreover, is it not in searching out the darkness in others that one may find the worst, the darkness, in oneself? He thought of Elizabeth's suffering. His mind returned to the Donne poem.

> Love, which in spite of darkness brought us hither,
> Should in despite of light keep us together.

Browne stepped away from the window and rearranged some of his papers. Then he chose a book to read as a better antidote to his speculations, which were of little use either to himself or to Elizabeth at this point. It was the fat octavo volume of the now obscure Herrick that his resourceful bookseller, one Hezekiah Usher of Boston, had discovered.

But soon his eyes troubled him in the poor light and he put his book down, made his usual rounds of the house, undressed, and went to bed. He realized that he would never get used to sleeping alone, even though it had seemed the most common of his experiences in all the years before his marriage. He had not even the faintest desire to marry again. And God alone knew how long he would mourn, the deeper mourning, even after he had again donned his scarlet coat lined with green sarcenet. He recalled the old men he had seen standing or sitting in the burial ground, visiting in lonely silence for an hour or more. Yes, he would be like them, alone until the end. It would not matter any more if he were the only man in a town of beautifully bosomed and bedecked widows.

He had opened a window before turning in and now the chill night air of May made him cold, but he knew he would not get out of bed to close the window. He sat up, not quite ready to lie flat, closed his eyes and breathed evenly, letting his mind run down toward sleep. Somewhere in a grove a lone thrush was ending its evening song later than the others, its trill growing less frequent and softer. Souls of the dead.

This one seemed the song of a child's shade. He felt a pang of love for his six grandchildren, saw each one's face and spoke their names, then prayed that each would survive him. He wanted a rest from death. He would go willingly himself, but please, he prayed, do not take the children. He was old, full of the petty corruptions and compromises and failures and successes of a long life as a man of fortune. He thought his worth must be roughly £10,000.

His memory suddenly ran to the Reverend Mr. Vaughan, who once insisted to him: "Nay, instead of looking to the Bible for the way of life, you merchants look to the English Gomorrah and ape courtly pomp and delicacy. Men are seen in the streets with monstrous and horrid periwigs, and women with their borders and false locks and such like whorish fashion, whereby the anger of the Lord is kindled against this sinful land."

Browne recalled now how he had protested and how Mr. Vaughan had left him, unregenerate man that he was, in disgust. They had had heated arguments on the subject from time to time, until Vaughan finally curtailed his visits to his friend Elizabeth Browne. But the minister's sermons would on occasion take up the refrain.

"My brethren," his voice boomed above the congregation, "this is never to be forgotten, that New England is originally a plantation of religion, not a plantation of trade. Let merchants and such as are increasing *cent per cent* remember this, that worldly gain was not the end and design of the people of New England, but religion. And if any man amongst us make religion as twelve, and the world as thirteen, let such an one know he hath neither the spirit of a true New England man nor yet of a sincere Christian."

Browne recalled hearing that the Reverend Vaughan had gone so far as to preach during the recent Indian war that God's judgment upon the greed and follies of the fathers had lighted upon the present generation. Elizabeth had received a gift copy of the sermon. "The woeful neglect of the rising generation is a sad sign that we have in great part forgotten our errand; and then why should we marvel that God hath taken no pleasure in our young men, but they have been numbered for the sword."

What would the minister have said, Browne thought, had he known of Browne's lucrative trade in provisions during that war and, worse, his reopening of the French trade while the blood of that war had not yet dried upon the ground! These opportunities had at the time troubled him briefly. Yet he, Browne, had seized them, just as he had seized the greater portion of Coffin's legacy.

He laughed at himself. "'Let no man seek his own; but every man another's wealth,'" he said aloud.

Yes, he was expendable. "'My substance was not hid from thee when I was made in secret, and curiously wrought in the lowest parts of the earth. Thy eyes beheld my unformed substance; in thy book were written, every one of them, the days

that were formed for me, when as yet there was none of them.'"
But not these children, he thought; they are not expendable.
Though in truth, like that brave infant of *Saguntum*, might not
any child creep back into its mother's womb than be borne into
the strife of its age?

> Where shame, faith, honour, and regard of right
> Lay trampled on; the deeds of death, and night,
> Urg'd, hurried forth, and horld
> Upon th' affrighted world:
> Sword, fire, and famine, with fell fury met;
> And all on utmost ruine set;
> As, could they but lifes miseries fore-see,
> No doubt all Infants would returne like thee.

Suddenly he recalled the death of a local man—was it nearly
twenty years ago?—one grandfather Shurtleff killed by lightning, the very reach of the Lord's arm, while his grandchildren
sat in his lap and a third stood between his knees. "Cast forth
lightning, and scatter them: Shoot out thine arrows, and de-
stroy them." The children remained untouched. Each generation a new innocence, a new chance.

Yes, he thought, *that* was the way to die. Cleanse me. Take
me. Leave these children untouched. Well, it would be enough
then to leave the grandchildren. Come what may.

Let them shun evil. Let them prosper. Let them, Oh Lord,
stand safe among the shafts of Thy fire.

About the Author

Robert J. Begiebing was born in Massachusetts and holds degrees from Norwich University, Boston College, and the University of New Hampshire. He is professor of English at New Hampshire College, where he teaches writing and American literature. He lives with his wife and their family in Newfields, New Hampshire.